THE LEGEND OF
PERLEY GATES

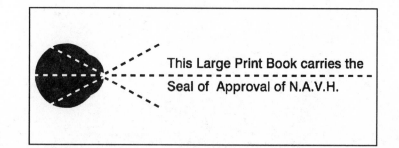

A PERLEY GATES WESTERN

THE LEGEND OF PERLEY GATES

WILLIAM W. JOHNSTONE
WITH J. A. JOHNSTONE

THORNDIKE PRESS
A part of Gale, a Cengage Company

Farmington Hills, Mich • San Francisco • New York • Waterville, Maine
Meriden, Conn • Mason, Ohio • Chicago

Copyright © 2018 by J. A. Johnstone.
A Perley Gates Western.
The WWJ steer head logo is a Reg. U.S. Pat. & TM Off.
Thorndike Press, a part of Gale, a Cengage Company.

ALL RIGHTS RESERVED
Following the death of William W. Johnstone, the Johnstone family is working with a carefully selected writer to organize and complete Mr. Johnstone's outlines and many unfinished manuscripts to create additional novels in all of his series like The Last Gunfighter, Mountain Man, and Eagles, among others. This novel was inspired by Mr. Johnstone's superb storytelling.
Thorndike Press® Large Print Western.
The text of this Large Print edition is unabridged.
Other aspects of the book may vary from the original edition.
Set in 16 pt. Plantin.

LIBRARY OF CONGRESS CIP DATA ON FILE.
CATALOGUING IN PUBLICATION FOR THIS BOOK
IS AVAILABLE FROM THE LIBRARY OF CONGRESS

ISBN-13: 978-1-4328-5306-8 (hardcover)

Published in 2018 by arrangement with Pinnacle Books, an imprint of Kensington Publishing Corp.

Printed in the United States of America
1 2 3 4 5 6 7 22 21 20 19 18

THE LEGEND OF PERLEY GATES

CHAPTER 1

"Howdy, Perley," Ben Henderson sang out when he saw the familiar figure walk into his general store in the little settlement of Paris, Texas.

"Ben," Perley returned. "I've got a list of things we need — some flour, salt, sugar, and such. It's right here on this list." He handed the list to Ben. "Reckon you can read it as well as me callin' 'em out."

"That I can," Ben said. "Looks like your mother's handwritin', and anybody can read that. How are your folks? Your pa still down on his back?"

"Never mind his pa." A harsh voice came from the other end of the store, where the hardware and ammunition were located. "You're supposed to be waitin' on me, and I don't see no .44 cartridges on these shelves."

Perley had not noticed the two men near the back shelves. He looked then to see them, neither of whom he had ever seen in town before. "Ma's fine," he answered Ben quickly, "but Pa's come down with something he can't seem to get rid of. You go ahead and wait on those two fellows. I'm not in any big hurry."

Henderson hurried over to the end of the counter. "Yes, sir, boxes of .44 cartridges right here on the shelf," he said and pointed to them. "If they'da been a snake, they'da bit you." He laughed good-naturedly but stopped when it was obvious the strangers didn't appreciate his attempt to lighten the atmosphere. "Yes, sir, how many boxes?"

While he was biding his time at the front counter, Perley remembered something he had promised his younger sister, Esther, he would ask about. Figuring he needed a woman's help with that, he asked Ben, "Is Mrs. Henderson around? I'm gonna need some help with some material."

"Yeah, Perley," Ben answered. "She's in the stockroom." He called out then, "Shirley!"

It obviously irritated Ben's ammunition customer, who said nothing, but the hard look he shot Perley's way was enough to send a message. Perley decided he'd better wait patiently, but it was too late, because Shirley Henderson popped through the stockroom door immediately.

"Perley's gonna need some help with some dress material," Ben said.

"Well, hello, Perley," Shirley said. "I haven't seen you in town in a long time. How's your mother and father? Is he over that fall yet?"

Perley started to answer but was interrupted before he was able to.

"His mama's doin' just fine and his papa's still in the damn bed," the gruff voice blurted. "Now, are you gonna get me those damn cartridges or not? Two boxes. I ain't wastin' my time all day in this store."

"No need to get cross, neighbor," Ben said as he hurried to get the cartridges. "Anything else I can do for you?"

While the stranger was paying Ben, Shirley gave Perley a raised eyebrow but carried on cheerfully. "That dress pattern came in. I suppose you want to pick that up."

"Yes, ma'am," Perley answered, trying to remember if Esther had given him any other instructions. "I need to see if you've got some dress material in a deep blue."

"We got some in," Shirley said. "Are you thinking about a navy blue, or something a shade lighter?"

"I don't know," Perley replied. Esther hadn't given him that much information.

9

He followed Shirley over to another counter where bolts of cloth and sewing things were kept. The two strangers, both trail-hardened cowhands, from the looks of them, turned to stare at him in open scorn.

"Will there be anything else?" Ben asked.

"No, reckon not," the big one replied. "I was thinkin' 'bout lookin' at some of your fancy lace or some pretty bows or somethin', but I reckon I'll do that some other time."

His friend cracked up over the remark, and they both roared with laughter. They were still laughing when they headed toward the door.

"Maybe I'll knit some booties to put on my horse," the big one said loudly as they went out.

"I'm sorry about that," Ben said.

"Sorry about what?" Perley asked.

Ben looked surprised. "Those two jaspers," he said. "They were a rough-lookin' pair, and I'm sorry they took to japin' you like that. But I'll be honest with you, they looked like too much for me to handle."

"Were they japin' me?" Perley asked. "I reckon I wasn't payin' enough attention to know it. Don't pay 'em no mind — just some cowhands in town to dust off some rust. They most likely didn't mean any harm."

Ben exchanged a puzzled glance with his wife and shook his head.

"I think this blue is more what Esther is looking for," Shirley said.

"Looks good to me," Perley said. "Cut off however much the pattern calls for. I've gotta pick up something from Patton's. I'll go do that while you're gettin' my order ready."

He left the buckboard at the rail in front of Henderson's and walked up the street past the post office to Patton's Saloon.

"Howdy, Perley," Paul McQueen, the blacksmith, called out when Perley walked by.

Perley returned the greeting but continued on to the saloon. As long as he was picking up a pattern and material for Esther, he thought he might as well surprise her with one of her favorite treats. Patton's was an odd place to get it, but in Paris, it was the only place. Perley might have considered having a drink while he was there, but it was a little early in the day for him. Another reason was of a more personal nature. Any time he came to town, especially if alone, he made it a point to eat dinner at the Paris

Diner, and he didn't like to have whiskey on his breath when he ate there. He wouldn't want Lucy Tate to smell it on him.

According to his railroad watch, he had about the right amount of time to make a quick stop in Patton's, then return to Henderson's to pick up his supplies. That should put him at the diner right when they opened for the midday meal. A picture of Lucy Tate, floating cheerfully around the dining room, immediately took over Perley's mind. Sometimes, he couldn't clear his brain of the diner's young waitress, and he was certain that she had similar feelings for him. She never failed to give him special attention when he came in, even to the point of sitting down at the table with him to visit. Perley was the only one of Nathaniel Gates's grown sons who was not married, and Perley felt that maybe it was time to think about things like that. Rubin and John were lucky that they had found good women to build their families with. He just hadn't met that special woman yet, but maybe Lucy was meant to fill that void in his life.

There were two saddled horses and one packhorse tied at the rail in front of Patton's. It was early for the afternoon customers and already late for the dedicated drunks who opened up the saloon. Perley stepped

12

up onto the boardwalk and went inside, where he found Raymond Patton sitting at a table against the wall, drinking coffee.

"Mornin', Perley," Patton greeted him.

"Mornin'," Perley returned with a nod, then went straight to the bar to speak to Benny Grimes, the bartender.

"Howdy, Perley," Benny said. "Ain't seen you in town in a while."

"Reckon not," Perley said. "We're kinda busy this time of year, gettin' the cattle ready for the drive up to Ogallala."

"I figured as much," Benny said. "Ain't seen much of any of your crew. What'll ya have? Whiskey?"

"Little too early," Perley answered. "I just came in to buy a couple of those big peppermint sticks you keep for Mrs. Patton."

At the other end of the long bar, Zeke Cotton nudged the man drinking beside him with his elbow. "Lookee there," he drawled, making no attempt to muffle his comment. "Damned if that ain't that sweet little girlie feller that was at the store buyin' some material to make him a dress."

They both turned to stare at Perley, who was just in the process of taking the peppermint sticks and wrapping them in a piece of cloth that Benny had torn from a clean bar rag.

"I swear, Lige, ain't that plumb precious?"

"It sure is," Lige replied, knowing there was going to be some fun to follow.

"Reckon he could do some sewin' for us? I've got some socks that sure need darnin', and he's the only seamstress we're liable to come across between here and the Red River."

"Maybe so," Lige said. "But what strikes me as kinda queer is, what the hell is he doin' in a saloon? There ain't nobody but men supposed to be in a saloon."

Their sarcasm became louder and louder, no matter that Perley ignored it.

"Wait a minute!" Zeke exclaimed. "Maybe *she* is supposed to be in here. *She* might just be dressed up like a man. I think it'd be a good idea to pull them trousers off her and see if she is a woman."

When they started to move down the bar toward Perley, who was now facing them, it finally became too much for Raymond Patton to ignore. He got up from his chair and walked after them.

"Hold on, there, men — there's no need for that kinda trouble in here."

Zeke turned to face him. "Who the hell asked you? You'd best set back down there and keep your mouth shut."

"I'm the owner of this saloon, and we

don't stand for any harassing of our regular customers, so you'd best sashay right on out that door, and don't come back."

"You're talkin' mighty big," Zeke said. "Maybe I ain't ready to get out till I take a look at what ol' Precious, there, has between his legs. Whaddaya think about that?"

"I think you'll be a mess to clean up," Benny answered for his boss. "And it's my job to clean up around here."

They turned back to see the double-barreled shotgun resting on the bar, with the bartender sighting in on them, both hammers cocked.

"Whoa, Zeke!" Lige recoiled. "I believe he means what he says. Maybe we'd best do what the man wants."

Zeke hesitated, unwilling to back down, but there was no chance against the cocked shotgun. He considered himself handy with a six-gun, but there was no use in committing suicide.

"All right," he finally conceded. "You got the jump on me this time, but this business ain't none of yours anyway. It's between me and Precious, here." He glared at Perley, who had said nothing up to that point. "And you'd better stay clear of my path, 'cause next time I see you, you might have to use that gun you're wearin'."

"Ain't no cause for you to threaten Perley," Patton said. "He ain't done nothin' to rile you. Now you'd best be movin' along before I send somebody to get the sheriff."

"We're goin'," Lige said and grabbed Zeke by the arm. "Come on, Zeke."

Zeke allowed himself to be pulled toward the door, while Benny's shotgun followed him all the way. When they passed close by Perley, Zeke growled, "What did he call you, Precious? Pearly? That's a good name for you — Pearly Precious."

"Looks like we got off to a bad start, friend," Perley replied. "Most likely the likker talkin'."

Zeke laughed at Perley's weak response. "You'd best stay outta my way if you see me comin'," Zeke threatened. "Next time, you might not have somebody there to save you."

"That makes sense to me," Perley said. "I know I ain't got any desire to see you again."

Lige pulled his friend out the door, and Benny followed to make sure they were leaving. In a few seconds, he reported that the two had gotten on their horses and ridden down toward the stable.

"Damn it, Perley," Raymond Patton said, "I'm sorry you had to have something like that happen to you in my place. Those two

16

drifters had no reason to start in on you."

"Just the whiskey talkin'," Perley said. "Don't think nothin' of it. I didn't. I can't blame 'em for japin' me a little about comin' to the saloon to buy peppermint candy." He picked his candy up from the counter and stuck it in his shirt pocket. "I'd best hurry on back to Henderson's now and pick up my order."

When he got back to Henderson's store, he saw that Ben had loaded his packages in the back of the buckboard. *I appreciate that,* he thought, for he was anxious to get down to the Paris Diner, and now all he had to do was go in and pay for the merchandise. That took only a couple of minutes, and he said good-bye to the Hendersons.

Back outside, Perley took a quick minute to say good morning to Jenny McQueen, the blacksmith's wife. She was in the process of scolding her six-year-old son for playing around an old unused shack next to the store.

"I told him he could stay with his daddy at the shop, but every time Paul turns his back, this little mischief-maker winds up in this old snaky-looking shack. I declare, I wish Ben would tear it down."

"Yes, ma'am," Perley replied, taking time to be polite, even though he was eager to

17

get to the diner. "Places like that old shack just naturally call to little fellows with a spirit of adventure."

The youngster sidled back over to the door of the shack while his mother was distracted and began pulling on it again. Perley was puzzled then by the inquisitive frown on Jenny's face as she seemed to be looking beyond him.

"Well, I'll be damned," Zeke Cotton drawled. "Look here, Lige — it's ol' Pearly Precious."

Perley turned to discover the two drifters, who had walked their horses slowly up behind him while he had exchanged polite conversation with the blacksmith's wife. He had hoped they had left town, but it appeared they were going to be impossible to ignore.

"Reckon what they're talkin' about, Zeke?" Lige mocked. "Maybe they're exchangin' recipes."

Perley knew he was going to be forced to deal with them, no matter how he tried to avoid it. Jenny seemed confused by their remarks, and Perley wished she would grab her kid and be on her way, but she remained.

"You fellows have had a good time japin' me, but I reckon it's time for me to say that's enough. So whaddaya say you just ride on outta here now, and we'll all get back to our business."

"Why you . . ." Zeke started. "I've had about enough of you. You wanna get back to business, do ya? Well, my business is takin' care of smart-mouth son of a bitches like you."

"I'll have to ask you to watch your language around the lady and the little boy," Perley said.

"You son of a bitch!" Zeke spat. "You're wearin' a gun, so you'd better get ready to use it, or I'm gonna shoot you down where you stand." He stepped down from his horse and handed Lige his reins.

"Go get him, Zeke," Lige jeered. "He ain't got the guts to stand up to you. He's most likely peein' in his britches right now."

Confident that Perley would turn and run instead of standing to fight, Zeke walked a few steps back toward the street and stood ready to duel.

"I asked you politely to watch your language. Now you're gonna force me to do something that there ain't no call for at all," Perley said. He looked at the woman, standing wide-eyed and stunned, and said, "Jenny, take your son and walk away from here."

19

Seemingly paralyzed moments before, she suddenly realized that all hell was about to break loose. She turned to her son and screamed, "Tommy!"

But it was too late. The huge rattlesnake coiled just beneath the rotted-out boards of the old shack was already set to strike the youngster poking around its nest.

With no time to think, Perley spun around, drew his .44, and fired, splattering the rattler's head onto the walls of the shack. It happened in less than a second and left the two drifters, as well as the shaken mother, stunned.

Perley twirled the pistol on his finger and dropped it back in the holster; then he turned to face Zeke again. Unable to believe what he had just witnessed, Zeke found himself virtually paralyzed. It took Lige no more than a moment to realize Zeke was facing instant death.

"We're done here, mister. Come on, Zeke, we've got no more business in this town." He tipped his hat to Jenny. "Beg your pardon, ma'am, for our language."

Zeke, still suffering from the shock of the draw he had come close to facing, needed no further encouragement. Almost stumbling, he climbed onto his horse and followed Lige out the south end of the street, wanting no part in a shoot-out against a draw too fast to see.

Still shaking, Jenny McQueen finally asked, "Who were those men?"

"Ah, nobody important, I reckon," Perley replied, greatly relieved that the trouble had gone no further. "Just some drifters passin' through town. I'm real sorry you had to hear their rough language. They most likely ain't been around civilized ladies like you in a long spell."

He looked at Tommy, clutching his mother's skirt now. "Reckon this old shack ain't a good place to play. Looks like a family of rattlesnakes has moved in." Perley looked up to see Paul McQueen running from his forge. "Here comes your daddy, now, so I guess I'll get along."

He climbed up in the buckboard, since some other folks were running to investigate as well, and he didn't want to hang around to answer questions. "Maybe your daddy will skin that snake — make you a nice belt, like the Indians do."

"What was that shot I heard?" Paul asked excitedly when he ran up.

"Just shot a snake, Paul," Perley answered. "That's all it was. I think Tommy's thinkin' about skinnin' it."

He popped the horse with the reins, and the buckboard pulled off toward the diner.

He tied the horse at the rail before the small frame structure with the sign that proclaimed it to be the Paris Diner. Most of the locals referred to it as Beulah's Kitchen, since it was owned and operated by Beulah Walsh. Perley stepped up onto the stoop, removed his hat, and brushed his hair as best he could with his fingers.

This was an important day for Perley Gates, for he had made up his mind to let Lucy Tate know that he was interested in the two of them getting to know each other better. The slight distraction earlier with the two strangers had already left his mind, banished by his thoughts of developing something between himself and the attractive waitress. Lately, it seemed she had not disguised her interest in him, so it couldn't hurt to let her know that he was attracted to her as well.

"You goin' in?" a voice behind him asked.

"Yes, sir, excuse me — I was just tryin' to remember something," Perley mumbled to the elderly man on the step behind him. He opened the door and held it for the man. "After you, sir."

Perley stood there in the doorway for a

few moments while he looked over the dining room. He didn't see either of the two waitresses, so he passed by the long table in the center of the room and sat down at one of the small tables against the wall. He usually sat at the long table, but on this day, he preferred the privacy one of the side tables offered. In a minute or two, Becky Morris came from the kitchen with a full dish of potatoes. She set it down on the big table, then came over to greet Perley.

"Howdy, Perley. I didn't see you sneak in. Whatcha doin' sitting over here by yourself? Did they run you off from the big table?"

"Howdy, Becky," Perley answered. "I just thought it'd be easier to talk if I wasn't sittin' in the middle of the big table. Where's Lucy? Ain't she workin' today?"

Becky smiled. "Yes, Lucy's working today. She's in the kitchen. I'll tell her you're here. First, I'll get you some coffee, though." She left to get his coffee.

"Thanks, Becky," Perley said when she came back with a steaming cup of coffee; then she left him to tell Lucy he was there. Perley watched the slight girl until she disappeared through the kitchen door.

He liked Becky. She was always pleasant and cheerful, and almost always took the time to ask how his folks were doing.

Thoughts of her were immediately lost a few seconds later, however, when Lucy Tate walked in from the kitchen.

"Well, hello there, stranger," Lucy called out as she approached his table. "I was wondering what happened to you, you haven't been in for so long. I brought you a plate of stew. If you don't mind waiting a few minutes, I've got a fresh batch of biscuits coming outta the oven." Her smile seemed to warm the entire dining room. "Whatcha been up to? Keeping out of trouble?" she teased playfully.

Standing in the kitchen door, Becky watched Lucy charming the unsuspecting young man, and it suddenly made her angry. Lucy was a friend of hers, and Becky didn't care how she turned her charm on the young men around the town. She just wished Lucy wouldn't lead Perley on. He was especially vulnerable to her flirting, seeing as how shy he was in a woman's presence.

"You know me," Perley said, "tryin' my best to stay outta trouble." He swallowed hard, his mouth having suddenly gone dry as he realized he didn't know how to tell her what he had come to say. "I wanted to come by to see you before we get the cattle ready to drive to market," he finally managed. "I'll be gone for a couple of months, so I figured I'd best come in to talk to you before I go."

"About what?" she asked.

"You know," he stumbled, "about one thing and another."

He had hoped she would know what he wanted to say. She had to know, and she wasn't making it easy on him, so he dived right in. "You know I think a lot of you."

"Why, I think a lot of you, too, Perley," she replied. "You're a good friend."

"Well, I'm thinkin' maybe we could spend more time together," he came back weakly.

"Are you trying to say what I think you are?" A mischievous smile parted her lips.

"Yeah, I reckon I am," he confessed. "I was just thinkin' maybe I could call on you sometime when you ain't workin'."

"Well, that's really sweet of you, but I'm not interested in you in that way, but thanks for the offer." She smiled sweetly and walked back toward the kitchen. "I'll check on the biscuits."

He felt as if he had been shot, and wished at that moment that he had been. He felt like a fool for having interpreted her flirting as genuine interest in him. Sick to his stomach, he stared at the full plate of stew before him and knew he could not eat anything. He pushed his chair back and stood up, feeling that every eye in the room was on him. Knowing he had to escape, he shoved his hand in his pocket, pulled out some money to leave on the table, and headed for the door, his face flushed with shame.

"Perley! Wait!" Becky Morris ran after him. "Wait, Perley," she pleaded, until he finally stopped to untie his horse from the rail.

"I left the money on the table," he said, "if that's what you want."

"I don't care about the money," Becky said. "I care about you. I know what just happened back there. You don't have to be ashamed of getting the wrong impression from Lucy's flirting. You're not the first. It's a game she enjoys playing, and it's a terrible thing to play on someone as decent as you."

He finally looked up to meet her eyes. "Thanks, Becky. I 'preciate you comin' to tell me. I just feel like a damn fool, and I wanna find me a hole somewhere and crawl in it. I ain't nowhere near ready to court a woman anyway. I don't know what I was thinkin'."

"I know how it feels to be attracted to someone and know they don't feel the same way about you," Becky said.

"You do?" Perley replied. "Then I reckon that gives you and me something in common."

"That's right," Becky said. "That's something we'll always have between us, so don't let this keep you from coming back to the diner when you're in town. I always look forward to seeing you."

"Why, thank you, Becky, I 'preciate it. Now I reckon I'd best haul this stuff back home, before John or Rubin sends somebody to look for me."

He climbed up on the buckboard seat and turned the horse toward the street. She stood out in front of the diner and watched him until she heard Lucy's voice behind her.

"Hey, are you gonna help with these dishes, or are you gonna stand out here all day?"

Becky looked around to see Lucy standing in the doorway.

"He'll get over it," Lucy said.

"Lucy, you really are a bitch," Becky said. "That's the most decent man in this county."

Lucy laughed. "You think so, anyway."

CHAPTER 2

Rachel Gates walked out to the back porch, where her daughter was shelling peas for supper. "Esther, go down to the barn and get your brothers. Tell them to come up to the house."

Esther was struck by her mother's grave manner. Spoken softly and calmly, her words conveyed a heavy sadness, causing Esther to drop the pan filled with peas and ask, "Daddy?"

Her mother nodded solemnly. "I'm afraid so," she murmured. "Go fetch your brothers."

Rachel hesitated a moment or two to watch Esther run toward the barn, oblivious of the spilled pan of peas, half shelled, lying on the ground at the foot of the steps. She turned then and went back to the bedroom where her husband, Nathaniel Gates, lay in eternal sleep.

His death was not totally unexpected, for

he had taken a turn for the worse over the last few days, when he appeared to have come down with a pneumonia-like fever that didn't seem related to his accident. Up until that time, the whole family assumed he would recover from being thrown by a horse, landing him hard on his neck. It was not the first time he had been thrown, and every time before he had recovered, like the indestructible man that he had always been.

Rachel placed her hand on her husband's cold brow, then gently closed the stark blue eyes that gazed into the world beyond the life he had known. She took a step back when her daughter-in-law appeared at the bedroom door.

"What's wrong, Mama?" Lou Ann implored. Having seen Esther running to the barn, calling out to the men, she had paused only to pick up the pan of peas Esther had dropped before rushing into the house. "Is Papa all right?"

"He's gone," Rachel whispered, struggling to hold on to her emotions. "I just came in to see if he felt well enough to drink some coffee, and he was . . ."

Unable to finish, she tried to hold back the tears that choked her. Lou Ann stepped close and took her in her arms. They were both crying when Rubin and John ran into the room, with Esther close behind.

Rubin, the eldest of Nathaniel and Rachel Gates's sons, moved at once to comfort the two women, with his arms around both of them. Right behind him, John paused to stare at his father, barely able to believe he was dead.

"Perley's down near the river, lookin' for a bunch of strays that wandered off after that thunderstorm last night," he said, his gaze still fixed on his father. "I sent Sonny to find him."

They were joined then by John's wife, Martha. "What is it, John?" she asked upon seeing them gathered in her father-in-law's bedroom. "I was feeding the chickens when I heard you shouting to Sonny to go fetch Perley."

He held his arm out to her, and she, seeing something wrong, stepped inside his embrace.

"It's Papa," John said. "He's gone."

She gasped in response, even though she had already feared that to be the cause of the sudden gathering of the family. It was almost impossible to believe that the powerful head of the Gates family had succumbed to a fever that none of the family thought a serious threat.

Nathaniel Gates, having grown up on the

small farm his father had abandoned when Nathaniel's mother died, took it over and built it into the giant cattle ranch it was today. A small empire carved out of the Texas plains, it continued to grow under the hard work and guidance of Nathaniel's family, who were all gathered now in this sorrowful room, with the exception of one. Rachel, his widow; Rubin, the eldest son, with his wife, Lou Ann; John, one year younger than Rubin, and his wife, Martha; and Esther, Nathaniel's only daughter, all stood in shocked distress. The one surviving son missing was Perley, the youngest of the brothers at age twenty.

The Gates brothers, all strong, hardworking men, were cast in the same mold but were not identical after the final polishing. Rubin was born a serious man of high morals, with a sense of responsibility and total dedication to the family. John was equally moral but somewhat less serious in his approach to hard work. He was the strongest of the three brothers, but not by very much. The youngest, Perley, seemed not to be bothered by much of anything, taking whatever was offered at the dawning of each new day with the same open mind that he had the day before. The only one of the brothers who had not married, Perley had never exhibited any urgency to find the right woman, although his brothers accused him of being particularly fond of a young woman who worked in the diner in town. He was awarded the unusual and often fight-provoking name Perley Gates, to honor his grandfather, the original Perley Gates. When his grandfather was born, his mother had named him Perley, in hopes that it might help guide him to a righteous life that would see him approach the Pearly Gates of Heaven at his life's end. She was not an educated woman, so she misspelled his name, but that made little difference to the family.

The name proved to have minimal influence upon the life of the original Perley Gates, for he was born with a lust for wandering and a constant yearning to see the far side of the mountain. To his credit, he tried to harness his adventuresome nature, even to the point of taking a wife and trying to scratch out a living on a hardscrabble plot of ground in north Texas. His wife died not long after giving birth to their one son, Nathaniel, who was named after his wife's father. The boy was raised there on the farm by his mother's parents after Perley reached the end of his patience for the hard work of farming and left Texas to seek the peace he sought in the mountains to the northwest. Some years later, Nathaniel learned that his father had actually made it no farther than the Sans Bois Mountains in the Indian Territory of Oklahoma and was rumored to be living with a Choctaw woman in a shack somewhere in that small range of mountains. Nathaniel had no desire to contact his father upon learning that. It was not until years later, when he started his own family, that he began to understand the nature of his father and truly forgave him for his wanderlust. It was this change of heart that inspired him to name his youngest son Perley to show his sincere forgiveness, unaware that of his three sons, Perley was the most like his namesake.

"Perley!" Sonny Rice yelled when he saw him near the edge of the river.

Perley looked back from the bank to see the young hired hand loping toward him on the little paint mare the boy most often rode. Perley turned his attention back to the steer on the end of his rope and continued to back his horse up the bank. By the time Sonny rode up to a stop beside him, the cow Perley was in the process of rescuing found solid footing and scrambled up onto the bank.

Perley dismounted and removed the rope from the cow before asking, "What's up, Sonny?"

"It's your pa!" Sonny exclaimed. "I think he musta died. Everybody went runnin' up to the house, and John sent me to fetch you."

Perley was immediately concerned. Like the rest of the family, he had expected to hear that his father was beginning to recover. "Are you sure?" he asked, for sometimes Sonny got things mixed up in his head. "Did anybody say Pa was dead?"

"No, but they was all actin' kinda worried, and John told me to fetch you in a hurry."

"All right," Perley said. "Let's get goin', then."

He looked back at the cow he had just pulled out of the area of quicksand, to make sure it didn't venture back toward the same section of riverbank. When the steer trotted away to join the other cows farther up the river, Perley climbed back onto his horse and started toward the house.

Perley was not prepared to deal with his father's passing. Nathaniel had always been a paragon of strength and endurance that all of his sons tried to emulate. Now, as Perley rode the two miles back to headquarters, as the ranch was referred to, he hoped and prayed that Sonny had leaped to the wrong conclusion — but he feared the worst.

As soon as he pulled his horse up to the front porch of the house, he guessed that Sonny's assumption had been correct. John and Martha were out on the porch talking, and they stopped abruptly to greet him when he came up the steps. Martha's eyes were red from crying, and she held tightly onto John's arm as he relayed the sorrowful news to Perley.

"Papa's dead, Perley," John stated solemnly. "Rubin and Lou Ann and Esther are in the bedroom with him and Mama."

Perley shook his head slowly but made no reply. Martha released John's arm long enough to step forward and give Perley a firm hug before stepping back beside her husband. She wondered if the youngest son had had a premonition of his father's death, because he had acted strangely ever since he came back from town a few days ago. John had told her that Perley wanted to work alone out on the range with the cattle. She would not be surprised if Perley had received some kind of message in a dream, or something. There were folks who got those sorts of messages, and Perley was strange in a lot of ways.

Nathaniel Gates was buried on a grassy slope fifty yards behind the main ranch house, just beyond the two small cabins that his married sons lived in. The funeral was short and simple, just as her husband would have preferred, according to the grieving widow. The three sons dug the grave and built the crude coffin their father was to spend eternity in, using some of the lumber bought to repair the bunkhouse.

On the day after Nathaniel was laid to rest, the family gathered to discuss the management of the ranch from that day forward. It was assumed that Rubin would inherit the role of overseeing the operation of the cattle ranch, with no objection from either of the two younger sons. There was no one better qualified. Near the end of the family meeting, another item was brought up for discussion by the widow.

"There is one wish I know your father would have," Rachel said. "He talked to me many times about his father and his desire to make amends with him. He came to forgive his father for leaving him with his grandparents after his mother died. His grandma who raised him had always told

Nathaniel that his father couldn't help himself for his desire to wander." Rachel paused to brush away a tear. "Well, your papa never found time to search for his father and tell him that he had named Perley after him. So now I think we should try to find your grandpa and let him know that his son has passed away. I think he should know this."

"I don't see how we're gonna do that," Rubin said, "unless we go lookin' for him. And we've got too much work to do here this time of year." All hands on the ranch were preparing for the spring cattle drive, planning to start out for the railroad in Ogallala in two weeks' time.

"One of you boys can go," Rachel insisted. "I think we owe your father that. He wanted so much to make things right with his father, so we can at least let your grandpa know about his death."

Rubin still looked uncertain, so Rachel continued. "I think Perley should go look for him. You and John have wives to take care of. Perley doesn't, so I think he should go."

"Mama's right," John said. "We oughta at least tell the old man about Pa's death." He looked at Perley then and asked, "Whadda you think, Perley? You wanna ride up in

Indian Territory to see if you can find Grandpa? If he's still up there in the Sans Bois Mountains, you oughta be able to get up there and back before we start the cattle out for Ogallala."

Perley shrugged indifferently. "I reckon, if he's still there and if Mama thinks that's best."

He didn't express it, but any chance to get away from the routine of the ranch was always welcome, even in unhappy circumstances like these. When there were no objections from anyone, he shrugged again and announced, "I reckon I can start out in the mornin'."

Rubin walked out of the room with him after the family meeting. When out of earshot of the women, he spoke to Perley.

"I think it's important what Mama wants to do, and I hope you can find the old man up in those hills. But Perley, if you can't find him in a week, come on home. We need you on that cattle drive."

"I will," Perley said.

Since no one in the family knew for sure how to find his grandfather, Perley determined to start out on his search the next morning. He'd follow the Kiamichi River up into Indian Territory until reaching the

Kiamichi Mountains. He figured when he struck those mountains, he would head north of the river, hoping to find the Sans Bois Mountains, where his grandfather supposedly had his camp. Once he knew he was in the Sans Bois Mountains, his plan was to find someone who might know his grandpa and be able to tell Perley how to find the camp.

"If that doesn't work," he told his brothers, "I reckon I'll just comb those mountains till I stumble on Grandpa."

"Well, don't keep lookin' for him forever," Rubin repeated. "If you don't find him after a week or so, come on home. He mighta moved on to God knows where."

Perley nodded in reply.

"You got everything you need?" John asked. "You're gonna be gone for a while. Make sure you're takin' enough bacon and hardtack and coffee. I reckon you've got plenty of cartridges for your rifle."

Perley couldn't help chuckling. His two older brothers were fretting over him like a couple of worried parents. "I reckon I'll make out all right," he said. "I think I've got everything I'll need, and as long as I've got my rifle and cartridges, I reckon I won't starve."

With everything ready, he threw his saddle

on the big bay gelding he favored most. Working cattle, he used many different horses, but the bay was his personal horse. He was named Buck after Perley's brother John bet him a dollar he couldn't saddle-break the horse. Perley not only won the bet, but in the process, gained a four-legged friend that bucked off every other rider who climbed on his back. It didn't take long before all the crew at the Triple-G Ranch learned that it was no use cutting Buck out of the remuda, because they wouldn't stay in the saddle for long before the horse came back to the barn looking for Perley. His brothers chided him for making a pet of the horse, but they could not deny the big bay's strength and stamina.

On hand to see Perley off, one of the older ranch hands, Fred Farmer, was there to offer his help. Fred had spent a great deal of his life in the mountains of Oklahoma and suggested the best way for Perley to start looking for his grandfather was to go to a trading post he knew about in that part of the country.

"What you oughta do," Fred advised, "since you don't really know that country, is to follow the Kiamichi River up through the Choctaw Nation. It's gonna be about sixty-five miles or so after you cross the Red, but if you stay on the river, you're bound to strike that store. It's run by a feller named Russell Byers — I reckon he's still there. If he ain't, his son's most likely runnin' the tradin' post. There ain't any other places up that way for folks to buy supplies, that I know of."

" 'Preciate it, Fred," Perley said. "That's just what I'll do."

Ready to ride, he held up when his mother came out on the porch and called to him. She walked down the steps to stand at his stirrup.

"Here," she said and handed him a small velvet pouch. "This is the locket your grandfather gave your grandmother when they were married. Your grandfather might not believe you if you tell him you're his grandson. Show him the locket inside this pouch and he'll know."

She stepped back then, and he put the pouch in his inside vest pocket.

"And son," she said, "you be careful and come back home safely."

"I will, Ma."

He said good-bye then and rode out of the yard on Buck, leading a sorrel packhorse, heading north toward the Red River, two miles from the ranch. Once he crossed over into Oklahoma Territory, he would start up the Kiamichi for about twenty miles or so before resting his horses. Behind him, his brothers stood watching him until he passed through the front gate.

"Damned if that ain't a waste of time," John commented after Fred Farmer had left them to return to his work and their mother went back inside. "There ain't nothin' up in that part of the country that woulda kept Grandpa there for very long."

"I expect you're right," Rubin replied, "but if it'll bring Ma some peace, I reckon it's worth wastin' a little of Perley's time. I don't know if that old man is still alive after all these years. If he was, he mighta come back to Texas before now." He shrugged and said, "Maybe Perley can at least come back and tell her that Grandpa's long gone from there."

"I hope he'll be all right," John said. There was a definite hint of concern in his remark.

"Grandpa?" Rubin asked.

"No, Perley," John answered. "He's got a natural knack for walkin' right in the middle of trouble, when nobody else even comes close, and he's been actin' kinda quiet the last few days."

His comment brought a chuckle from Rubin. "He didn't tell you?"

When John looked puzzled, Rubin continued.

"He thought that little gal in the diner in town was shinin' up to him, and he found out she's been shinin' up to every other bachelor in the county. So, he's been feelin' kinda foolish for thinkin' about courtin' her." He chuckled again. "I told him he just ain't learned enough about women yet."

"Well, I swear," John chuckled. "I told him that he's gonna hafta start goin' to church to find the kind of gal he's lookin' for. Hell, Lucy Tate shines up to me every time I go in there."

Although his brothers felt a little sorry for him to have been saddled with a futile endeavor, Perley was of no such frame of mind. In fact, he was looking forward to what he perceived as an adventure and a welcome break from the usual mundane ranch chores. He had always held a curiosity about the man he had been named for, so who could be a better choice to go in search of his grandpa? As for the subject of Lucy Tate, he was grateful now that he had found out what a flirt she was before he made an even bigger fool of himself.

It was toward the middle of the second day when he came to the trading post Fred had

43

told him about. A low log structure sitting in a clearing close to the riverbank, the store appeared to have had two additions built onto the back of it. *No doubt to accommodate a growing family,* Perley thought. *He must be doing fairly well.*

As if to attest to that fact, there were three horses tied in front of the store at the hitching rail. In addition, there was a barn to one side of the store with several horses in the corral. Perley dismounted, looped Buck's reins over the end of the rail, and walked inside.

He paused at the door to allow his eyes time to adjust to the dimly lit room. A fire in the stone fireplace at the far end of the room was the only light, other than a lamp on the end of the counter.

"Well, howdy, stranger," a tall, thin man behind the counter greeted him. "It's gettin' a little raw outside, ain't it? I reckon the Good Lord ain't ready to call it summertime yet."

"That's a fact," Perley replied. "That fire yonder looks mighty friendly."

He glanced toward a table near the fireplace to see three men seated and obviously warming their insides with the contents of a glass jar. All three paused to take a good look at him. He turned his attention back to the man behind the counter.

"Would you by any chance happen to be Russell Byers?"

"No," he said, smiling. "I'm Bob Byers. Russell Byers is my pap. What can I do for you?"

"You know a man named Perley Gates?"

"Pearly Gates?" Bob replied. "Can't say as I do. Is that really a man's name?"

"Yes, sir. He's my grandfather, and last we heard of him, he was roamin' these parts — thought you mighta seen him down this way."

"Well, like I said, I ain't ever heard of anybody named Pearly Gates, but maybe my pap has," Bob suggested. "You wanna ask him?"

"Yes, sir, I surely would. Is he round about?"

"He's settin' in the kitchen, drinkin' coffee," Bob said. "Come on and you can ask him."

He led Perley to a door in the corner of the room that led to the kitchen and a white-haired old man seated at a long table.

When the door opened, the old man looked up quickly and asked, "Bob?"

"Yeah, it's me, Pa," Bob answered. "I've got a feller come to see you, lookin' for the Pearly Gates."

"Well, he ain't likely to find 'em lookin' in here," Russell Byers replied.

"I'm lookin' for a man *named* Perley Gates, Mr. Byers," Perley said. "I'm hopin' you might know something about him." It occurred to him that the old man was almost blind, judging from the way his gaze seemed to have trouble finding him. "My name's Perley Gates, too. The man I'm lookin' for is my grandpa."

"Perley Gates," Russell responded. "That's a name I ain't heard for a while, and that's a fact. Perley used to show up here every now and then, but not since my boy took over the store. And that's been over a year ago, ever since I got so damn blind I can't see what I'm doin'."

He reached for his coffee cup, just managing to grab it before he tipped it over. "You want some coffee? I would offer you somethin' stronger, but I never sold any likker. It's against the law here in the nations."

"I don't ever turn down a cup of coffee," Perley replied. He figured that Russell's son must have branched out into the whiskey business unbeknownst to the old man after he went blind. Thinking of the three men he had just seen in the store, he doubted that was apple juice they were drinking.

"Ruby!" Russell yelled. In a few moments,

a woman walked in from a back room. "Pour Mr. Perley Gates a cup of coffee."

Ruby, who Perley guessed to be a Choctaw, went to the cupboard at once to fetch a cup. She filled it and placed it on the table before Perley, giving him a faint smile before turning and leaving the room.

"Now, about your grandpappy," Russell continued, "did you look in that camp of his?"

"No, sir," Perley replied. "That's my problem. I ain't ever been to his camp, so I'm hopin' to find somebody who can tell me where it is."

He went on to explain why he had never seen his grandfather and the purpose of his search for him after so many years. "I need to tell him that his only son, my father, just passed away. We heard he had a place up in the Sans Bois Mountains, but I ain't got no idea where in those mountains. To tell you the truth, I ain't sure how to find the Sans Bois Mountains. I don't know much about the Oklahoma Territory this far east. The only time I've ever been in Oklahoma is on cattle drives up through Indian Territory on the Western Trail up to Kansas."

Russell slowly shook his head and scratched his beard thoughtfully before responding. "Well, I ain't never been to ol'

Perley's camp, myself," he said. "But I reckon I can tell you how to get to the Sans Bois Mountains."

"That's a start," Perley said. "I'd appreciate it — save me a lotta time."

"It's a pretty far piece from here," Russell started, "about fifty miles, but it's an easy trail to follow. Just make sure you take the right one, 'cause there's quite a few trails branchin' off from the river track that brought you to my store. They're goin' to different little settlements and farms, but the one that runs straight north to the Sans Bois is easy to find, if you know what to look for."

He went on to tell Perley to continue following the river trail for about another four miles until he came to a long, low ridge running parallel to the river. "There's a gap in the middle of that ridge, and the trail you want runs right through it. You'll know it; there's a big old cottonwood bent over almost to the ground right next to it. At least, there was. I reckon it's still there."

They talked for another twenty or thirty minutes before Perley took his leave, because Russell was happy to talk about Perley Gates. Listening to much of what Russell remembered, Perley learned that his old grandpa was somewhat of a character.

"I surely do appreciate your help, Mr. Byers," Perley finally declared, "and I thank you for the coffee."

"Not a'tall, Perley," Russell said, extending his hand. "You stop back to see me — let me know if you found your granddaddy."

Back in the store, Perley thought to thank Bob Byers as well on his way out. Before he reached the counter, he heard the taunting call of his name.

"Pearrrrleeee," one of the three sitting at the table called out, sounding close to a birdcall, causing his two companions to chuckle.

This was not the first time Perley had encountered someone mocking his name, so he ignored it and kept walking.

"Pearly Gates," one of the other two called out then. Evidently finding it to be hilarious, they all laughed heartily.

With no desire to rise to the bait to defend his name, especially with three drunks, Perley continued to the bar to thank Bob for his help. He was a little irritated to see Bob with a wide grin on his face and knew at once that he had informed the drinkers that his name was Perley Gates.

"Wanna thank you for your help," Perley said anyway. "I enjoyed talkin' to your pa."

Behind him, he heard the unmistakable

49

sound of chairs being shoved back from the table, and he knew he was going to be unable to avoid a confrontation. He turned to face the challenge, relieved somewhat to see that there was only one man walking toward him. The other two had just pushed their chairs back in order to more comfortably watch the fun certain to come.

A fairly tall man, although gangly in his build and walk, favored Perley with a drunken grin. It was easy to guess he and his friends were most likely small-time outlaws, maybe cattle or horse thieves. Aided no doubt by the courage found in a jar of whiskey, the man strode up unsteadily, stopping almost in Perley's face.

"Is your name Pearly Gates, like them gates up in Heaven?"

Aware then that the man was even drunker than he had first appeared to be, Perley took a step back to avoid his breath. "Yes, sir, it sure is, only it ain't spelled the same," he answered. "What's yours?"

This seemed to confound the belligerent drunk for a moment. "Ain't none of your business what my name is," he finally slurred.

"I reckon you're right," Perley said, favoring him with a friendly smile. "It was mighty neighborly of you to come over to say

50

howdy. I'd like to stay and chew the fat with you, but I expect I'd best get along."

"What's your hurry, friend?" The drifter took a step closer.

Forced to take another step backward, Perley was still determined to avoid the trouble the bully was just as determined to provoke. "I've got a ways to ride today, so I'd best get started. Otherwise, I'd enjoy hangin' around and jawin' with you and your friends."

He took a step to the side, thinking to walk around his antagonist, but the drunken drifter stepped in front of him again. Seeing he was not to have a choice, Perley exhaled a long sigh of resignation and said, "All right, friend, you've had your laugh makin' fun of my name, but I've wasted all the time I plan to on the likes of you. Now, if you'll step outta my face, I'll get on my way and you and your partners can get back to suckin' foolishness outta that jar."

Perley's remarks served only to draw another drunken grin across the bully's face, evidence that Perley had finally responded in a fashion that was going to call for the drunkard to fight or back down. Too late, Perley realized that the man was now even more encouraged to call him out, if only to avoid any appearance of backing

51

down in front of his companions.

"Mr. Pearly Gates," he slurred, "you're wearin' a gun and I'm callin' you a low-down yellow boot-lickin' dog. We'll settle this thing out in the yard, and if you don't come out to face me, I'll come in and send your sorry ass to them Pearly Gates you're named after. If you ain't man enough to stand up to me, you can get down on your knees and lick my boots. And just maybe I'll let you live." He looked back at the table. "That'd be all right, wouldn't it, boys?"

"Yeah, boy!" one of his friends blurted. "That'd do it all right, Poss — down like a dog!" Both men roared with delight at the prospect.

Perley, you've stepped in another cow pie, he thought, remembering what his brothers would say when he found himself in a mess. He stood gazing at his challenger, who appeared to be getting drunker by the moment. Perley had to wonder if the man would be able to walk out in the yard without falling on his face. As disgusted as he was, Perley had no desire to shoot the belligerent ass. It would be like shooting a bird in a cage.

"All right," he decided. "You want to shoot it out, so that's what we'll do. But we're gonna do it fair and square, Poss." He paused. "Is that your name?" He received no more than a foolish grin in response. "Bob, here, can be the judge — make sure everything's on the level. All right, Bob?"

Bob nodded, anxious to see the shooting, and Perley continued.

"We'll both empty our handguns and leave one cartridge in the chamber, just like a real duel, so we'll both get one shot. Is that agreed?"

"Yeah, yeah," Poss mumbled. "One shot, let's get started."

"Empty your gun," Perley said, but Poss made no move to do so.

"That's right, Poss," Bob Byers said, taking enjoyment in his role as judge of the duel. "Empty 'em all but one. Them's the rules." He watched as both participants emptied cartridges out of their cylinders.

"This duel is between Poss and me," Perley said, glancing at the two still sitting at the table as he spoke. "Whoever's left standing gets to walk away without any trouble from anybody else."

"Sure," one of the men replied. "You don't have to worry 'bout that." He nudged his friend beside him and laughed. "He don't know how fast ol' Poss is."

"All right, then," Perley said. "Let's go." They all went outside to witness the shoot-out between the two antagonists, some a little more unsteady than others. Unnoticed by the group, Perley pulled Buck's reins off the hitching rail as he walked past and flipped them over the saddle horn. Bob, still acting in his official capacity as judge, laid down the rules. The duelers stood back-to-back, their guns holstered while he gave them instructions.

"When I say go, start walking. I'll count to ten, and when I say *ten,* that'll be the signal to turn and shoot. The fastest gun will decide the winner, I reckon."

When both participants nodded agreement to the rules, Bob said, "All right — one," and they started pacing off the distance.

At the sound of "ten," both men turned. Confident but not above cheating, Poss anticipated the count early, actually reaching for his .44 a fraction of a second before Bob yelled *ten,* firing the shot as he turned, before Perley's gun cleared his holster.

As Perley had gambled upon, however, Poss's shot was wide by a good five feet because he was too drunk to shoot accurately. His miss served to suddenly sober Poss up considerably, especially since Perley had not taken his shot as yet and seemed in no hurry to do so as he carefully took aim.

Frozen in a paralyzing panic, Poss thought to turn and run, but didn't seem capable of making his feet move. The few onlookers seemed just as shocked, as Perley cocked the hammer back and drew down on the helpless man. With no real desire to kill a man, even this fool, he lowered the pistol, pulled the trigger, and shot Poss in the foot. The shocked silence was broken by the sound of the .44, followed by a painful howl from Poss, as he hopped around in a circle on his good foot.

Perley pressed a thumb and a finger against his lips to blow a sharp whistle. In a matter of seconds, the bay gelding trotted up beside him, leading the sorrel. Perley holstered his .44 and stepped up into the saddle. Pausing only long enough to bid them all good day, he nudged Buck and was on his way at a lope. When he reached the river trail, he looked back to see Poss sitting on the ground, trying to get his boot off while the three witnesses stood around gaping.

With Perley out of sight, Poss's two friends helped him up onto the porch and sat him down on a bench. While they got his boot and sock off, Bob went inside to find something to treat the wound with. He was searching under the counter for some rags when his father came from the kitchen.

"You in here, Bob?" Russell asked. When Bob replied, Russell added, "What was the shootin'?" When Bob told him what had just happened, the old man chuckled. "Shot him in the foot?" Bob said he did, causing his father to chuckle again. "Perley Gates," he said, "just like his grandpa."

CHAPTER 3

Relieved to finally be on his way, Perley held Buck to a steady lope for a good mile or so before reining him back to a comfortable walk. It was getting along in the afternoon, and he had already spent more time at the trading post than he could have foreseen. In a little while, he saw the long ridge paralleling the river, so he started watching for the trailhead Russell Byers had told him to look for.

As the old man had said, there were several small trails cutting away from the more traveled river trace, but as he had also predicted, the one Perley sought was easily identified. The gap up the middle of the ridge was obvious, and there was still a tall cottonwood that appeared to have been bent and almost uprooted by a high wind. Perley paused for only a few moments to look back the way he had come, not really expecting any pursuit from Poss or his drunken friends, before starting again. Then, leaving the river behind, he took the trail through the gap, heading almost straight north.

The country he rode through became more hilly and heavily forested the farther he went, but with no mountains in sight. He reminded himself that Russell had said it was at least fifty miles to the small mountain chain called the Sans Bois. He hoped he could cut that distance in half before having to make camp that night. There were no signs that the trail he was following was heavily traveled. In fact, he began to wonder if it was used by anyone, for it was narrow and grown over in places by bushes and tree branches. He suspected it was an old Indian trail that was no longer used after the relocation of the tribes.

It was almost dark by the time the trail crossed a narrow stream, so he decided he'd best make camp there since it was the first water he had come across in the last two hours. He turned Buck upstream and followed the water for about fifty yards before settling on a spot where the stream widened a few feet and there were a few patches of grass on the banks. He couldn't help thinking that he could have probably built his fire in the middle of the trail and nobody would know the difference, for he had seen no sign of anyone else having used the trail in a long time.

In the afternoon of the next day, the narrow trail ended at a wagon road running east and west along the southern side of a mountain range. He felt sure the mountains were the Sans Bois, and the road had to be the trail to Fort Smith, Arkansas, because it was obviously well traveled. Russell Byers had told him that he would be about a mile east of the joining of two roads, one from McAlester and the other from Atoka.

He took a long look at the mountains before him. They were not high mountains, but they seemed high in contrast to the flatter land around them, and the heavily forested slopes showed no signs of inhabitants. *Well,* he thought, *I think I found the Sans Bois. Now how the hell am I going to find Grandpa?* He nudged Buck with his heels and started up the road toward Fort Smith.

He hadn't traveled far when he came upon what looked to be a wide creek, and he was happy to see a trading post beside it. It was a small affair, little more than a shack actually, but a roughly lettered sign over the porch proclaimed it to be Brown's Store.

There was a dark-haired man with a bushy gray beard sitting on the porch in a rocking chair, smoking a corncob pipe. Perley turned Buck off the road and pulled up before the porch. The man watched him intently as he dismounted but didn't bother getting up from his chair.

"How do, young feller? Ain't never seen you pass this way before. Dewey Brown's the name. Welcome to my store. Maybe I've got whatever you're short of."

"Howdy," Perley returned. "Mostly I just need a little information. I could use some help findin' somebody."

Dewey frowned at that, his dark eyebrows lowering in a squint. "You a lawman? I know most of the deputy marshals that ride this territory, but I don't recall seein' you. What's your name?"

"Perley Gates," he answered and was interrupted before he could say more.

"Hell, no, you ain't," Dewey replied. "I know Perley Gates, and you sure as hell ain't him."

Perley smiled, happy to hear his response. "I expect that's my grandpa you're talkin' about. I was named after him, and I sure ain't a lawman."

Dewey paused to consider that, not yet sure he could believe him. He got up from his chair and stood at the edge of the tiny porch to study Perley as he dismounted. "Perley's your grandpa, huh? You don't favor him none."

"Reckon not," Perley said. "Folks say I don't favor anybody in my family, but we're pretty sure I ain't a bastard. So, my pa named me after my grandpa, and that's who I'm lookin' for."

He went on to tell Dewey why he was trying to find his grandfather and why it happened that his family didn't know where to look for him. "Last we heard, he's got a place around these mountains somewhere."

Dewey listened, somewhat fascinated. "I'll be go to hell," he remarked. "Perley never said nothin' about havin' a family down in Texas. Closest thing to a family I ever heard about was a Choctaw woman that stayed with him for a spell, and I think she run off on him." He paused to scratch his head while he thought about it. "I was thinkin' about ol' Perley the other day, wonderin' why I ain't seen him in a while. Come to think of it, I bet it's been six or eight months since I've seen him. He used to show up here every month or so, lookin' to trade some hides for coffee and flour. Hope he ain't come to no bad luck — run into some of them damn outlaws that like to hole up in these hills, or somethin'.'"

Perley listened patiently before pressing for the information he came for. "I'd like to find him to see if he's all right. Maybe you can tell me how to get to his place."

"I know about where it is," Dewey said. "I never been there. I never go anywhere, matter of fact. I ain't got nobody to watch my store for me. There's a cave up in them hills that's a favorite place for outlaws to hole up. It's right in the middle of this mountain range, and I've heard Perley say his camp ain't too far from it. Matter of fact, he said it was too damn close to suit him; said he'd run into some of them jaspers once in a while."

"I'd appreciate it if you would tell me how to find that cave," Perley said. "At least, that would give me someplace to start lookin' for Grandpa."

"Sure," Dewey replied. "What I said about Perley's camp, it's the same thing for that outlaw cave. I know *about* where it is, but not exactly. Like I said, I don't get away from the store very often." He started to give directions but stopped when it became clear the way was more complicated than Perley would likely remember. "Come on inside," he said. "I'd best draw you a map."

Perley followed him inside and waited

while Dewey tore off a piece of wrapping paper and found a pencil. Then he proceeded to sketch a rough map, which Perley was grateful for when he saw the many turns and trails he would have to recognize.

Feeling he should buy something from Dewey since he had made such an effort to help him, Perley bought a sack of coffee beans with some of the money he had brought with him. Even though he didn't really need them, it was always a good idea to have extra coffee. He thanked Dewey then and set out on the road to Fort Smith, planning to go as far as he could before darkness caught him.

He had ridden only about two miles when he reached the first turn on his map, a trail that forked off between two hills. The trail took him deeper and deeper into the mountains, winding through slopes of oak, pine, and some hickory, until he came to a fork where Dewey had indicated he should turn off to take a new trail. He continued until darkness began to threaten the slopes, and when he came to a stream, he decided to call it a day and make camp while he could still see.

As he unloaded his horses and prepared to build a fire a couple of dozen yards from the trail, he thought about the solitude of his surroundings. He wondered if this was what his grandfather had needed most, and while Perley might understand it, he knew for sure he hadn't inherited that trait from his namesake. Solitude might be good every once in a while, but he couldn't remember meeting a man who had lived alone for many years without getting funny in the head.

After a peaceful night, morning found Perley studying his crudely drawn map. He wished it would have been possible for Dewey to note the distances between points, so he might have some idea how long it was going to take to reach the rough circle at the end. The circle represented no place in particular, since Dewey didn't know exactly where his grandfather's camp was located. But it would tell him where to start looking, so he saddled up to continue his search.

He had not ridden more than a few minutes when he heard a rifle shot. He pulled Buck up at once to listen for more shots, but there was just the one. It sounded to be no more than a mile or two away, and in the midst of hills now surrounding him, he could only guess from which direction it had come.

Most likely it was someone hunting, he figured. Deer, maybe, and he wondered if he should try to find out for certain. If it was a hunter, as he suspected, the man might know where his grandfather's camp was. If it was a shot fired for some other reason, it might be in his best interest to know that as well, so he decided to find out.

Judging by the sound and the echo of the shot, he guessed that it may have come from the west of him, so he turned Buck toward a narrow gap between two hills in that direction. Finding a game trail between the hills, he followed it cautiously, lest he suddenly expose himself to whoever had fired the rifle.

After about fifty yards, the game trail led down a gradual slope toward a wide stream. He pulled up short just before starting down when he suddenly spotted the shooter. Perley had guessed right, for the man was securing a young deer on his horse, preparing to step up into the saddle. He was dressed in animal hides, so it was hard to tell at that distance if he was looking at an Indian or a white man, so Perley decided to watch him for a little while before making contact.

He held Buck and the sorrel back in the cover of the trees until the hunter started up the trail on the other side of the stream. Then he signaled Buck to go forward. Once across the clearing and the stream that bisected it, the trail climbed gradually for about seventy-five yards before starting back down again. About to follow, Perley reined Buck back when he realized he had lost sight of the man. Afraid he may have been spotted, he backed the bay gelding a few paces to take advantage of some bushes crowding the game trail.

He was thinking that he might have gotten himself spotted by following too closely, so he considered doing an about-face before the hunter took a shot at him. Then he noticed the top of a narrow ravine beyond the bushes, with a rocky path down the middle of it. That was why he had lost sight of the hunter! The man had evidently ridden down the ravine; the loose gravel disrupted at the start of the path verified it.

Determined to be a little more cautious now, Perley dismounted and led his horses down the steep path, alert for anything resembling an ambush. Even as he did this, he kept telling himself he should have hailed the hunter as soon as he came upon him at the stream. If the man discovered him now, he might naturally think he was being stalked. *Rubin and John would be ragging my ass if they saw me,* Perley couldn't help thinking. If there wasn't but one cow pie on the entire ranch, Perley would step in it, John liked to say. He decided to look a little farther, anyway. *After all,* he reasoned, *if I'm close to Grandpa's camp, this fellow most likely knows where it is, if he hunts around here.*

He continued down the path until reaching the bottom of the ravine, where it opened upon a grassy clearing. Looking across the clearing, he saw a cabin built up against the face of a cliff. In front of it, the man he had been following was in the process of taking his deer carcass off his horse. With his back toward the ravine, he had not as yet seen Perley.

Close enough now to see the hunter clearly, Perley realized that he was older than he had appeared from a distance. At the moment, he was struggling to pull the deer off, his short legs bowing under the deadweight.

"Hello the camp!" Perley yelled.

Thinking to call out a neighborly greeting, Perley instead scared the hell out of the little old man, causing him to jerk backward, pulling the carcass off the horse in the process. Although he landed on the ground with his deer on top of him, the sprightly old man rolled out from under his doe and scrambled up to draw his rifle from the saddle sling.

Startled when he realized the old man was set to defend himself, Perley called out frantically, "Whoa, mister! Ain't no call for that!" When the old man cranked a cartridge into the chamber, Perley suddenly came to the conclusion he was about to get shot.

The first thought after that initial panic was that his horses were in danger, since he was standing beside them, so he took off running toward a large oak stump thirty yards off to his left. He still had ten yards to cover when the bullets began kicking up clods of grass and dirt around his feet, stopping only after he reached the safety of the stump.

After a few moments without rifle fire, Perley yelled, "What the hell's wrong with you? You coulda killed me!"

"I still could!" the man yelled back. "Sneakin' up on a man like that . . . whadda you want with me?"

"I wasn't sneakin' up on you," Perley replied. "You just didn't notice me passin' by. That's why I yelled to you — tryin' to say howdy."

"Passin' by?" he responded. "Passin' by? How the hell could you be passin' by my cabin? You had to follow me down that damn ravine to get here!"

He had him dead to rights on that one, Perley thought. "You're right," he yelled back. "But I was just tryin' to catch up with you. I ain't out to cause you any trouble. I just figured you could help me find somebody I'm lookin' for. Hell, if I was set on doin' you any harm, I woulda just shot you when you had your back turned to me instead of hollerin' at you like I did."

Evidently, the old man considered the possibility of that being the fact of the matter, for he didn't reply for a long moment. When he did, he called out, "Who you lookin' fer?"

"My grandpa," Perley answered. "He's supposed to live around here somewhere."

"Grandpa, huh?" It was obvious that he was still wary of the stranger. Finally, he said, "All right, come on out from there, but I'm still holdin' this rifle, in case you ain't tellin' me the straight of it."

"I ain't lookin' to cause you any trouble," Perley said. "I'm comin' out. You ain't gonna shoot me, are you?"

"Not if you're tellin' me the truth."

The man stood watching Perley as he came out from behind the cover of the stump and walked toward him. When Perley stopped beside the carcass of the doe, the old man asked, "What's your name,

69

young feller?"

"Perley Gates," he answered, not expecting the violent reaction it caused.

"Perley Gates!" the old man erupted, and swung his rifle up again to aim at Perley's belly. "You got no right to this cabin!" he charged. "You abandoned it for good and all, and I've still got the paper to prove it. You might as well git on your horse and clear outta here right now before I put a couple of holes in your belly."

Perley suddenly feared he had once again stepped in the cow pie. Convinced he was facing a man with a severe case of mountain fever, he couldn't imagine what he had said to set him off to rant like a crazy man. "Hold on a minute," he said as calmly as he could affect. "You've got nothin' to fear from me. I ain't lookin' to steal your cabin. The only thing I wanted was to know if you might be able to tell me where I might find my grandpa. He's got a camp in these parts somewhere. If you don't know where it is, then I'll say I'm sorry to have bothered you, and I'll be on my way. And I'd appreciate it if you'd lower that rifle. It's givin' me an itch in my belly button."

There was a certain sincerity in the young stranger's manner that prompted the old man to wonder if he had misjudged him.

Still holding the rifle on him, an unlikely possibility suddenly struck him. "What is your grandpa's name?"

"Perley Gates, same as mine," Perley answered.

The old man slowly lowered his rifle to his side and paused, still wary. When Perley made no move to take advantage of it, he said, "Looks to me like we got off on the wrong foot. My name's Merle Teague. I never met your grandpa, but I've got somethin' you need to see. Wait on the porch, there, while I fetch somethin' from the house."

Reasonably sure that he was no longer in danger of getting shot, Perley did as Merle asked and stepped up onto the tiny porch. In a matter of seconds, Merle came back from inside, holding a piece of cardboard.

"Can you read?" he asked.

When Perley said that he could, Merle handed the cardboard to him and watched him while he read, *Whoever finds this place is welcome to it. This is a good warm cabin. I bilt it and it has served me good. I won't be back.* It was signed *Perley Gates.*

Merle continued to study Perley as he read it again. "Like I said, I never had the pleasure of meetin' your grandpa, so I ain't got no idea where he was headin' when he

left here. But you found his cabin, all right."
He hesitated before adding, "*My* cabin now.
I wish I could help you, but I can't."

Reading the obvious disappointment in
Perley's face, Merle offered an invitation.
"You any good at skinnin' a deer?"

Perley said that he was fair to middling.

"If you ain't in a big hurry, why don't you
help me butcher this deer, and we'll roast
us up a mess of it?"

"That sounds to my likin', for sure," Perley said, a smile now replacing the frown
the news of his grandpa had brought. "I
wasn't figurin' on eatin' breakfast till it was
time to rest my horses, but I can't see myself
passin' up fresh-killed deer meat."

"Good," Merle replied. "It'll be a pleasure
to have some company for a change. I'd offer to boil us up some coffee, but I've been
out for a spell, now."

"I reckon I can bring that to the feast,"
Perley said, thinking of the extra coffee
beans he had just bought from Dewey
Brown.

Perley couldn't deny a feeling of closeness
with his grandfather once he realized that
he had found the old man's cabin, the cabin
that he had no doubt built himself. After
Perley had taken care of his horses, he
helped Merle hang the deer carcass from

the limb of an oak tree that looked to have been used for that purpose many times. Merle built a fire outside in the yard, and before long, there was freshly butchered venison roasting over the flames. While they worked, Perley took special note of everything about the camp — the cabin, the corral, the shed that substituted for a barn — and he imagined his grandfather's existence there. He thought that he could almost feel his presence.

While they ate, Perley told Merle the purpose of the quest he had undertaken, to tell the original Perley about the death of his only son.

"Now that you found out he ain't here no more, whaddaya gonna do, go on back to Texas?" Merle asked.

Perley hesitated only a moment before answering, because he suddenly realized that he wasn't ready to return to the ranch. Maybe he had more in common with his grandfather than just the name. There were a lot of places he hadn't seen, and he felt a hankering to see what was beyond the horizon. He was at once mindful of what his brother Rubin had told him, and he knew the obvious thing to do was to get on his horse and head back home. He was needed on the cattle drive, but Perley was reluctant to give up after the first setback. It seemed a lot of bother to ride all the way up there only to turn around without looking any further.

"No, I reckon not," he answered, "but danged if I know where to go from here. My pa told me that Grandpa had always regretted that he had never gone to see the Rocky Mountains before he settled down with a wife. Maybe he took off to go there, but the Rockies cover a lot of territory, and they're a helluva long way from here. I wouldn't know where to start lookin'."

"I don't know how old your grandpa is," Merle said, "but I'd guess he must be about my age, don't you reckon?" Perley shrugged and Merle continued. "I figure I'm too damn old to set out to see the Rocky Mountains, but if I had the itch so bad I couldn't stand it, I reckon I'd head to Denver. Maybe he felt the same way. Maybe he set out for Colorado Territory, someplace like that. That's still a far piece — about two weeks of hard ridin' from here, I expect — but it's closer'n Montana."

He studied Perley carefully, as if truly interested in what his decision might be. It was obvious that Perley was thinking hard about it. "If I was a little bit younger, I'd think about goin' with you. I ain't never

74

seen the Rockies, myself."

"Hell," Perley finally blurted, reminding himself that he had obligations to his family. "I can't go ridin' off to the Rockies. I've gotta help my brothers push a herd of cattle up to Ogallala."

"Well, I reckon that settles that," Merle declared. "Cut you off another slice of that meat."

Perley ate his fill of the roasted venison and drank a couple of cups of coffee before he thanked Merle for his hospitality and prepared his horses to leave. He left the rest of the sack of coffee beans with him, for which Merle was extremely grateful and apologized for shooting at him. Perley assured him that he hadn't taken it personally. They shook hands, Perley gave Buck the signal to start with a gentle nudge of his heels, and he rode back up the ravine to retrace his tracks. He felt like he now had a friend in Merle Teague, which was not unusual. Perley made friends easily.

When he got back to the Fort Smith road, he turned Buck to the west, thinking he still had plenty of time to return to Texas. He might as well go home by a different way, just in case he had a streak of good luck and ran into someone who had seen his grandfather — maybe as the old man was on his way west. According to what Dewey had told him, this road would lead him to Atoka. He could cut back south from there. He had asked Merle how far it was to Atoka, and he had said about sixty miles, so Perley figured to make it by midday tomorrow.

Common sense told him that if his grandpa had gone to Denver, he would most likely have taken the road to McAlester instead of going through Atoka. But although Perley didn't know much about Atoka, he did know it had a railroad station, so there might be someone who could recall an old man on his way to the Rockies. Even as he thought it, he knew the odds of that were zero. As he was about most endeavors, however, he started out with a positive attitude and an expectation for good luck.

The road he traveled took him in a steady southwest direction through a range of high hills that might even be considered low mountains. It was evidently an often-traveled trace, judging by the tracks of hooves and wagon wheels, but he met no one along his way.

Since there seemed to be frequent streams, he decided to ride on after the sun began to sink on the horizon before finally making his camp beside a slow-moving creek. Guiding Buck along the creek bank, he rode about twenty-five yards from the road before settling on a wide patch of grass that offered grazing for his horses.

With plenty of wood for a fire, he unwrapped the cloth holding a piece of venison that Merle had insisted he should take with him. As he held it over the fire to cook, he thought about the gray-haired little man in buckskins and his remark that if he was a little younger, he'd go to see the Rockies. Perley could understand that urge, and he wondered if he would one day find himself lamenting the fact that he had never gone when he was young enough to do it. *Maybe not,* he thought as he turned the piece of venison over when it began to sear.

CHAPTER 4

He rode into the town of Atoka close to noontime, sooner than he had expected to, a result of having pushed Buck and the sorrel a little farther before making camp the night before. He crossed the railroad tracks at a slow walk, then rode the length of the short street to look the town over. There wasn't much to see — a few stores and shops, a general store, stables, and at one end, close to the shack that served as a train station, there was a rooming house. His interest was caught by a building next to it, proclaiming itself to be Mabre's Diner.

"I might wanna do a little business there," he said to Buck. "But first I'll stop at the general store in case Grandpa stopped there on his way through here." The big bay gelding seemed not to be impressed one way or the other, so Perley said, "Then I'll let you rest a bit while I sample the victuals in that diner."

"Good day to ya," Tom Brant called out from behind the counter when Perley walked into his store. "What can I do for you?"

"Good day to you," Perley answered. "I don't reckon I need any supplies. I was just wantin' to ask you if you mighta noticed an old man passin' through town a few months ago. His name's Perley Gates. He's my grandpa, and I'm tryin' to catch up with him." As soon as the question left his lips, Perley realized how foolish it was, and he was not surprised by the answer he got.

Brant didn't reply immediately, as he took a brief moment to think how to respond without sarcasm. "I can't rightly say," he started. "We get strangers passin' through town right along. Not a whole lot of 'em, but too many for me to see every one of 'em. So, I don't remember seein' anybody with a name like that. I think I mighta remembered that. Anything else I can help you with?"

"No, sir," Perley replied. "I'm sorry to have bothered you." He turned and walked back out the door.

Brant's wife, Eva, walked to the end of the counter, having caught a glimpse of Perley as he went through the door. "Who was that?" she asked her husband.

"Damned if I know," Tom said and chuckled. "Just some fellow looking for his grandpa. I've never seen him before."

She went to the front window in time to see Perley climb into the saddle. "Nice-looking young man," she commented.

His next stop was at the stable, where he negotiated with Stanley Coons to leave his horses there to rest and water. Coons quoted him a reasonable price for a full portion of oats for both horses as well. When asked what brought him to Atoka, Perley simply said that he was trying to track his grandpa, without going into detail. Coons didn't recall anyone named Perley Gates and wasn't interested enough to pursue the subject. He left Perley to unpack the sorrel and pull the saddle off the bay. After he turned the horses out in the corral, Perley walked back up the street to the diner.

"Howdy, young fellow," Lottie Mabre greeted him when he walked in. "You lookin' for some food?"

"Yes, ma'am," Perley answered. "Something smells mighty good in here."

He glanced at the long table in the center of the room. There were half a dozen men seated at the table. All paused momentarily to eyeball the stranger before resuming a concentrated attack on the plates before them.

"I reckon I'd better take a seat before it all gets ate up."

"Don't you worry," Lottie said. "I'll make sure you get fed."

"Thank you, ma'am." Then, in an effort to be friendly, he asked, "Are you Mable?"

She responded with a puzzled look. "No, my name's Lottie. Who's Mable?"

"I don't know," he fumbled. "I mean, I was just readin' the sign out front, and I figured you were the owner, or something."

"I am the owner," she said, still curious. Then it occurred to her. "The sign! Did you think it said Mable's Diner? It's Mabre's Diner. I'm Lottie Mabre. My husband and I own this diner and the rooming house next door. We used to call it the Atoka Diner. Maybe I shouldn't have changed the name on the sign." She favored him with a benevolent smile before going to the kitchen while the diners at the table chuckled.

"I reckon I didn't take a close enough look at it," he mumbled.

Feeling much like a backward child, he nodded politely toward a man and woman seated at a small table on the side wall who were also smiling at him. Then he sat down, to be confronted with several smiling faces from the men at the table.

In a few moments, Lottie was back at the table with a plate filled with stew for him. She picked up the empty bread plate from the center of the table.

"I'll be back with some more bread," she said, then paused. "I believe this is the first time you've eaten with us."

"Yes, ma'am, first time," he replied, already over the embarrassment for having bungled her name. "This is fine stew," he said after one bite.

"Best in town," she replied with a wide smile.

"*Only* stew in town," one of the other diners said.

"You'd best watch your mouth, Rob," she came back at him, "else I might have to refuse your business. You eat too much for the price anyway." She looked back at Perley. "What's your name, honey?"

"Gates," Perley replied. Having already embarrassed himself, he thought to avoid any more discomfort over his name.

"Well, Gates, I appreciate your business," she said. "I hope we'll see you in here again."

"Thank you, ma'am. If I'm back this way again, I'll surely stop in to see you."

Feeling he was in friendly company, he

finished his meal. Just to make sure he didn't miss any possible clue, he asked Lottie if she'd seen an old man named Perley Gates. She hadn't.

After saying so long to his diner friends, he paid for his meal and returned to the stable. When he was saddled up and ready to leave, he asked Stanley Coons for some help.

"I never got up this far in this part of the Nations, but I have come up a little north of Durant on Clear Boggy Creek. I'm on my way back to Lamar County in Texas, and that's southeast of here. Instead of riding on south to Durant, I'd make a shorter ride if I follow Clear Boggy Creek back to the Red River. What I'd like to know is, how far south of Atoka do I have to ride before I strike Clear Boggy Creek?"

"Clear Boggy is about ten miles south of Atoka," Coons said. "You'll know it when you strike it. It's a pretty good-sized creek."

"Much obliged," Perley said and started out on the road along the railroad tracks to Durant.

He had ridden for what he estimated to be at least ten miles when he came to the creek. As Coons had predicted, it was easily recognized, wide enough to have a railroad bridge across it.

Perley left the road and took a game trail following the creek to the southeast. It was almost dark and past time to rest his horses when he reached the confluence of Clear Boggy and another large creek. He figured it had to be Muddy Boggy Creek, and he made his camp there for the night. Suppertime the next night should find him back home on the Triple-G Ranch.

"Perley's back," Sonny Rice announced to John Gates when he looked out the barn door and saw Perley approaching. "Wonder if he found your grandpap."

John looked up from the bridle he was mending. "I doubt it," he answered and placed the bridle aside.

He and Sonny walked out to meet Perley.

"Did you find him?" John called out before Perley reached the barn.

"Nope," Perley replied and rode on in before continuing. "I found his cabin, though," he said, stepping down from the saddle. "He'd abandoned it. Left a note tellin' whoever found it they were welcome to it. I met the fellow who's moved in, and he said he'd been livin' there for about six months. He showed me the note, and that's what it said, all right. 'Course, he mighta wrote it himself. I don't even know if

Grandpa could write, but this fellow seems like an honest man — name's Merle Teague. I hate to disappoint Ma, but I didn't have any idea where to start lookin' for Grandpa, and I told Rubin I'd be back to help with the cattle."

"Hell, I knew it was a waste of time for you to go ridin' up there," John said, "especially when there's plenty of work here if we're gonna start those cows out for Ogallala this week. I'm glad you got back when you did."

"You boys ain't got everything ready to go?" Perley asked as he pulled the saddle off Buck. "I didn't think you could without me," he joked. "Is Ollie goin'?"

"Yep," John said. "He said he reckoned he had at least one more good trail drive in him before he hung 'em up. He's been workin' on his chuck wagon, gettin' it ready to roll."

Perley smiled. "That's what he said last year, and I expect he'll say the same thing next year."

Ollie Dinkler drove the chuck wagon and was not only a top-notch cook but took care of all the injuries that needed tending during the cattle drive — and there were usually plenty.

"Me and Rubin talked it over and decided

ol' Sonny, here, was old enough to take on the job of wrangler this year." John nodded toward the grinning young man. "We might lose half of our remuda, but he thinks he's old enough to handle it."

"Shoot, John," Sonny huffed. "I coulda rode wrangler last summer, and I expect I'll be good enough at ropin' next summer to herd cattle."

"We'll see after we get to Ogallala how good you are," John said and winked at Perley.

"I reckon the women are gettin' kinda sad, since their husbands are ridin' off to the North Platte River, gone for a couple of months or more," Perley said, his eyes twinkling.

"You'd expect so, wouldn't you?" John responded to Perley's teasing. "Hell, they can hardly wait for me and Rubin to get gone. It's the only vacation they get."

"Fred and his boy gonna take care of things?" Perley asked.

Fred Farmer and his young son, thirteen-year-old Jimmy, had stayed behind the year before to take care of the ranch, and it had worked out all right. There had been no complaints from the women, so Perley assumed they would do the same this year. John confirmed it with a nod.

"Good," Perley said. "Now I expect I'd best go on up to the house and tell Ma I couldn't find Grandpa."

"I'll go with you," John said. "It's about suppertime already."

As Perley expected, his mother was disappointed to hear that her father-in-law had not been found, but she still held hope that he might be alive.

"If the Lord wants us to find him again, then He'll make it happen in His own way," she had declared.

It was early Sunday morning when the drive got under way, with Rachel Gates, her daughter and two daughters-in-law, and their young children all saying their goodbyes. Fred and his son, Jimmy, stood by to see the men off as they rode out to the herd. Ollie Dinkler followed in the chuck wagon. The cookshack was closed up, with Fred and Jimmy the only occupants in the bunkhouse. They would be enjoying most of their meals at the ranch house till the men returned.

This first day was planned to get the cattle started to move as a herd, probably traveling no farther than eight or ten miles, depending on how soon they became adjusted to the constant pressure by the cowhands to keep them on the move. The second day would be when the drive was actually considered under way, starting at three or four o'clock in the morning and stopping at noon to let the cattle graze. They typically drove the herd about fifteen miles a day. Any more than that would take too much weight off the animals, bringing a lower price in Ogallala.

In earlier days, the Triple-G herds would take the Chisholm Trail up through Indian Territory to Wichita, but the Kansas legislature kept pushing the Texas herds farther west to accommodate the farmers. Now Perley and his brothers had to drive their cattle about two hundred and fifty miles west to Doan's Crossing at the Red River in order to take the so-called Western Trail to Dodge City. Stopping at Dodge City for supplies and to let the cattle feed, they would then drive the herd another three weeks to the buyers in Ogallala.

With Ollie and his chuck wagon out front and Rubin riding point, the Triple-G crew started two thousand cattle west, young Sonny Rice following behind with the remuda. It would take them seventeen or eighteen days to strike the Western Trail at Doan's Crossing. From there, they drove the cattle north, up through Indian Territory, reaching Dodge City, Kansas, after thirty-five days of coaxing the bawling, reluctant longhorns over the Kansas plains. Anxious to deliver their cattle to the holding pens at Ogallala, the Gates brothers allowed a rest of only two days before pushing on to the North Platte.

It was the second week in June when they arrived in Ogallala. The drab, unpainted collection of businesses was all on one street, running parallel to the railroad tracks. Only a block long, it was enough to include two saloons and a hotel. It was in these establishments that all of the entertainment as well as the cattle buying took place.

The men from the Triple-G settled their cattle north of the city to await the buyers and were met almost immediately by several who rode out to look the stock over. Perley, always prone to let his older brothers handle the business end of the ranch, elected to stay with the crew, watching the herd while John and Rubin went into town to negotiate the price. It didn't take long to sell the cattle, with the beef market at its highest, and the Gates brothers were soon ready to pay the cowhands.

As he paid each man, Rubin encouraged them, especially the younger ones like

Sonny Rice, to avoid the traps waiting for them in the bustling town of Ogallala. It was not uncommon for some of the younger boys to ride back to Texas with no more money than they had started out with. It was advice he offered every year, knowing that his warning would be ignored, just like the year before. The hardships and sacrifices of the long cattle drive were begging to be compensated for, and there were loose women, whiskey, and gambling eager to provide that service. As a rule, those foolish enough to spend all they had earned were satisfied that it was money well spent.

Perley was not above the temptation of a stiff drink and some friendly conversation with the bawdy women who worked the saloons, looking to relieve the suddenly liberated cowhands of their money. It was not like talking to regular women, like the kind a fellow would meet in church, or any of the women in the families that settled around the Triple-G. Perley was always shy whenever he came in contact with women like that. But with the rough-edged women who worked the saloons, it was different. It was just like talking to another man.

With the ownership of the herd success-fully transferred, he went with Rubin and John to celebrate the completion of their venture. They picked the Cowboy's Rest to burn the trail dust out of their throats and were lucky to find an empty table in the busy saloon. Perley and Rubin secured the table while John went to the bar to buy a bottle. When he returned with bottle and glasses, he poured the celebratory drink, and the three brothers drank to the success of another cattle drive.

"I reckon we'll start back in the mornin'," John said and glanced at Rubin to see if there was any reason not to.

"I reckon so," Rubin agreed. "Some of the boys are talkin' about waitin' a couple of days here before they start back." He shook his head as if perplexed. "Most of 'em won't have a dime by the time they get back home. I figure we've got good reasons to get on back home, but that doesn't mean we don't deserve a good supper and a night in the hotel, if they've got an empty room. If they don't, at least we can have the supper. Whadda you say, Perley? You care one way or the other?" he asked, knowing that Perley was likely to go along with whatever his brothers decided.

To prove him right, Perley merely shrugged to show his indifference. He couldn't help thinking that Rubin was already beginning to act like his father, now that the old man was gone.

"Then that's what we'll do," Rubin said and poured himself another drink.

It wasn't long before the three men caught the eye of a full-figured woman who had been watching a card game on the other side of the room. Ready to give up on the Kansas cowhand who had bought her a drink before his luck changed, she was looking around for better prospects. Her gaze lingered on the table and the three Texas cowhands — one especially, who looked to be younger than the other two. She decided she was losing money, standing by the man in the card game. Her decision was validated when he threw in another losing hand, cursing his luck. It was obvious to her that he was going to run out of money long before he thought about spending any on her.

"I'll see you a little later, sweetie. It's plain to see I ain't bringing you any luck," she said and started to step away.

"Where the hell are you goin'?" he demanded. "You ain't leavin' after I done spent my money on you."

"You bought me a drink, Riker," she replied sarcastically. "That ain't hardly enough to buy my whole evening."

"Why not? You sure as hell ain't the prettiest whore in the place."

His insult was all she needed to justify her decision. "Good luck with the cards. I'll see you some other time." With that she walked away, leaving him to stare threateningly after her.

"You ain't got no luck at all tonight, Riker," one of the card players said, causing the others to laugh at the scowling cowhand.

"Looks like them boys from Texas is gonna be partying with ol' Liz tonight," another one commented when he saw her stop at their table.

"We'll see about that," Riker replied. "The night ain't over yet."

"Howdy boys," Liz greeted Perley and his brothers as she approached the table. "You must be some of those Texas fellows that came in with that big herd yesterday."

"That's right," John responded and gave her a smile.

"Looks like you could use some company, since you've got an empty chair," she said. "Maybe you might buy me a drink."

"Why, sure," Rubin said. "Set yourself down over there by Perley. I know he could use some female company." He winked at John. Knowing how shy Perley was around women, he thought he'd have a little fun.

"Why, thank you, sir. I knew you were gentlemen when I spotted you, so I brought a glass with me. My name's Liz." She sat down, placed her glass on the table, and turned at once toward Perley. "What did he say your name was? It sounded like Pearly."

"Yes, ma'am," he replied, "Perley."

"Well, nice to meet you, Pearly. That's an unusual name." She took a sip of the whiskey John poured into her glass.

"Gates," John stated, unable to resist. "That's his last name. Perley Gates."

Liz howled, almost spilling her drink. "You're joshing me now." She looked from John to Rubin, both of them grinning like mischievous imps. "Pearly Gates," she repeated, then turned back to Perley. "Well, that's a dandy name. I'll drink to that. You might be inclined to go upstairs with me. Might turn out to be a heavenly experience for both of us."

"Yeah, Perley," John said, "that might be a heavenly experience at that. It might be just the thing you need."

Even though ready to throttle his brothers for ganging up on him, Perley did not want to hurt the prostitute's feelings. As the cowhand named Riker had observed, Liz was not the prettiest woman in the saloon. In fact, she was quite homely, but he was sure she had feelings like everybody else, so he didn't want her to feel rejected.

"I have to say, it would be a real pleasure to go upstairs with you," he said, "but it wouldn't be a kind thing to do to infect you with a deadly disease just so I could have the pleasure of your company for one night." When she responded with a puzzled stare, he continued. "You see, ma'am, I've got a real bad case of hoof-and-mouth disease from workin' in too close with the cattle."

Confused, Liz looked from him to Rubin and John, to witness their ever-expanding grins. Then she looked back at Perley and asked, "Just how close were you working with 'em?" The loud guffaws that followed told her that they might be japing her, but she wasn't sure.

"You ain't in no danger catchin' it just sittin' here havin' a drink," John said, "else I wouldn't be sittin' here, myself. Ain't that right, Rubin?"

"That's right," Rubin said. "You just stay there and have another drink. You ain't got nothin' to fear from Perley just talkin' to him. He ain't even broke out with spots on his lips or under his arms yet. When that happens, I reckon we'll have to put him down before he spreads it to the rest of the cows back home."

Certain that she was being japed then, she

laughed and asked, "Are all you boys from Texas full of shit?"

"Most of us," Rubin replied with a chuckle. "Me and John are married —"

"To each other?" Liz interrupted, showing them she could joke as well. It brought a laugh from Perley and John.

"Me and John have wives at home," Rubin tried again. "That's what I meant to say. Otherwise, we mighta been tempted to go upstairs with you. Perley, there — well, he's on his own. He ain't got a wife."

"Wives at home, huh?" Liz responded, then smiled. "Like I said, I knew you fellows were gentlemen, and I thank you for the drink." She looked directly at Perley then. "I'm sure I could show you a good time, but I don't wanna catch hoof-and-mouth disease."

Certain they were putting her on about that, she figured he would now set her straight if he was a potential customer for her services. Before Perley had an opportunity to respond, they heard a loud outburst at the poker table she had recently left.

"Damn the luck!" the Kansas cowhand named Riker exploded as he watched another large portion of his recent payday disappear. "And damn this game!" He pushed his chair back and stood up. "That's it for me. I've got better things to do with the money I've got left." With a firm idea what that was, he stormed over to the table where Liz was sitting and grabbed her arm. "Come on," he ordered, "I'm ready to get outta here."

In spite of having decided to get up only seconds before, Liz changed her mind immediately. "Get your paws offa me!" she demanded and jerked her arm free. "You lost all your money playing cards, so now you come to me with empty pockets? Ain't nothing free around here. Besides, I'm busy visiting with some gentlemen friends now. Go bother one of the other girls."

"The hell I will!" Riker roared back and tried to grab her arm again.

Again, she snatched it away. "Go away, Riker. I don't want anything to do with you."

Still, he refused to leave her.

The three Gates brothers sat immobile for a long moment, fairly astonished by the unexpected encounter between Liz and Riker, but before Riker could grasp her arm again, Rubin spoke.

" 'Pears to me the lady doesn't very much wanna go with you, Riker. Least, it looks that way. Whadda you think, John? Does it look that way to you?"

"Well, now that you brought it up, it does kinda look that way," John answered. " 'Course, they might not be too good with the English language in Kansas. Maybe if he thinks about it a minute, he'll understand she doesn't wanna go with him, and he'll go away. Whadda you think, Perley?"

"I think when he realizes she doesn't wanna go with him, he'll be wantin' to apologize for treating her so rough," Perley said. "He seems like a nice enough fellow when he ain't had too much to drink."

Riker looked in disbelief from one brother to the next as they spoke. "This ain't none of your business," he growled. "This is between me and her, and if you're thinkin' about makin' it your business just because there's three of you, then maybe you'd best think again. There's three of my partners settin' at the table over there, so that makes it four to three."

John nodded slowly as he appeared to be thinking over what Riker had just pointed out. "By Ned, he's right. Four Kansas cowboys against three Texans. That's an even match, all right."

"I'll go with him," Liz said. "I don't wanna be the cause of getting you boys in a fight. You didn't call any of this down on yourselves. I invited myself to your party."

"Well, now," Perley said, reluctant to see her having to submit to the crude cowhand, "we've been enjoyin' your company, so why don't you stay here with us? I'll pay you whatever you charge for a tussle, and all you'll have to do for it is sit here and talk. That'd be all right, wouldn't it?"

When she looked undecided, Perley nodded toward Riker, who was obviously fuming.

"Look at ol' Riker, there. He's thinkin' he's a gentleman, too, and wants to do the right thing by you. Ain't that right, Riker?"

"Why, you crazy son of a bitch," Riker blurted, and lunged toward Perley.

Perley's chair toppled over under the sudden weight of both men, landing them on the floor with Riker on top. With one hand grasping for a choke hold around Perley's neck, Riker drew his right hand back, cocked to land a wild haymaker. Before he could throw it, his wrist was locked in the powerful grip of John Gates. He was forced to let go of Perley's throat when his arm was bent backward, threatening to break, effectively peeling him off Perley. The painful yelp that bellowed from Riker's mouth served as a call to his three friends at the poker table. Truth be told, none of the three were enthusiastic about participating in a brawl started by Riker, since he was a troublemaker by nature. But seemingly bound by what some might call cowboy honor, they responded to his cry for help and came out of their chairs on the run.

John silenced Riker for a brief time with a hard right that sent him skidding on his back, then stood ready with Rubin to meet the charge. In seconds, the two Triple-G men were exchanging punches with the men from Kansas. Having seen more than one saloon brawl, Liz backed away quickly, thinking to grab the whiskey bottle from the table as she did.

With no time to scramble up from behind the table before the onrush from the three Kansas cowhands, Perley dived under it and grabbed the first pair of unfamiliar boots he could get his hands on. Taking a firm grip, he jerked the boots toward him, pulling the surprised cowhand off his feet, to land hard on his back. Stunned for the moment, the cowhand was helpless to prevent Perley from pulling him out from under the table.

"You take care of that one, Perley!" Rubin yelled when he saw the man disappear just as he was throwing a punch at him.

"I got him!" Perley yelled back.

Before the Kansan could collect himself,

Perley pinned him to the floor with a chair clamped over his chest, sitting on it to keep him trapped. When his opponent tried to fight his way out of his predicament, Perley responded with a series of rights and lefts. After a few minutes of this punishment, Perley could see the fight draining out of the Kansan, so he asked, "You had enough?"

"I've had enough," the man gasped, clearly helpless to defend himself.

"Fair enough," Perley agreed. "If I let you up, we're done, right?"

"We're done," the cowhand agreed. "I didn't want no part of Riker's trouble in the first place."

Perley got out of the chair, removed it from the cowhand's chest, then extended his hand to help him up. The timing was such that the contest between the man's two friends and Perley's brothers also came to a halt, with both sides calling it a draw. The hostile air seemed to have cleared entirely, with even a grin from a couple of the participants, and there appeared to be a desire for a truce from both sides. The circle of patrons that had formed to watch the brawl dispersed to return to their drinking. The event was passed off by all as a harmless fistfight to vent the hardships of a long trail drive — with the exception of one participant.

His head cleared now, after the flush punch that sent him reeling, Riker sought revenge — revenge that would not be satisfied in a fistfight. While the others were distracted in the process of shaking hands, he quietly drew the .44 Colt he wore and raised it to take aim. He had not yet cocked the hammer back when the whiskey bottle wielded by Liz caught him upside his head, and he collapsed to the floor again.

"Well, I reckon that about signals the end of the drinkin'," Rubin declared when he realized what Liz had just done. "I expect everybody's worked up an appetite for supper, so we might as well go on over to the Ogallala House."

"I think we're gonna call the card game done," one of the Kansas cowhands said. "We'd best get Riker outta here before he starts more trouble." He turned to Rubin and said, "None of the rest of us was even thinkin' about pullin' a gun."

"I know," Rubin replied. "No hard feelin's a'tall. It was nice gettin' to know you boys."

That brought a laugh from both sides.

Perley gave Liz the price of her standard service, telling her that it was worth it in exchange for her action to prevent Riker from shooting one of them.

"You can keep the bottle, too," he said. It was still over half full. "That's a good bottle. Didn't even break when you hit him in the head."

They stopped to talk to the bartender on their way out of the saloon. Rubin wanted to make sure they left on good terms.

"My name's Rubin Gates. These two are my brothers, John and Perley. We set the table and chairs back up," he told him. "I didn't see that anything got broken."

Billy Fowler, a slim little man with snowy white hair and beard, responded cordially enough. "I 'preciate you tellin' me, Mr. Gates. Most of my customers wouldn't care whether they broke up the furniture or not."

When he said that, something triggered his mind. "Gates," he repeated. "Did you say one of your brothers is named Pearly?"

"That's Perley," Rubin said, nodding toward him.

"Pearly Gates," Billy said. "That's a name you ain't likely to forget. If that don't beat all, and I've heard it twice in the last six months." He took another look at Perley. "Only the first one was a helluva lot older than you." He couldn't help noticing the look of surprise registering on their faces. "Is he kin of yours?"

"Our grandpa," Perley said. "As a matter

103

of fact, we've been tryin' to find him. Has he settled around Ogallala somewhere?"

"No," Billy replied. "He was just passin' through here. Nice old feller — said he was on his way to see the high mountains while they were still there." He chuckled when he recalled it. "I don't know where he thought they might be goin'."

"Did he say where in the mountains he was headin'?" John asked.

"Well, no, not exactly, but I think he was talkin' about Colorado, 'cause he was askin' about the South Platte River. You know — whether it went to the mountains, or should he be on the North Platte."

They talked a while longer to Billy, but soon realized that he had told them all he could about their grandpa's plans. So, they thanked him for his help and walked to the Ogallala House to discuss it over supper.

"Whaddaya figure the odds of that happenin'?" John remarked. "Ride over eight hundred miles, and strike Grandpa's trail in a saloon." He shrugged. "Well, we know now he ain't dead." The question before Rubin and John was what to do about it, if anything.

They were not certain, but Perley was. "I figure this was a sign, just like Mama was talkin' about. She said we'd find him if we're supposed to, and this is too unlikely to be a coincidence. I'm thinkin' I'm supposed to ride the South Platte to Colorado, just like Grandpa did. Maybe I'll find him in that town we heard about, on Cherry Creek — what's the name of it?"

"Denver," Rubin said. "There were a lot of people lookin' for gold around there. Maybe Grandpa's gone out there to strike it rich. I know you're thinkin' about what Mama said, tellin' him about Pa dyin', but I don't think she'd expect you to go that far."

It was hard to explain his feelings to his brothers. They wouldn't understand, but he had an overpowering desire to find the old man. The cattle drive was over, so now would be the best time to be away from the ranch, and he was already hundreds of miles closer to Denver here in Ogallala. It was just too much of a coincidence to strike his trail here, and it would have to be a mistake not to continue on.

His mind made up, he informed them. "Come mornin', I'll be headin' west. Reckon you two can find your way back to Lamar County without me?"

"You're crazy — you know that, don't you?" John replied. "There ain't no tellin' where that old man ended up."

"Yeah, but I've gotta look anyway, to suit

105

myself," Perley insisted.

Rubin knew better than to try to dissuade him. "So be it," he said. "I'll explain to Mama why you didn't come home. She'll appreciate you still lookin' for him."

"I'll take Buck and cut out a packhorse in the mornin'," Perley said, already thinking about the supplies he would need.

"Make sure you take extra cartridges for that Winchester," John said. "And you keep a sharp eye about you."

They spent the night with the rest of the Triple-G crew, beside a small creek, since there were no rooms available at the hotel. After breakfast the next morning, John and Rubin started back to Texas with most of the men, while Perley visited Louis Aufden-garten's general supply store to outfit himself for the journey he was determined to take.

When he had completed his purchases, he started out on the road, right beside the store, that led to the South Platte River. Once again, he was looking forward to the adventure, much like he imagined his grand-father had felt as he started out on the same trail.

CHAPTER 5

With a new spirit of adventure, Perley set out to follow the South Platte to the west as the river wound its way across the seemingly endless prairie. The clerk in the general store where he bought his supplies told him that he would have to travel close to one hundred seventy-five miles before he would likely see the mountains on the horizon. The little town called Denver was over two hundred miles from Ogallala. Perley didn't care. He was in no hurry, the cattle had been delivered to market, and he had a good horse under him and enough money to buy any supplies he might come to need.

According to the store clerk, he would come to a fork in the road about thirty miles west of Ogallala, where another trail on the north side of the river headed out a little more to the north.

"Make sure you don't take that one," the

clerk had said. "You do and you'll end up in Cheyenne, in Wyoming. About ten miles beyond that fork is where the town of Julesburg was, before the Indians raided and burned it. You'll know you're on the right trail when you see what's left of it."

Perley figured the fork in the trail might be a good place to rest his horses. He started the bay gelding out at an easy lope for a couple of miles before letting him settle back to a comfortable walk. He usually let his horses rest after riding about twenty or twenty-five miles, but it wouldn't be any strain on Buck or the sorrel packhorse he was leading to continue another five miles. Neither horse showed any signs of tiring.

Although there was a common trail running along the river, he met no one else as he rode. When he approached the spot where the other trail the clerk had mentioned forked off, he could see that it led directly to the riverbank. Perley decided to follow it down to the water, but pulled Buck up short when he spotted a couple of horses grazing near the bank. He scanned the trees that lined the river, but saw no one. He decided to proceed, but with caution, so he drew the Winchester from the saddle sling and nudged Buck to move slowly into the trees.

He had not gone more than a few yards when a woman suddenly popped out from behind a cottonwood, with a pistol aimed at him. He reined back hard, almost making Buck rear up, but the woman didn't shoot.

"Stop right there!" she commanded.

A few feet away, someone stepped out from behind another tree, also holding a gun. Perley started to slowly back Buck away.

"I said stop," the woman said.

"Perley Gates!" the second person exclaimed. "It's all right, Stella — I know him." She dropped the pistol down to her side. "You remember me, don't you? I'm Liz, from last night."

It struck him then — it was Liz, all right, but she was dressed in men's clothes and boots, and her hair was pulled up under a hat. Sizable woman that she was, she looked like a man, standing in the shadow of the tree.

"Well, I'll be . . ." he started. "Why were you fixin' to shoot me?"

"Because we thought you were Kenny Lamb, coming back to see what else he could steal before he killed us," Stella said.

"Who's Kenny Lamb?" Perley asked as he

stepped down from the saddle.

Liz explained. "He's a no-account drifter who's been hangin' around the saloon. We paid him to take us to Cheyenne. He said he could protect us from any outlaws or wild Sioux renegades — only trouble is, we needed somebody to protect us from *him*. He was gettin' free service to boot, but I reckon that wasn't enough. He wanted to clean us out, and I know he was plannin' to leave us out here with our throats cut. He didn't figure on us havin' guns, did he Stella?"

Stella held her pistol up again for him to see, grinning as she did.

"He sneaked up on me when I was down in the bushes, yonder," Liz continued. "He didn't know that Stella was over behind another bush, and she had her pistol with her. I let out a yell when he grabbed me by the throat, and Stella came to my rescue." She paused to chuckle over the memory. "When Kenny saw her gun, he ran for it."

"I shot at him three times," Stella said, "but I reckon I can't hit doodley-squat with a pistol."

"Anyway," Liz went on, "I guess he decided to settle for what he could take on the run. The son of a bitch took off with our packhorse. When we heard your horse whinny, we thought it was him coming back."

Perley was amazed to hear the women's story. "What were you goin' to Cheyenne for?"

Liz had said nothing about planning to take an early morning trip when she sat with them the night before. He thought he would have remembered it.

"Well," Liz began, "that's another story, one you already know something about. Seems like I bought a whole lot of trouble for myself when I hit Riker upside the head with that bottle. After they left last night, one of his friends came back to warn me that Riker swore he was gonna come after me. His friend, I think his name is Red, said Riker wasn't foolin', and he thought I'd best find a place to hide. I thought I'd be better off somewhere besides Ogallala, and Stella has a friend that runs the Cattleman's Saloon in Cheyenne, so she said she'd go with me."

"Is that why you're dressed up like a man?" Perley asked, since she hadn't offered to explain.

"Yep. It was Stella's idea. She figured if Riker happened to catch sight of us, he'd think she was with a man."

"I was plannin' to go to Cheyenne anyway," Stella said. "It's a bigger town than Ogallala. Me and Liz oughta do real well there."

"I reckon we'll just have to make it to Cheyenne on our own," Liz said. "I know I ain't goin' back to the Cowboy's Rest. Hell, we'd most likely be leavin' there in a couple of months anyway. Ogallala gets pretty dead in the winter after the last herds are brought in."

"I swear," Perley responded, "that's enough bad luck to last for a good while. Did you say this fellow ran off with your packhorse?"

"He did," Liz replied. "And it was already packed up ready to start out, and that's a problem." She looked at Stella, who nodded in agreement. "All our food and cookin' supplies were on that horse — our clothes, fryin' pans, coffeepot . . . didn't leave us anything to start out with. I reckon we oughta thank our lucky stars that our ridin' horses were down at the water, or we'd be on foot."

Perley thought about their plight for a long moment before commenting. "I expect it's a hundred and fifty miles from here to Cheyenne."

He paused again, thinking about his quest to follow his grandfather into Colorado, before reluctantly volunteering. "You can't make that trip without anything to cook — or even to cook with, if you had it. I reckon I can see you to Cheyenne. I've got enough bacon and such for the three of us, and if we're lucky, we might run up on something to shoot. 'Course, that's if you want me to come along."

The expressions displayed on both of their faces were answer enough.

"I declare!" Stella exclaimed. "I might better drop down on my knees right now and thank the Good Lord for sendin' us an angel. Me and Liz was wonderin' what in the world we was gonna do."

"We coulda rode back to Ogallala," Liz said. "But I was scared to go back there. I was set on ridin' to Cheyenne even if I starved to death on the way. I'll figure some way to pay you back for takin' us. Were you headin' that way anyway?"

"No, ma'am," Perley replied. "I was gonna stay on that other trail into Colorado, headin' to Denver."

His remark caused Liz to remember his talking to Billy Fowler, so she asked, "Is that where you were goin' to look for your grandpa?"

"Yep, that's where I was aimin' to *start* lookin', anyway. That bartender said that's where Grandpa was talkin' about."

"I reckon we're messin' up your plans." She said it as if to apologize, but she was not about to refuse his help.

"No matter," he said. "I'll see you ladies to Cheyenne, then I'll head south to Denver from there. It's gonna be a little while before we start out, though. I've gotta rest my horses."

While the horses were drinking from the river, Perley rebuilt the fire the women had built to cook their breakfast and put his coffeepot on to boil. While they enjoyed his coffee, Stella sought to make his acquaintance.

"I ain't sure I heard right when you first rode up, me gettin' ready to shoot you and all. What did Liz call you?"

"Perley," he answered. "Perley Gates."

She paused, not sure, so he said, "Like the gates up in Heaven, just not spelled the same."

Stella couldn't help chuckling. "Your mama and papa musta had a real sense of humor to put a name like that on a young'un."

"I was named for my grandpa," Perley said patiently, then repeated the story of how he came to be called Perley Gates, an explanation he had given a hundred times or more.

When he had finished, Stella commented, "Well, that's a right good name for an angel, and that's what me and Liz are gonna call you — Angel." She grinned at Liz and Liz grinned in agreement.

"I reckon I'd rather you call me Perley," he said.

It was not yet noon when they crossed over the South Platte and set out on the trail to Cheyenne. Perley couldn't help but wonder how he happened to decide the fork in the trail was where he wanted to rest his horses. He had been following the river all the way, he could have stopped anywhere to rest the horses, but he decided to push them another five miles. Had he not, he would no doubt never have run into Liz and Stella and would be on his way to Denver. *Another damn cow pie,* he thought, but as soon as he thought it, he chastised himself. It was a lucky thing for them that he had come along. They would have been in a hell of a fix on their own.

He looked back now at the two women trailing along behind him. They were riding side by side, talking casually, as if out for a Sunday ride or on a picnic. Evidently, they felt their worries were over, with him to take care of them.

Of some concern were the horses they were riding. They counted themselves lucky that Kenny Lamb had not had time to steal their riding horses when he absconded with their packhorse. After a quick examination of the two horses, Perley was of the opinion that Kenny didn't figure the two nags were worth the effort — and Perley agreed with him. He suspected the fellow at the stable who sold them to the women was glad to be rid of them. If they were lucky, the horses would make it to Cheyenne with no trouble. They weren't carrying much of a load, but it was a good one hundred and fifty miles to Cheyenne. Normally, he would figure that would take about three and a half to four days if he was not in a hurry to get there. He decided he'd best figure a day longer, so as not to make it too hard on their horses. Of the two, Liz's horse, a flea-bitten gray, was in better shape than Stella's sorrel, although it showed signs of aging. The sorrel was pretty gray in the muzzle as well and had an awkward gait, as if it had sore feet.

He had loaded his packhorse with supplies enough to carry him for a long trip, but at the time, he hadn't counted on feeding two women. Maybe he might be lucky enough to find some game to supplement the sowbelly he packed. Water would seem to be no problem, for the trail they rode followed a strong creek. The clerk at the general store had told him it was called Lodgepole Creek, and a traveler could follow it all the way to Cheyenne.

Hoping to make twenty miles before resting the horses, Perley was forced to stop after what he estimated to be about fifteen or sixteen. Stella's sorrel began to limp soon after they started out, but she wasn't aware that anything was wrong. She said the horse always had a rough gait, ever since they started out from Ogallala, so she didn't say anything about it. No matter, Perley told her. There wasn't anything he could do about it except to rest the miserable horse.

"That horse is so old, he's probably got a case of rheumatism or something," he said.

"He was the cheapest horse Walter had," Stella said, referring to the owner of the stable in Ogallala. "I had to buy one in a hurry. I didn't own a horse like Liz did."

"I let Walter take it out in trade for the price of that horse," Liz said. "This is the first time I've actually rode the damn thing. Walter was still comin' to see me three or four nights a week to pay for the saddle. Said I still owed ten bucks on it. I told him I didn't have time to fool with him — I would just tell his wife how I was payin' for my horse and saddle." She looked at Stella and giggled. "He yelled 'paid in full' quick enough then."

"Well, we'll let the poor old horse rest and see if he's able to go again after that," Perley said. "I'll pull the saddle offa him. Maybe that'll help a little."

Before turning the horse loose to go to the water with the others, he took a close look at its hooves and legs. He could only come to the same conclusion as before — the horse was old. The two of them might be riding double before they reached Cheyenne, he thought.

The women still had some concern about the possibility of another visit from Kenny Lamb, since they thought he couldn't know that Perley had come to their rescue. Perley didn't share their concern, because Kenny hadn't left them with anything worth coming back for — unless, he allowed, they were in possession of enough cash money for Kenny to risk getting shot at.

"I know it's a little too soon to eat," Perley said when he walked back from the edge of the creek to join them. "But would you ladies like to have a cup of coffee, since we're gonna be here for a while?"

"I was thinkin' about how good a hot cup

of coffee would be right now, with the wind whippin' offa that prairie like it is," Stella replied at once. "I didn't say nothin' about it, 'cause I didn't know how much coffee you've got."

Perley assured her that he had enough to have a little extra while the horses were resting. The problem, he said, was the shortage of coffee cups. He always carried one extra cup, but they would still be a cup short.

"Me and Liz can share a cup. Can't we, Liz?"

Liz nodded. In a short while, they had a fire going and Perley's coffeepot working up some fresh coffee. Stella took on the chore of fixing the coffee, and when she poured the two cups, Perley insisted that he would wait for his; he had to tend to the horses first. She knew he was just being polite, even though he walked over to the horses and busied himself checking his packs.

"First man I've run into in a long time that don't automatically think God put women on earth to serve men," she commented to Liz.

"Perley's different, all right," Liz replied.

"Reckon how long it'll be before he takes a notion that he wants to jump under the blanket with one of us?" Stella asked. "And when he does, reckon which one of us he'll pick?"

"I don't know," Liz said. "Seein' as how you're so much younger and dainty, might be you — might be both of us. But I wouldn't be surprised if he don't come sniffin' around either one of us at all."

"Shoot!" Stella scoffed. "He's a man, ain't he? He can't help hisself."

Liz shrugged, causing Stella to challenge, "I'd bet a dollar he asks one of us before we get to Cheyenne."

Liz smiled. "I'll take that bet, but on one condition . . . it's no fair for either one of us to ask him if he wants a free one. All right?"

"All right, it's a bet," Stella agreed. "I wish to hell he had some sugar to put in this coffee, though."

She took another swallow, then refilled the cup and walked over to the edge of the creek and gave it to him. She walked back to the fire to find Liz grinning at her.

"You ain't cheatin' on me, are you?" Liz chided her. "I hope you ain't afraid of catchin' hoof-and-mouth disease."

Stella responded with a puzzled frown and waited a moment for an explanation. When there was none, she shrugged it off, thinking Liz said a lot of things that didn't make sense, and answered the question.

"Hell, no," she replied, grinning. "I ain't cheatin' on you. I thought about it, though."

"Something about him, ain't there?" Liz remarked. "I think I'd just like to take him home with me and mother him, more than anything else."

"Well, when you pay me that dollar, you can mother both of us," Stella said.

When Perley decided the horses were rested enough, they started out again, hoping to make this segment of the trip longer than the first one had been. Stella's sorrel looked to be traveling better and maintained a decent pace for over ten miles before it began to show a pronounced limp in its walk. Still it held to the pace.

The critical moment came when the trail crossed a swift stream. In crossing, the horses had to drop down from one bank and scramble up the short bank on the other side. Buck and the packhorse behind him managed it with no difficulty at all, as did Liz's flea-bitten gray.

But when Stella urged her sorrel to cross, the horse refused at first. Then, when it decided to jump down the short bank, its front hooves landed solidly on the creek bed. It almost sounded like a rifle shot when the bones in both front legs broke. The injured horse collapsed headfirst into the stream, sending Stella flying over its neck to land on her back on the other side.

Liz and Perley dismounted as fast as they could to come to her aid. Relieved to find that she had only had the wind knocked out of her, Perley went at once to the stricken horse. With no way to comfort the injured sorrel, he was faced with the undesirable task of ending its misery. Seeing the pain in the old horse's eyes, he didn't hesitate to pull his .44 and put a bullet into the sorrel's brain. Startled by the gunshot, both women flinched, with Stella suddenly sitting upright. Liz helped her to her feet, and they both rushed to the fallen animal.

"You shot my horse!" Stella exclaimed. "He didn't mean to throw me!"

"I know he didn't," Perley said, realizing she still wasn't sure what had happened. "I shot him to put him outta pain. He broke both his front legs, and there wasn't nothin' to do for him except shoot him."

"Oh —" Stella started, then checked herself. "Well, I understand. You had to do it." Embarrassed by her outburst, she recovered a moment later when another concern occurred to her. "I don't have a horse now . . ."

She looked to Liz for help, but even in a

moment of tragedy, Liz couldn't help japing her.

"That's mighty tough luck, gal. It's a long walk to Cheyenne," she said. "Ain't it Perley?"

"You and Liz will have to ride double," Perley said to Stella. "As light as you are, that gray of hers can handle it without noticin' the extra weight."

He waded out of the shallow stream to get a rope, then returned to the dead horse and put a loop of the rope around its neck. He tied the other end around Buck's withers, then dragged the carcass out of the stream.

"Ain't no use in foulin' the water," he explained to Liz when she asked why. "I'll get your saddle off of him," he said to Stella. "You can sell it when you get to Cheyenne. I can load it on top of my packs."

It took a little more help from Buck before Perley managed to get the saddle out from under the horse. Then, with Stella up behind Liz on the gray, they got under way again.

Gray Wolf pulled his pony to a stop when he saw the dead horse lying on the other side of the stream. He paused there in the trees until he was sure there was no one else around before he called out to his friends.

"Over here," he yelled, then urged his pony forward to cross the stream.

He took another quick look around him before sliding off the horse, and was kneeling beside the carcass of the unfortunate sorrel when Cripple Horse and Walking Man rode up beside him. Gray Wolf pointed to the bullet hole in the sorrel's head.

"This was the shot we heard. The horse is very old; maybe that is why they shot him."

"White man," Cripple Horse said when he saw the horseshoes on the sorrel's hooves. A moment later, he said, "The old horse broke his legs. That is why they shot him." He looked up, as if searching for the white men. "This horse has not been dead for very long. They cannot be very far away. They dragged the horse up out of the water and took the saddle. They cannot be far."

"How many are they?" Gray Wolf wondered. "Maybe soldiers?"

Walking Man, who had been studying the ground around the carcass, answered him. "Not soldiers — soldiers don't ride old horses like that one. I see tracks that tell me there were probably three more horses, all wearing iron shoes."

"Only three," Gray Wolf murmured, thinking out loud. "Maybe we have found something better to hunt than deer or antelope," he said then. "Where do the tracks lead?"

"They are riding the trail west," Walking Man answered.

"Then I say we are wasting time looking at a dead horse. Let's find these white men and kill them and take their horses and guns," Cripple Horse suggested.

"I think maybe they have guns and plenty of bullets, if they waste one on this worthless horse," Walking Man said. "They will see us long before we can get close enough for our bows."

He received grunts of agreement from both of his friends, for the trail ahead of them was barren of trees, except for those that lined the creek. The possibility of acquiring guns and ammunition was too great to be ignored, however.

"Walking Man is right," Gray Wolf said. "We must wait until they camp and strike them at night."

"We're wasting time standing here talking about it," Cripple Horse said. "They're getting farther away while we talk."

Gray Wolf looked up at the sun. "It is still a long time before the sun goes down. We have plenty of time to catch up with them." When his two companions looked skeptical, he said, "They will still be on this trail. There are no white-man settlements between here and Duck Bend."

"I think you are right," Cripple Horse said, "but it would still be a good thing if we could get close enough to see them before it gets dark."

There was no disagreement with that, so they jumped on their ponies and started up the trail after the white men.

The three lone hunters were but one small group of many Sioux warriors who had refused to go to the reservation after their defeat at the Battle of Wolf Mountain. Vowing never to surrender to the soldiers, the three friends had joined with a few other Lakota Sioux and Cheyenne warriors to live as they had always lived. But the near extinction of the buffalo and the constant pressure from army patrols forced them to retreat into the Rocky Mountains and the harsh winters they found there. Before a year had passed, the band of Indians began to break apart, with most of them reporting to the reservation. Still defiant, Gray Wolf and his two friends moved into the plains of Nebraska and Wyoming, still seeking the buffalo, even after ammunition for the two rifles among them was depleted and bows were their only weapons.

They had not met with much success, so they decided to scout the wagon road between Ogallala and Cheyenne, hoping to prey on settlers heading west. Happening upon this small party of whites might give them the opportunity to gain precious cartridges and other supplies, as well as three horses.

The warriors started out after them at a spirited lope, hoping to catch up enough to spot them in the distance. In the treeless prairie they rode through, it was necessary to remain far enough behind so as not to be discovered by their prey. It was certain that the white men carried rifles, and the warriors would be no match for them if they were spotted.

Walking Man, noted for his sharp eyes, rode a little ahead of his two friends, his focus concentrated on the trail ahead as it disappeared into the horizon.

"There!" he exclaimed after they had ridden for half an hour. He pulled up and waited for Gray Wolf and Cripple Horse to catch up to him. "I see them." His companions nodded, seeing the tiny images on the road far ahead. "We must fall back, so they don't see us."

For any chance of success, they had to wait until the party had camped and darkness had set in. To attack before then would be suicide against their rifles.

"We should keep up with them if we cross over to the other side of this creek and use the trees beside it for cover," Walking Man said.

His suggestion was met with approval, for the trees along the creek were the only trees for as far as the eye could see. And even with the many winding curves the creek took, they could easily shorten the distance between themselves and their targets.

The sun was starting to settle down upon the horizon by the time Perley decided both the horses and the women had traveled enough for that day. So, when they came to a point where the creek left the trail to take a wide bend before rejoining it, he decided it would be a good place for their camp. There was a large patch of grass within the loop of the creek bend that promised good grazing for the horses, and there were cottonwoods on both banks that provided an abundance of firewood. A couple of hundred yards north of the trail, a long grass-covered ridge rose above the rolling prairie beyond.

The women went to work immediately, gathering wood for the fire, while Perley took care of the horses. He hobbled the packhorse and Liz's gray to make sure they didn't stray during the night. He never hobbled Buck. It wasn't necessary, because the big bay gelding never strayed far from him. Perley's brother John used to say the horse had a foolish crush on Perley, even claiming that Buck would break away from the remuda on a cattle drive and chase after Perley when he was working another horse.

In short order, Liz and Stella had coffee boiling and sowbelly frying in the pan. Using Perley's supplies and the few utensils he owned, Liz mixed up some pan biscuits to go with it.

"If we had one more cup, we'd be dinin' in style," Stella declared.

"And maybe a little sugar," Liz added.

"Maybe tomorrow I could ride in the saddle and you ride behind," Stella commented.

"We'll see," Liz teased. "You're mighty lucky I was kind enough to let you ride behind me."

Perley shook his head, amazed by the carefree air of the two women, when only a few hours before they were stranded on the prairie, fearing for their lives. Thoughts of a return by Kenny Lamb were forgotten, and the Kansas cowhand named Riker was growing even fainter with each mile traveled from Ogallala.

Watching from the cover of a clump of laurel bushes on the other side of the creek, Walking Man was surprised to see two men and a woman as they made their camp for the night. From his angle, he could see three saddles, and one of them appeared to have a rifle stock showing. *Cripple Horse will be happy to hear this,* he thought, *since he does not have one.* His next thought was to hope they had plenty of cartridges, and that he and his friends could kill them before they had a chance to use them.

Walking Man was careful to take in every detail of the camp — where the bedrolls were positioned and where the horses were left to graze. Again, he was pleased with what he saw. The patch of grass where the three horses were peacefully grazing was close to the road, and they would be easy to steal. He was sure that, had they not planned to kill the white men, it would be a simple thing to slip in that night and ride away with the horses without the owners knowing they were gone. One of the horses, especially, caught his eye — the big bay. *That is the one I will steal,* he thought.

Already, the shadows were growing long,

so he thought he should get back to his friends. They were sure to be getting impatient by now. Slowly, he started to back carefully away from the bushes, when he suddenly stopped and lay as flat as he possibly could. The woman and one of the men had gotten up from the fire and started walking toward him. Had they seen him? He was trapped if they continued to advance his way! They both wore handguns, but neither one had drawn one, so maybe he had not been discovered.

A few moments later, he breathed a sigh of relief, for they turned toward a larger group of laurel bushes directly across the creek, no more than twenty yards from where he lay hiding. He realized then that they were simply seeking privacy from the other man to perform their calls to relieve their bowels. He watched as they made their preparations and was further surprised when he realized they were both women. One of them, a large woman, was simply dressed as a man.

Walking Man almost blurted out his surprise upon discovering their attack was to be against one man and two women. It was too much to have hoped for. Of course, there was still some caution to take because of the guns, but the odds were now heavily in the warriors' favor. In his excitement, it was difficult to remain still until the women had finished and walked back to the fire. When they had gone, he made his exit back into the cottonwoods where he had tied his horse. Then, shielded by the cover of trees along the creek bank, he rode back about a quarter of a mile to report his findings to Gray Wolf and Cripple Horse.

CHAPTER 6

"Only one man?" Gray Wolf questioned. "When we spotted them on the road, they were too far away to tell. Are you sure the other two are women?"

"I saw them when they went to the bushes," Walking Man insisted. "I know the difference between a man and a woman," he added sarcastically.

"Are you sure?" Cripple Horse couldn't resist joking. "We have been away from the village a long time, now." When Walking Man ignored him, he asked, "Are you sure they have only one rifle?"

"I can't be sure," Walking Man said. "But the saddles were all easy to see, and there was only one that had a rifle showing in the strap where they usually carry them." He went on to tell them that the only problem would be if one of them remained alert while the others slept. "The creek is wide where they camped, and we would have to cross it to attack them. If we were discovered before we got across, it would be bad for us." He gave them a few moments to consider that before continuing. "If we were interested only in stealing their horses, it would be an easy thing to sneak in and take them, because they are not far from the road."

"But that does not give us what we need," Cripple Horse said. "They will still have their guns."

"If the horses are as easy to take as you say," Gray Wolf said, "maybe we should steal them first and leave the white devils on foot. Then, they could never run very far from us, and we could watch them for a chance to get close enough for our bows to be effective." He looked at Walking Man and repeated, "If their horses are as easy as you say."

"There is a high ridge on the north side of the trail," Walking Man replied. "Now that it is almost dark, we can ride up the back of that ridge and see the camp. After they have gone to sleep, it will be easy to go down and take the horses."

Cripple Horse looked at Gray Wolf and nodded. It seemed the safest way to attack the camp. If, afterward, they had failed to kill their prey, at least the warriors would have three fine horses. So, they jumped upon their ponies and rode east far enough to cross over the road and circle around to the back of the ridge.

Unaware of the danger threatening them, the occupants of the camp took their time to wash the frying pan and spoons. The women, apparently free of worry over who might be chasing them from Ogallala, were enjoying the last of the coffee. There was no thought in Perley's mind concerning the threat of an Indian attack. It had been a fairly long time since there were reports of any hostile activity in the area, most all of the surviving holdouts against the reservations having been captured.

Luckily for the women, their bedrolls were tied behind their saddles, so they didn't lose them when Kenny Lamb rode off with all their other supplies. Using the saddles for pillows, they turned in for the night, planning to get an early start in the morning. As a matter of practice, Perley kept his Winchester handy, plus he counted a lot on Buck's senses to alert him in the event of an emergency. It wasn't long, however, before all three were surrendering to the music of the crickets and other creatures that dwelt along the creek bank.

At some point late that night, Perley was awakened. He did not realize at once that he had been alerted by the faithful gelding, hearing only the low mumbling of Liz, apparently in a deep dream. He lay there listening for only a moment more before he heard the unmistakable sounds of alarm from Buck.

He reacted immediately. Grabbing his rifle and rolling away from the fire, he scrambled up to his feet and ran to the horses. What he discovered in the darkness of a moonless night might be considered humorous later on when retelling it. But at the time, it was a desperate attempt to save the horses from being stolen.

In the moments before, Walking Man had leaped upon the back of the bay gelding he admired, while Gray Wolf and Cripple Horse had jumped onto the other two horses. Buck promptly screamed his defiance and launched a stiff-legged dance of the devil, making short work of the would-be thief's ride. The surprised Indian was thrown head over heels, to land on his back, while the bay ran toward the camp and his master.

While Walking Man was being introduced to Buck, Gray Wolf and Cripple Horse, not having noticed that their mounts were hobbled, began flailing and kicking them frantically when they refused to gallop. When the first shot from Perley's rifle cracked over their heads, it was incentive enough for them to come off the horses. Perley's second shot inspired them to run for their lives and their own horses, waiting at the foot of the ridge. Walking Man followed close behind, in spite of extreme difficulty in getting his breath, a result of landing solidly on his back.

Perley followed for a little way until convinced the thieves were not stopping in their escape. To encourage them, he fired one more shot over their heads, then he gathered the horses and led them back closer to the camp and tied them there.

"Thanks, partner," he said to Buck as he rubbed the big bay's neck. Then he prepared to give an accounting to the two women, who were both lying flat on their stomachs, their pistols out, and using their saddles for cover.

Not waiting for his explanation, Liz blurted, "What the hell was that? Was it Kenny?"

"No," Perley answered. "It was just some Indians, doing what Indians do. They were figurin' on stealin' our horses, but they didn't know Buck was on duty. I reckon I shoulda been on the lookout for somebody tryin' to take the horses, but I didn't figure on any trouble with Indians. I'll try to be a little more careful from now on. Sorry it spoiled your sleep, but I think you can go on back to it — you won't be bothered the rest of the night. I'll stay awake, just in case."

"The hell you say," Stella immediately responded. "There ain't no way I'm gonna go back to sleep with those bastards sneakin' around in the dark."

"The same goes for me," Liz declared. "I'm up for good. I've heard some tales about what those savages do to white women." She held her pistol up. "And this ain't goin' back in the holster till daylight and I can see a mile around me."

"Well, I reckon I might as well liven up this fire a little and we'll make another pot of coffee," Perley said. "Might be a good idea to set back a ways from the fire, though — don't wanna give 'em too good a target, just in case." He scratched his head thoughtfully. "They didn't put up any fight at all. I figure they don't have any guns, and all they had in mind was stealin' the horses."

While the victims of their attack prepared to wait out the night, the vanquished raiders pulled their ponies to a halt after galloping to the north side of the ridge, where they stopped to review their ill fortune.

"This was a foolish plan," Cripple Horse complained. "We are lucky one of us is not dead. We should have attacked the camp. They were all asleep. We could have killed them all while they slept."

"I don't think so," Gray Wolf disagreed. "The one with the rifle rolled out of his blanket immediately. We would have all been killed if we had rushed in." He looked to Walking Man for confirmation. "You saw him grab his rifle, didn't you?"

"No," Walking Man answered. "I was watching the horses." This was true. Because he was so eager to get to the bay gelding first, he wasn't watching the camp at all.

"I think we would have gotten away with the horses if Walking Man had not caused that bay horse to buck and make the noise that gave us away," Cripple Horse said. "Maybe Gray Wolf or I should have ridden that horse."

"I ride as well as any man," Walking Man retorted in anger. "That horse is crazy. You and Gray Wolf could not even make those other two horses run."

"Their legs were tied!" Gray Wolf exclaimed in their defense. "They could not run."

"Anyone knows a horse can't run if his legs are tied," Walking Man replied. "You should have untied them before you tried to ride them."

"It was too dark to see that they were tied," Cripple Horse replied. "There was no time, anyway, with all the noise when that horse threw you off."

"It is done," Gray Wolf asserted. "Our plan didn't go well, and it does no good to argue among ourselves. We must talk about what we will do now."

"Gray Wolf is right," Walking Man said. "Let's make our plans to kill those three whites and take their horses and guns. I want to teach that crazy horse to obey."

They talked it over for a short time, and all three agreed that there would be no honor in abandoning their original plan to kill the whites. And they desperately needed their guns and ammunition. Since there was very little time left before sunrise, they decided to ride farther up the trail to get ahead of the white party. Then, when it became light enough to see, they could find a good spot to ambush them. All agreed, so they rode along the back of the ridge to the end of it before returning to the wagon road and continuing west.

When the first rays of the sun began to melt the shadows near the creek, Perley saddled Buck and told Liz and Stella that he wanted to make sure the Indians were not still hanging around.

"You didn't get much sleep last night, so you might wanna go ahead and have a little breakfast before we start out this mornin'," he said. His suggestion was well met by both women. "I think our visitors from last night have decided we're not worth the risk, but I'd like to see some sign of that. I won't be gone long, but keep your pistols handy anyway. I've been wrong a heap of times before."

"You don't have to worry about us," Liz said, "as long as it's daylight and we can see."

Stella nodded in agreement and patted her .44 on the grip.

"I figured," he said, then gave Buck a little nudge and loped off through the grassy area toward the road. He had no trouble following the trail the three raiders left after they crossed the road and ran through the tall grass toward the eastern edge of the ridge. On the north side of the ridge, Perley found the spot where they had left their horses, and a trail leading west after they left. He was immediately concerned with the possibility that they might have in mind moving on ahead of him to set up an ambush somewhere along the trail.

Faced now with the same problem the three Indians had when they first started trailing him, he decided to take the same precaution they had taken. It was easy to spot someone from a great distance away on the gently rolling prairie. So, when the horses were saddled and his packs loaded on the packhorse, Perley led his group across to the south side of the creek and set out for Cheyenne, using the trees along Lodgepole Creek to keep from being seen by anyone looking for them. He didn't see that as much of a loss of time, since the creek ran almost straight east and west. There were no objections from the women when he explained his reasons for leaving the plainly marked road.

It was after the first stop to rest the horses, and they had been under way again for only about half an hour, when Perley signaled with his hand and reined Buck to a stop.

"I got a funny feelin' about that clump of trees up ahead," he told the women. He pointed to what looked to be a thick grove of trees that stood out like a sore thumb when compared to the almost treeless prairie. "It's hard to tell from here, but I think there's a stream flowin' down the middle of a shallow draw, and it empties into this creek. And there are trees and bushes along it, just like this creek. And what's got me thinkin' is, what a good place to wait to ambush two nice ladies and a fine-lookin' gentleman like me."

The women were at once alarmed.

"Whadda we gonna do?" Stella asked. "Do you think they've seen us comin'?"

"I don't know," Perley said. "Maybe, but if they ain't got nothin' but bows, they can't do nothin' about it if we take a wide swing around that spot and keep outta range of their arrows."

With that in mind, he led them south toward a line of low hills a couple hundred yards distant, until they reached a shallow draw. It offered enough cover to allow them to pass on westward without being seen by anyone who happened to be in the grove of trees by the creek.

When Perley estimated that they had ridden far enough to have passed the area he suspected, he dismounted and went to the top of the hill to take a look back. Kneeling in the grass, he watched for a few minutes, but there was no sign of anyone that he could see. He descended again to report to the women.

"Can't say if I was right or wrong," he said. "If they are in that bunch of trees, they must have their eyes on the road."

His report was at first reassuring to Liz and Stella, but it did nothing to dispel the sense of danger awaiting them at every point in the trail that looked suitable for an ambush.

No choice but to keep moving. The farther they rode, the more Perley's curiosity worked on his mind. There was nothing to base his suspicion of an ambush on other than the notion that the spot was a perfect setup for one. Finally, he couldn't deny his curiosity any longer. He pulled Buck up and waited for the women to come along beside him.

"I'm gonna go back and take a look at that place," he said. Seeing immediate concern register on both faces, he tried to reassure them. "I don't wanna have to worry about playin' leapfrog with those three Indians all the way to Cheyenne. You keep on ridin'." He turned and picked out a round slope in the distance. Pointing toward it, he said, "Just keep your nose on that point, and I'll catch up with you."

"Damn it, Perley," Liz replied. "Are you sure that's a good idea?"

"Well, no," he said. "But if they are hidin' in those trees, I might find a way to stop 'em from comin' after us."

"You might find a way to get your scalp lifted, too," Stella commented. "You'll be a helluva lot of good to us then."

"There is that to consider, I reckon," he replied. "But I've always been kinda lucky." *Unless you ask my brothers about it,* he thought. "And I'll be careful."

"You be damn careful," Liz ordered.

"I aim to be," he said and handed her the lead rope on his packhorse. Then he wheeled Buck and headed off to intercept the creek west of the area he suspected, thinking to himself, *Hope I ain't getting ready to step in another cow pie.*

Once he reached the creek again, he looked back the way he had come and felt pretty confident that he would not have been seen by the Indians if they were at the fork where the stream emptied into Lodgepole Creek. He estimated he was a hundred and fifty yards above that spot. He walked Buck slowly back toward the fork, holding him close to the trees that lined the banks until within about fifty yards of the potential ambush. Dismounting then, he dropped

145

Buck's reins to the ground instead of tying him to a tree branch as he might ordinarily have done. In the event he did find trouble and got himself scalped, he wanted Buck to be free to escape.

Straining to be as alert as possible, he made his way cautiously along the creek on foot, stopping every few yards to look and listen. There was no sound, save that of a lonely hawk circling above, no doubt curious as to what purpose the man in the bushes had in mind. He was inching closer now to the potential ambush spot, with still nothing in sight to indicate there was anyone there but himself. About to rise from his kneeling position again, he stopped halfway up when he heard a horse whinny.

He froze at once, his rifle ready to fire, but there was no other sound. Kneeling again, he scanned the trees and bushes ahead of him, searching for the horse. He was about to dismiss it as a sound he had imagined when a movement of branches in a clump across the creek caught his eye. When he moved a few feet to get a better angle, he got a glimpse of a horse beyond the bushes. He was sure then that he had been right about the ambush. They were waiting. It occurred to him that they might have purposely left their horses far enough behind them that the animals wouldn't nicker when he and the women approached.

Knowing now that the three Indians were still farther along the creek, he moved even more cautiously through the clumps of laurel bushes and cottonwoods, his finger resting on the trigger guard of his Winchester. Finally, he reached a point where he could see the road where it passed through the trees. *This would be the place,* he thought, but he saw no one on either bank of the creek.

Then he glanced up. There, lying in the fork of a cottonwood tree limb, he made out the form of one of the Indians. Having discovered him, Perley looked toward the trees on the far side of the trail and soon spotted another one. A further scan turned up the third warrior. All three had their eyes on the road, watching for the arrival of the man with the two women. *Well, I'll be . . .* he thought. *They're in the trees.*

He had found them, but the question now was what to do about them. The advantage was definitely his. He was sure he could easily pick off two of them before they had time to react, and maybe get a shot in the third one if he had any trouble getting down from the tree. Perley drew the Winchester up to his shoulder and lined the sights up on the first warrior he had seen.

He hesitated, not sure he was set on killing them. He should be satisfied just to stop them. He fretted over the question until the front sight on his rifle began to waver. Relaxing his arms, he let the rifle lower slowly to his side. *Ah, to hell with it,* he told himself. *I've got a better idea.*

He moved carefully back from his position and backtracked the way he had come. When he reached the point where he had seen the horse, he waded across the creek. Behind the clump of laurel bushes, he found three horses tied to the branches. Each horse had a deerskin sack tied around its neck. He figured each sack probably contained a warrior's personal property, and was what an Indian called his war bag. He started to untie the sacks, then decided he'd take the sacks with him. Working quickly, he untied each horse and gathered their reins up, then led them back to the spot where Buck was waiting. The big bay greeted the three ponies with a soft nicker.

"Look here, Buck," Perley said, "you got company." He climbed up into the saddle and started out after Liz and Stella at a lope. Thinking about the three Indian raiders he left behind, he allowed, *It might not stop you, but it'll damn sure slow you down.*

After a short time, Stella looked back to discover a group of horses catching up with them.

"I'll be doggoned," she uttered. "He stole their horses."

She and Liz pulled up then to wait for him, still some three hundred yards behind.

"I didn't hear any shots," Liz said. "So, I reckon he didn't shoot 'em." She threw her head back to release a hearty chuckle. "Damned if he ain't somethin'! Turned the tables on 'em — stole the horse thieves' horses."

When he caught up with them, Stella said, "Looks like you've been shoppin'. I don't reckon we have to worry about those Indians anymore."

"Maybe not," he answered. " 'Course, I don't know how fast those boys can run, so I expect we'd best put some ground between us and them. At least we can cut back on the road again."

"Doesn't look like you had any trouble," Liz commented as he was fixing lead ropes for his newly gained horses.

"Got my feet wet when I had to wade across the creek," he complained.

"Why do they have those hide sacks tied around their necks?" Stella asked.

"Those are what they call their war bags,

where a warrior keeps all his personal stuff — same as our saddlebags," he answered.

They set out again, with Perley leading the three captured horses, Liz and Stella still riding double, and Perley's packhorse trailing behind their horse. As Perley had said, the object was to get far away from the three hostiles. Their horses were fresh, since they had traveled only a few miles before reaching the ambush. Stella was a bit wary when Perley said she would no longer have to ride behind Liz's saddle, but he assured her he would check the horses over before she tried one out.

"We'll wait till we stop to rest 'em," he said. "They won't be too spunky then."

Easing Buck up to a comfortable lope, a pace the horses could maintain for a while, he intended to gain a little on the hostiles. To keep from tiring their mounts too soon, he would then pull them back to a fast walk and an occasional trot. He was only guessing, but he figured a man in good condition could walk as fast as a horse's normal walk, and he wasn't sure how fast an angry Indian could trot, or how long he could keep it up.

Walking Man climbed down from his perch in the tree and walked across the road to where his friends were hiding. "Where are they?" he complained. "Are they still sleeping? They could have walked this far by now. My bottom was starting to grow to that tree."

Feeling much the same as he, Cripple Horse said, "There is still no one in sight. Maybe they have turned around and gone the other way."

Gray Wolf had other thoughts. He climbed down from his perch to join Walking Man. "I think they have outsmarted us," he said. "While we sat here in the trees like birds, I think maybe the white man led his women off the road and rode around us. There are hills on either side of this place in the trail. We would not see them."

"I think you're right," Walking Man said. "If they were going to continue on this trail, they would have been here long ago. Let's get the horses and split up to scout the hills on both sides of this creek. Maybe we can pick up their tracks where they went around us."

"To be cautious," Gray Wolf said, "I'll stay here to watch the road, just in case they have lolled in their beds. You and Cripple Horse go and get our ponies."

Cripple Horse dropped down from the tree and went with Walking Man to bring the horses.

They had not been gone but a couple of minutes when Gray Wolf heard Walking Man's screeching outburst. Thinking his friends had been attacked, he notched an arrow on his bowstring and ran to their assistance. When he got to the spot where they had tied the horses, he found the men both scouting the tiny clearing for tracks, but there were no horses.

"They stole our horses!" Cripple Horse exclaimed when he saw Gray Wolf. "While we were waiting to ambush them, they stole our horses."

"This cannot be true," Gray Wolf replied. "The horses must have pulled loose from the branches and wandered off."

"He stole them," Cripple Horse insisted. "See for yourself. Here are tracks from a white man's boot where he untied the horses, and the tracks here show where he led them across the creek."

All three ran splashing across the creek then to look for the tracks on the other side.

"Here!" Walking Man exclaimed, and followed the hoofprints for a few yards before stopping to take a line of sight. "He led them away in that direction," he said, pointing toward the southwest.

His two friends ran up to stand beside him, and all three peered out in the direction he had pointed, desperately hoping to catch sight of the horse thief in spite of knowing there had been too long a lapse of time.

The loss of their horses was devastating, and when the humiliation of having been so outfoxed by a white man compounded it, the occurrence was unbearable. Along with their horses, they also lost their blankets and the war bags each one carried, with most of the things essential for cooking food. They had but one choice, so they set out to follow the tracks, running at a trot, setting as fast a pace as they could maintain for any length of time.

The tracks led them to the spot where Perley had caught up with the women. From that point, they saw the tracks lead again to the west. There was yet another problem to consider, and Gray Wolf reminded them of it.

"We must overtake them before they reach the place the white man calls Duck Bend," Gray Wolf said. "It is no more than a day's ride from here, so we have to move quickly."

Duck Bend was a wide place in the creek where it became a small pond, formed when the creek almost doubled back upon itself. A man named Lou Temple had built a trading post beside the pond, and a few settlers had staked out acreage for farms close by. Hostile Sioux raiders avoided Duck Bend because Lou Temple and his three grown sons were heavily armed.

"They will probably stop to rest their horses when they are about halfway there. That is when we must catch them," Gray Wolf continued. "If we don't, we will be walking from now on."

There was no need for further encouragement. Already far behind, they wasted no more time in starting out again, with Walking Man setting the pace.

Back on the common wagon road to Cheyenne again, Perley and his two female traveling companions held their horses to a steady pace. Reduced now to a fast walk, Perley's bay showed no undue strain; however, Perley saw signs of fatigue in Liz's gray as well as in his packhorse.

"I reckon we'd best rest these horses for a while," he told the women, and he turned off the road at the next suitable place to water and graze them.

If there had been time to spare, he would have liked to work with the three Indian ponies so they could alternate mounts and cover more ground at a faster rate. But he had a notion that there were three irate

Sioux warriors wearing their feet out in an effort to rescue those horses. Perley felt confident that the pace he had set would gain his group some time to rest, and he planned to at least try to pick out a horse for Stella to ride. He knew that she didn't think much of the fact that there were blankets but no saddles on the horses, so he would have to see if one of the ponies would tolerate the heavy single-rigged saddle she had ridden before her old sorrel cashed in.

"Have we got time for coffee?" Liz asked when they dismounted beside Lodgepole Creek.

"I reckon," Perley replied. "We ain't gonna be here as long as we usually would, though." He looked at Stella. "Which one of those fine-lookin' horses has caught your eye?"

"None of them," she answered at once. "They all look wild as coyotes. And why don't they have any bridles?"

"These fellows didn't use saddles," Perley said, "but they've got bridles." He held up a piece of rope for her to see. "They call 'em war bridles. They just loop a rope around the horse's lower jaw and guide the horse by turning his head one way or the other." When Stella looked skeptical, he said, "The horse works fine that way, especially if he ain't ever heard of a bridle."

She shook her head. "I think I'm gonna need a bridle, and I know damn well I can't ride bareback."

"Well, that might be a problem," Perley said, scratching his head. "We can try throwin' your saddle on one of 'em, but I ain't got the time to saddle-break a horse right now."

In the face of imminent danger trailing them, Liz still found humor in Stella's predicament. "You oughta give bareback ridin' a try," she said. "Hell, you've been ridin' bareback behind my saddle. You just had me to hold on to, is the only difference."

"Yeah, but there's nothin' but a rope to hold on to," Stella came back. "Why don't *you* ride with nothing but a rope to hang on to?"

" 'Cause I ain't the one walkin'," Liz said, grinning.

"I'll try a bridle on one of 'em," Perley said. "Which one do you like?"

"Like I said, none of 'em, but if you're gonna try it, try that one." She pointed to a paint that was a little smaller than the other two.

"Let me borrow your bandana, there," he said, so she took it from around her neck and handed it to him.

Then she watched with a great deal of apprehension as Perley walked up to the horse, talking softly in an effort to keep from making the horse nervous. Naturally wary, for the man smelled strange to it, the paint started to shuffle its feet slightly as if about to rear up. Perley held its head and gently rubbed the horse's neck and face with Stella's bandana. In a little while, and to Perley's surprise, the horse settled down.

After the paint seemed content to tolerate the strange smell of the bandana, Perley draped the bridle across its neck. When it appeared to tolerate that as well, Perley slipped the bit into the horse's mouth and pulled the bridle on and fastened it. The horse showed no sign of rejecting it. Liz and Stella watched with fascination and newfound admiration for Perley and his apparent ability to charm the wild horse.

It was spoiled a moment later when he stated, "That horse has been rode with a bridle before the Indian stole him. Might as well throw the saddle on him. He's had one of them on his back, too, I reckon." He handed Stella's bandana back to her as he walked past to fetch the saddle, giving Liz a puzzled glance when she started laughing again.

Stella sniffed her bandana and made a face. "I'm not puttin' that around my neck after you rubbed it all over that horse," she complained, bringing another hearty chuckle from Liz.

As Perley suspected, the horse had been saddle-broken before. It stood calmly while the saddle was placed on its back and the girth was drawn up tight.

"You feel like you're back home again, now, don't you?" Perley asked the paint.

When he was finished with the horse, he took the cup of coffee Liz handed him and walked back to the road, where he stood sipping it while gazing back the way they had come.

There was no question in his mind that they had created a lot of space between themselves and the hostiles they had left behind. But he also knew that if it was him who had been left on the prairie on foot, he would run-trot as fast as he could to catch the people who had stolen his horse. A man can walk alongside a horse when the horse is walking, and he can walk-trot a little faster when he has to. Although he wouldn't be as fast as the horse, the horse would have to be rested after about twenty miles, while a man with the right motivation can walk straight through the day and night without stopping. For that reason, Perley was not willing to rest the horses as long as he usually would have.

He was also thinking that he had better take more care when he selected a place to camp that night. *I reckon I should have just shot the damn Indians and not had to worry about them catching up.* He walked back to ready his little party for the trail again. While Liz washed the cups and pot, he untied the deerskin war bags from each horse and left them in a neat stack by the ashes of their fire.

"Are you ready to try your new horse?" Perley asked Stella when it was time to go.

She gave Liz a doubtful glance before walking over to the paint pony with him.

"Say hello to him," Perley said. "He ain't gonna bite you."

Not so sure, Stella kept her hands well away from the horse's mouth as she gave it a couple of pats.

"Up you go," Perley said and put his hands together to make a step for her.

When she put a foot in his hands, he popped her straight up in the air, leaving her no choice but to throw her other leg over to land in the saddle. The horse took a couple of quick steps in surprise, but then stood patiently waiting for commands.

Stella grinned, relieved that she was not flying through the air like on her last ride with the old sorrel.

Perley turned and pointed. "That way," he said and gave the paint a little slap on the rump.

It was late in the afternoon when three weary Lakota braves came to the place where those they pursued had stopped to rest their horses. There was no doubt the man and two women they followed had stopped there, for waiting in a neat stack by the ashes of a fire, they found their deerskin war bags.

The sight infuriated Gray Wolf. He felt as if the bags were left there to taunt them. "He seeks to shame us," he said. "I will find this white devil and kill him, and I will kill the crazy horse he rides."

Equally frustrated, Cripple Horse and Walking Man were glad to see their war bags, however, and immediately looked into them to see if their possessions were still there. When they found that the contents were undisturbed, Walking Man said, "Now at least we can make a fire and cook something to eat."

"First, we must find something to cook," Cripple Horse reminded him.

"Forget about filling your bellies," Gray Wolf snapped. "This white man has stolen our ponies, and left our war bags to show us how little he thinks of our belongings."

"I think we have lost this race with him," Cripple Horse said. "I am tired. I can't walk another step until I have rested. We are already close to the place the white men call Duck Bend, and there are too many guns there." He stirred the ashes of the fire with his finger. "These ashes are almost cold. They have been gone from this place a long time, so they will surely get to Duck Bend before we could catch them, even if we were not tired."

"What Cripple Horse says is true," Walking Man said. "What we must do now is find some horses. There are white farmers that have settled not far from here. Perhaps they will have horses."

Gray Wolf knew they were right. He was as tired as they were, but he was still reluctant to admit they had been defeated, outsmarted by the white man riding the crazy horse.

"We will rest for a little while, but then we must keep going. They have our horses!" he exclaimed, as if to remind them. "They will probably stop at the trading post for only a little while. We will strike them when they

161

leave, kill the white man, and take the women, if we want them."

Walking Man looked at Cripple Horse and shrugged. He was met with the same gesture from Cripple Horse, so they both nodded, and Walking Man said, "We will do as you wish."

CHAPTER 7

With still some time left before having to stop for the night, Perley was surprised to see what appeared to be a building sitting close to a pond up ahead. They were not close enough yet to determine if it was a trapper's shack or a farmhouse. As they drew closer, he could see the outline of the building more clearly through the trees between it and the road. It turned out to be larger than it had first appeared, with a barn and a couple of small outbuildings as well.

"I hope one of 'em's an outhouse," Liz commented. "I'm gettin' a rash on my behind from squattin' in the bushes so much."

When they approached the house, they saw a small sign nailed on a corner post of the porch, proclaiming the place to be a store.

"Well, that's a welcome sight," Stella said. "Maybe they've got a few things we could use, like another coffee cup, some sugar, and some bakin' soda for those poor biscuits."

With concern about the three Lakota warriors they had left behind, Perley suggested that it might be a good place to camp that night. "We can give the horses a good rest," he said. "And if those three Indians show up, they might think again about attackin' this place."

His suggestion was met with undisguised enthusiasm, so they turned off the road.

"Well, howdy, folks. Welcome to Duck Bend. My name's Lou Temple. This here's my store. You folks travelin' to Cheyenne?"

He came out from behind the counter to meet them. A short, plump little man, bald on the top of his head with long gray hair hanging to his shoulders on the sides, he nodded to Perley but took a closer look at Liz and Stella. It was fairly obvious that he was speculating on the reason for a man and two women on horseback to be riding the road — and one of the women dressed like a man. He glanced out the door to see the extra horses they were leading.

"That's a fact," Perley said, answering Temple's question. "I never traveled this road before, so I didn't expect to see a tradin' post between here and Cheyenne."

"That so?" Temple replied. "I built this place before the railroad got to Cheyenne. It wasn't even called Cheyenne then — it was Crow Creek Crossin', and to tell you the truth, I used to do a lot more business back then."

"I don't suppose you sell anything for women, do ya?" Liz interrupted. "I'd sure like to get outta these men's clothes."

"No, ma'am, I wouldn't have much reason to carry stuff like dresses and such, if that's what you're talkin' about. I've got some material, if you wanna sew yourself a dress. That's what my wife does."

"I ain't much for sewin'," Liz said. "How 'bout some sugar, and a coffee cup?"

"And we need some more coffee," Stella piped up. "We've been usin' a helluva lot of that."

"I can fix you up with those things," Temple said. Based on the brash attitude of the two women, he was coming to a quick conclusion that they might be "working ladies." Addressing Perley again, he commented, "You're gonna find a lot of competition when you get to Cheyenne, but from what I hear, they can always use more."

His remark puzzled Perley, so he asked, "Competition? Competition for what?"

"You know, for you and your ladies,"

Temple said with a wink. "They're whores, ain't they?"

Perley suddenly realized what he meant, and he felt the blush that burned his cheeks. "No," he blurted. "Well, yes, they are, but I ain't got nothin' to do with that. I'm just takin' 'em to Cheyenne because they ran into a little trouble."

Thoroughly enjoying Perley's blushing, and far past giving a damn what Lou Temple thought of her or her occupation, Liz made a proposition to Temple. "That's right. Ol' Perley, here, ain't got nothin' to do with our business. He just happened to come along when we needed help and agreed to take us to Cheyenne. Me and Stella don't need nobody to take care of our business. That bein' said, those supplies we need . . . maybe we could work out a little trade for what we want. Whaddaya say, Lou?"

Astonished by her boldness, Temple could say nothing for a long moment, but the little man's mind was working fast, thinking this might be an opportunity worth taking. To Liz's surprise, he answered, "Maybe we can."

He took a quick look over his shoulder, just in case his wife may have come in from the kitchen. Then he motioned for Liz to walk over to the far end of the counter, where he made his own proposition in hushed conversation. "I've got three grown sons that ain't never had any experience with a woman, and I'm afraid if they don't find out what to do with one pretty soon, they're liable to dry up and die before their time."

"Well, now, you're right about that, all right," Liz agreed in her most professional manner. "I've seen it happen. And this is your lucky day, because there ain't nobody with more experience in startin' young men on the right path to full manhood than me and Stella."

"It's gonna depend on the price," Temple said. "I figure I oughta get a discount, seein' as how I'm bringin' three customers to the party."

Their negotiations were interrupted for a few moments when a young man came through the door.

"You want Elam to shoe that mare tonight, Pa? He told me to ask you. I think he wants to do it in the mornin'." While he waited for his father to answer, he gaped openly at the two women as if never having seen one before.

"You tell him he can wait till tomorrow," Temple said, and the young man turned and went back out the door. Temple winked at

Liz when he had gone. "He might need his strength tonight."

"Is that one of your sons, the ones that need an education?"

"Yep," Temple replied. "That's Jonah, the middle boy."

"You mighta just got yourself a reduction in the price," Liz said with new enthusiasm for the task at hand. "Do your other two sons look like Jonah?"

"Pretty much, I reckon. They favor their mother more'n they do me," he said.

"Well, all I can say is, your wife must be a fine-lookin' woman," Liz replied.

"She was in her day," Temple said. "So, tell me what you're needin' to buy and we'll see if we can strike a deal."

Liz called off a list of the things they were short of, plus another coffee cup as well as a coffeepot she saw on a shelf behind the counter. It was larger than Perley's small pot and would save a lot of time in the mornings. When she had finished, Temple thought about it for a few moments, realizing he was going to be giving away more than he cared to.

"I don't know," he finally said. "How 'bout if I give you everything you wanted but the coffeepot? And you give me three dollars for that pot?"

"Done," she said and extended her hand.

He shook it, and there was nothing left but to make the arrangements for his sons' classroom.

"I kinda get the idea that you don't want your wife to know what's goin' on, so where are we gonna do this?" Liz asked. "We're fixin' to camp here tonight, ain't we, Perley?"

She looked at Perley, who had been listening to the negotiations dumbfounded, barely able to believe what he was hearing. Naturally shy around women to begin with, he was astonished by the man's interest in his sons' introduction to women. If anything, it would severely damage their attitude toward any young women they might happen to meet in the future.

When he seemed to be stuck in a trance, Liz prodded him. "Ain't we, Perley?"

"Yeah," Perley finally answered. "We'll make camp up the creek a ways, if that's all right with you, Mr. Temple. That's as far as I wanna push the horses today."

Still somewhat astounded by the negotiations he had just witnessed, Perley's thoughts returned to the realization that he might still have to deal with three angry Indians.

"There's something else I need to let you

know," he said and went on to tell Temple about the encounter with Gray Wolf and his friends.

"I wouldn't be surprised if them three weren't the ones snoopin' around here about a week ago," Temple said. "My son Elam spotted 'em sneakin' up close to the corral, but they skee-daddled quick enough when him and his brothers got their rifles after 'em." He paused then to chuckle. "So, you stole them three horses from the Injuns while they was tryin' to steal yours, huh? I reckon that set 'em off, all right. What's your name, son? Did she call you Pearly?"

"Yes, sir," he said. "Perley. Perley Gates."

"Say what?" Temple asked, thinking he had heard wrong.

"Perley Gates," he repeated. "Like the gates up in Heaven, only it ain't spelled the same."

Temple paused for a moment, so Liz interrupted. "So, where are we goin' to entertain your sons?"

Brought back from the curiosity over Perley's name, Temple answered. "I figure in the barn's the best place. I'll have the boys throw down some fresh hay — make you a nice bed." *That's where we breed the hogs,* he thought but resisted saying it aloud.

"Sounds like a good place to me," Stella

commented, content up to that point to let Liz handle the bargaining but wanting to make one stipulation. "You understand this is for just one ride apiece for each one of your sons," she emphasized.

"Right," Temple agreed. "One ride oughta be enough to give 'em an idea — make 'em think about findin' a wife, startin' a family — so there's somebody else around here to do the work. Me and Ma ain't gettin' no younger."

"Well, as soon as we load up those supplies, we can go set up our camp," Liz said. "Then give us a little time to eat supper and we'll set up in the barn."

"I don't reckon there's any chance you'd load up these goods and take off on me," Temple said.

"You don't have to worry about that," Liz said. "If your other two boys look as handsome as Jonah, I wouldn't miss it."

She might have said more, but Temple's wife walked in from the kitchen at that moment. A tiny, pleasant-looking woman, her gray hair pulled back in a neat bun, Joanna Temple met them with a warm smile.

"I thought I heard Lou talking to someone out here," she said. "My hearing's not as good as it used to be, so I wasn't sure."

"This here's Perley Gates and his two

ladies, Ma," Temple said. "They're on their way to Cheyenne."

"Pleased to meet you, ma'am," Perley quickly replied when she seemed puzzled by her husband's introduction. "They're not my ladies — they are Liz MacDonald and Stella Pender, and they ran into some hard luck, so I'm escortin' 'em to Cheyenne to live with a friend of theirs."

"Oh," she replied, still somewhat confused by Liz's trousers and jacket. "Well, I hope my husband can take care of your needs."

"Oh, yes, ma'am," Liz responded. "He's takin' good care of us."

"I wish you a safe journey for the rest of your trip to Cheyenne," Joanna said and promptly returned to her kitchen, making a mental note to inform her innocent-minded husband that the two women looked like prostitutes to her.

Still reeling mentally after the contract he had just witnessed, Perley led his party upstream a couple dozen yards to a place that looked to be satisfactory for their camp. He wanted to stay close to the trading post, in the event the three Indians were still on his tail, so he went only far enough to ensure he was upstream from the barn.

Having caught a glimpse of the older son,

Elam, coming out of the barn, the two women were chattering away in anticipation of the coming evening. Even though Perley felt it not the best way for a young man to be introduced to the opposite sex, he kept his opinions to himself. It was a business deal between Temple and the women.

It occurred to him then that Elam looked to be about the same age as he, and like Elam, he had not as yet crossed that mysterious threshold himself. Shy as he was around women, he sometimes wondered if he ever would. *But when I do,* he promised himself, *it won't be with a three-dollar whore in a barn.*

While he took care of the horses, Liz and Stella prepared supper, eager to try out their new coffeepot. Perley figured the women must have accumulated some cash in Ogallala, since there was no hesitation on Liz's part to fetch the three dollars from a purse inside her jacket.

As no one felt the need to talk quietly, Perley was subject to overhearing some rather lewd comments regarding the coming evening. Before long, Liz couldn't help but notice that he appeared to be in a constant blush, and while eating the bacon and biscuits they had cooked, he seemed to be sitting farther away than he normally did.

Finally, she commented.

"You know what? I may be wrong, but damned if I don't think ol' Perley ain't ever took a ride himself, just like the Temple boys. What about it, Perley? You think you might oughta get in line down at the barn tonight, too?"

Perley almost choked on a large piece of bacon he was in the process of swallowing. He had a coughing fit for a few seconds before recovering.

"I don't reckon so," he finally managed. "I think I'd best stay here and keep my eye on the horses. We might have visitors tonight." He could have put their horses in the corral with Temple's but decided he'd rather have them near him. And they could graze by the creek and drink freshwater.

Liz chuckled, amused by his reaction. "I know me and Stella will have visitors tonight," she said, "so I reckon we'd best clean up the pan and the coffeepot and get along to the barn."

"I'll clean up here," Perley insisted. "Why don't you and Stella just stay there and sleep in the barn when you're through? It'll be a better bed than sleepin' here on the ground. I figure we've got another day and a half from here to Cheyenne, so we'll get started again in the mornin'."

"That sounds like a good idea to me," he heard Stella say to Liz as they walked away. "I'd give a lot for my hairbrush. I hope Kenny is enjoyin' usin' it."

"Yeah, too bad Temple didn't have one to sell," Liz replied. "I don't reckon these boys tonight are gonna spend much time lookin' at our hair, anyway." They both laughed then.

Perley was happy to have them gone for the night. He was uncomfortable with the lewd jokes. That was the kind of language a man heard from women in a saloon, or among men on a cattle drive. It just didn't seem right, out on the prairie, for women to talk like rough cowhands. *I reckon I'm just too soft in the head,* he confessed to himself.

He put it out of his mind and went to work building himself a low firing position to sleep behind in case the three Indians showed up that night. He found a couple of logs that served his purpose quite well, so he dragged them over and fit them one on top of the other. By the time darkness descended upon the creek, he felt he was ready for any late-night visitors.

He was not long in his blanket when he realized he should not have made his camp so close to the barn, for he could soon hear sounds coming from there. The voices became louder as the evening progressed and were nearly all those of the excited young men. *What the hell,* he decided, *I need to stay alert anyway.*

"I don't see my pony in that corral by the barn," Cripple Horse whispered. "I don't see yours or Walking Man's, either. They are not here."

"How can they not be here?" Gray Wolf growled. "We saw their tracks where they left the road and came here." Cross and weary after their long trek on foot, he was in no mood for another frustrating defeat.

"Maybe they have left already," Walking Man suggested, "and might be camped somewhere farther along the road."

"We need horses," Gray Wolf said, looking at the horses moving about in the corral, already aware of the Indians' presence. "We can slip in and open the corral and steal these."

"You forget when we tried to steal horses here before," Cripple Horse reminded him. "Too many guns — we were lucky to get away alive."

"It was almost daylight then," Gray Wolf said. "*They* were lucky to have seen us. Now it is dark. They will be in their beds."

He rose from his kneeling position and

moved in closer to the barn. Cripple Horse and Walking Man had no choice other than to follow him. As soon as they moved up beside him, he motioned for them to listen. In a moment, they understood why, for they could hear loud voices, men's voices, whooping and hollering.

"This is not good," Walking Man whispered. "It sounds like a war dance."

"I think you are right," Cripple Horse agreed. "I think this is a very bad time to steal their horses. They have more men with guns than they did before. We should leave this place before they come out of the barn."

Gray Wolf scowled and bit his lip in angry frustration, almost to the point of rushing in to open the corral in spite of what they perceived to be a war party inside the barn.

Such thoughts were abandoned in the next few seconds when they heard a low, threatening growl emanating from a stand of bushes a few yards away. A large dog, as black as night, pushed its head through the branches, its teeth bared, causing the warriors to freeze for a long moment. All three had but one thought, so as one, they slowly withdrew. It was enough to set the dog to barking, and the canine was joined almost immediately by two more dogs. There were no longer any decisions to be made — the three warriors turned and ran for their lives, with the three dogs in hot, noisy pursuit.

Up through the cottonwood trees that lined the creek the warriors ran, but the dogs were right behind them. Already weary from the journey that had brought them to Lou Temple's trading post, they began to falter, until Gray Wolf, in a fit of rage, stopped, turned, and notched an arrow on his bowstring. Waiting until the lead dog was almost upon him, he released his arrow and quickly notched another.

His first arrow struck the large black dog in the chest, and it crashed to the ground almost at his feet. His second arrow struck a brown-and-white hound just in front of its rear leg, and the wounded dog howled out in pain and limped away. That was enough to stop the third dog. It turned and retreated to the barn.

Releasing his anger and frustration, Gray Wolf threw his head back and yelled out his victorious coup to the heavens. A dozen yards ahead of him, Cripple Horse and Walking Man came to a sudden stop, both shocked to hear Gray Wolf's war cry.

"He has lost his mind!" Walking Man gasped, struggling to get his breath. "They know we are here now! They will all come down on us."

In complete agreement, Cripple Horse called out, "Gray Wolf, come! We must get away from here!"

"I must get my arrow out of the dog," Gray Wolf called back.

"Leave the arrow!" Cripple Horse yelled in anger and turned to run again. "He has gone crazy," he panted to Walking Man.

Back in the barn, the "passage to manhood class" was abruptly halted, with only Elam and Jonah having crossed over the bridge. Fearing an Indian attack, the boys grabbed their rifles and spilled out of the barn. At the same time, their father ran out the kitchen door. All were primed to defend their home. On the other side of the barn, Perley leaped up over his log breastworks and ran to help the others.

"They musta been after the horses again!" Lou Temple shouted.

"Look!" Jonah said, and pointed to the hound, limping back to the barn with Gray Wolf's arrow protruding from his rear leg. "They shot Beau!"

"There's Belle!" Lou exclaimed. "Where's Bear?"

With a pretty good idea who the raiders were, Perley felt an obligation to go after the Indians. "I think they musta run off up that way," he said, pointing in the direction the dogs had come from. "I'll go after 'em. Maybe you'd better stay here to make sure the women are all right."

"I'll go with you," Jonah volunteered. "Elam and Josh can stay with Pa."

They had not gone far when they came upon the body of the large black dog. Jonah dropped to his knees beside it. "Bear," he moaned. "They shot Bear."

Fully distraught, he started to pull the arrow out of the dog's chest, but it was buried deep and was not easy to dislodge. That told Perley that the dog was shot at very close range. But he was more interested in how much farther the Indians had run and whether or not there might be another arrow coming their way.

When Jonah seemed unable to leave the dead dog, Perley scanned the edge of the trees before them but could see no one in the darkness beyond. Satisfied that there was no immediate danger of attack, he knelt beside Jonah and checked the dog.

"He's dead. Ain't nothin' you can do for him now." When Jonah still refused to move, Perley said, "I'm goin' on up to the other side of the trees." He rose to his feet again and left Jonah to mourn his dog.

After scouting all along the tree line by the creek and finding no trace of the Sioux raiders, Perley had to conclude that they had flown. When he returned to the spot where he had left Jonah, Perley found him still kneeling beside the dog. He said, "You musta thought a heap of that dog, but I reckon it's best to go on back now and let your folks know you're all right."

"It's him!" Gray Wolf had gasped when he saw Perley searching for them along the trees lining the creek. "I knew he was still here. I could feel it!"

Hiding in a gully near the wagon road, he notched an arrow and started to rise up but was held back by Cripple Horse and Walking Man.

"He is too far for your bow!" Walking Man charged. "You will bring them all down on us. You have let this white man get into your head."

"Have you no iron in your blood?" Gray Wolf scorned. "One white man has made us like women, with no horses, and afraid to fight."

"I think this white man has big medicine," Cripple Horse argued. "And now he has the other white men to help him. All of them have guns. Our bows are like nothing against them."

"What Cripple Horse says is true," Walking Man said. "It is foolish to fight when there is no chance to win. It is best to leave this white man alone and go from this place. There are many white settlers moving into this country. It is much easier to steal horses and ammunition from those who come to make their farms on our land."

"I agree," Cripple Horse said. "We have wasted too much time trying to kill this man and take back our horses. I say we should go back north to the big river the white man calls the North Platte, where the wagon trains roll across the prairie. We will find horses and food there."

Gray Wolf could plainly see that Cripple Horse and Walking Man were no longer willing to follow him against the white man with the crazy horse. Realizing he had little chance of success if he attempted to attack the trading post by himself, he followed reluctantly when they climbed up from the gully and slipped back across the road to disappear into the night.

Back at the trading post, no one was inclined to go to bed after the scare of an Indian raid, so Joanna Temple fired up her iron stove again to make coffee for her menfolk. Stella and Liz were invited to bring their bedrolls inside the store for the night, as was Perley. He, however, graciously declined, saying he felt he should guard his horses during the night. Even though they felt sure the Indians would not be back, Temple's sons were sent to keep watch on the barn and the corral.

Liz and Stella were pleased to accept the invitation, since it was warm inside the store and Temple closed the wooden shutters on the windows to guard against an attack. The one person who was distraught to see the two women move from the barn was Temple's youngest son, Josh, who was left with nothing beyond his youthful imagination when it came to the mystery of women.

In spite of her suspicions regarding the two women with Perley, Joanna attempted to make them feel welcome. "We're so sorry you had the bad luck to suffer an Indian raid," she said to them. "I surely hope you don't have any more before you reach your friend in Cheyenne."

"It wasn't really much of a raid, Mother," Temple said to his wife, "just some renegade Injuns tryin' to steal horses." He wanted to discourage conversation between his wife and the two whores, afraid she might pick up a clue as to what was going on in the barn just before the raid.

He cringed a few moments later when she

noticed some pieces of hay on Stella's back and reached over to pick them off her blouse. "My gracious, dear, you look like you've been rolling in the hayloft. How did you get hay all over you?"

Stella started, then paused when she heard Liz giggle. "Why, I don't know," she answered. "It musta been when I took some hay outta the barn and carried it back to our camp to use under my blanket."

"You shoulda had one of the boys do that for you," Joanna said. "I think they were in the barn doing something. I thought I mighta heard 'em, but Lou said they were fixin' to go to bed. You know, my hearing ain't as good as it used to be."

"It was no trouble at all," Stella said, doing her best to keep a straight face while ignoring the sheepish grins in place on the faces of Elam and Jonah. "The boys have been eager to help Liz and me," she couldn't resist adding, and smiled, herself, when she saw Perley roll his eyes upward.

Although Perley and Temple's sons remained alert for the rest of the night, it was obvious that the Indians had been discouraged from making another attempt. In spite of no sleep, Perley was ready to get his little party on the road early and was knocking on the front door of the store soon after sunup.

Having spent a comfortable night indoors, Liz and Stella were not enthusiastic about getting an early start, especially since Perley didn't plan to let them eat breakfast until it was time to rest the horses.

"You ain't on a cattle drive," Liz complained. "We don't have to start in the middle of the night."

Perley opened one of the window shutters to let in the gray light of dawn. "It ain't hardly the middle of the night," he pointed out. "You and Stella get your blankets up, and I'll saddle the horses. We need to get on the road."

He said his good-byes to Lou and his wife and left to get the horses ready.

With the packhorse loaded and the saddles on three of the six horses, Perley led them back to the trading post to pick up the women. Elam and Jonah seemed especially attentive to the women's needs, carrying their bedrolls for them and tying them on behind their saddles. Joanna Temple watched her two sons and was pleased to see their polite attention to the women's needs. She felt proud to know she had raised them to respect women, and decided she wouldn't tell them that the two women were probably prostitutes. *Wouldn't hurt for Josh to learn a lesson from his older brothers,* she thought, noticing that he made no move to help the ladies.

With a final tip of the hat, Perley turned Buck's nose toward the road and headed west once again, hoping to reach Cheyenne in a day and a half.

About twenty miles due north of Duck Bend, the three Sioux renegades sat by a small fire and shared one rabbit, the only game they had come upon that morning. Having walked through the night, they were not in a jovial mood.

"I hope we can find more than a rabbit to eat sometime today," Cripple Horse complained. "It is not easy to travel when my stomach is so empty. It growled all night while we walked."

"You do not eat," Walking Man said to Gray Wolf.

"I am not hungry," Gray Wolf spat. "I cannot think of eating when that white devil is still alive. I will eat again when I cut his heart out of his body."

Walking Man and Cripple Horse exchanged worried glances. "You must eat to keep your body strong," Walking Man said. "We might never cross paths with the white man again."

"I will cross his path again," Gray Wolf stated firmly. "Until I do, you eat the rabbit." He tossed the rabbit leg on the ground between them, then turned over on his side to sleep.

Walking Man picked up the rabbit leg, brushed the dirt off, took a healthy bite of it, then handed it to Cripple Horse.

Cripple Horse looked at Gray Wolf as he lay there with his back to them. Then he looked up at Walking Man and slowly shook his head. "We should sleep a little while before we start walking again," he said.

They were sure they had covered two thirds of the distance between Lodgepole Creek and the North Platte River during the night. And if they were correct in their figuring, they would strike the river before noon that day. The last time they were there they were lucky — they found some antelope. Maybe they would be lucky again. With that to hope for, they lay down and went to sleep.

"Wake up," Cripple Horse said and shook Walking Man on the shoulder.

"What is it?" Walking Man asked.

"Gray Wolf," Cripple Horse answered. "He is not here."

Walking Man sat up and looked all around

him and saw no trace of Gray Wolf, but he was not concerned. "He has gone to relieve himself," he decided, even though there were no bushes of any size near the tiny stream they had stopped by. He could think of no other explanation.

"The white devil has made him crazy," Cripple Horse insisted. "While we slept, he went back to kill the white man."

Walking Man was reluctant to believe that and said as much, so Cripple Horse walked a dozen yards back the way they had come the night just passed. He studied the ground until he found Gray Wolf's tracks heading back south. "See!" he cried. "The tracks do not lie. He said he would find him. He has gone back."

"We must hurry and catch him!" Walking Man exclaimed. "He will be shot!"

Cripple Horse did not share in his friend's anxiety for Gray Wolf. "I will not go back to try to stop him," he stated firmly. "One man cannot tell another man what he must do. Gray Wolf's mind has gone. We have told him what we think, and still he is determined to find the white man. He will be killed. I will go on to the big river. You must decide what you must do."

Walking Man thought about what Cripple Horse said. He could not deny the truth in his friend's words. After a few moments, he said, "Maybe you are right. We have done our best to save him from killing himself. There is no reason for us to commit suicide with him."

CHAPTER 8

The morning passed without incident as they followed the common road to Cheyenne. When Perley deemed it time for a rest, he picked a spot beside the creek where there were plenty of trees before he stopped for breakfast. By this time, they had traveled together enough to have settled into a routine for making camp, so there was little time wasted in gathering wood, starting a fire, and preparing breakfast while Perley took care of the horses.

"I sure will be glad to eat something besides sowbelly and pan biscuits," Stella commented as she tended the meat in the pan.

"At least we got a couple of oven-baked biscuits at Duck Bend," Liz said. "I don't think ol' Temple's wife was too tickled to give 'em to the likes of us." She chuckled when she pictured the tiny woman.

"Took an Injun raid to do it," Stella said

and joined her in laughing.

She was distracted then when her gaze lit on Perley stroking Buck's face. "Look at ol' Perley down by the creek. He talks more to that horse than he talks to us." She looked at Liz and grinned. "We're runnin' outta time on our bet — ain't but one more night before we get to Cheyenne, if he's right about the distance."

"Uh-huh," Liz replied. "Gettin' a little worried about payin' me that dollar, are you?"

"Shoot, no," Stella insisted. "Mark my words, he's gotta be thinkin' about tonight being his last chance. He'll come callin' — you just get that dollar ready to hand over."

Perley was the topic of their conversation for a while then. It occurred to them how little they knew about him, for he never volunteered any information about himself. They knew that he worked cattle, and that was only because Liz had sat down at the table with him and his two brothers in the saloon in Ogallala. Other than that, they knew he had come this way in hopes of finding his grandpa, who was the reason for his peculiar name. It was easy to see that he was bashful and shy around women.

"You reckon he's as green as those Temple

boys when it comes to women?" Liz wondered.

"I wouldn't be surprised," Stella said. "I'd like to be the one to break him in — be more fun than those boys last night."

Unaware that he was being discussed, Perley looked up toward the campfire when the aroma of boiling coffee reached his nostrils. A fresh, hot cup of it was the only temptation he had on his mind, so he gave Buck a final pat on his face and walked up to the fire to join his traveling companions.

"Just about ready," Liz greeted him. "Set yourself down. Stella, pour the man a cup of coffee."

"Here you go, Perley," Stella said, handing him a cup. "Got your own cup — don't have to wait for me or Liz to finish with one."

"Reckon not," Perley said. "Thank you."

He took the cup, wondering why both women had such silly grins on their faces. If he didn't know for a fact that there was none with them, he might have suspected they had gotten hold of some whiskey.

They relaxed under the trees until Perley figured the horses were ready to go again; then they were back on track, with Perley leading and the women riding side by side behind him.

When the afternoon grew long and the sun began to sink lower on the horizon, Stella rode up beside him. "How much longer do you figure we'll be ridin' before we camp for the night?"

"We can stop anytime now, I reckon, if you women are gettin' tired. I haven't seen a real good spot in the last couple of miles. Not many trees."

"That's a fact," she said. "Let's keep goin' till we find one, 'cause this is the last night we'll be campin' together. Tomorrow our trip will be over, so tonight's spot oughta be a good one."

"Oh," he replied. "Well, I reckon you're right. We'll try to find us a good one. I don't wanna push the horses too far anyway." He had planned to travel farther that day to get a little closer to Cheyenne, but if they wanted to stop early, he'd go along with it.

"Dumb as a stump," Stella said to Liz when she dropped back beside her again.

"I told you," Liz said. "Havin' a roll in the hay with a woman doesn't ever cross his mind."

"That ain't normal," Stella insisted. "There's something mighty wrong with him." She paused, then added, "Or with us."

"I expect it's with us," Liz said. "And I reckon I don't blame him."

"We'll see," Stella said. "The night ain't over yet."

They traveled on for close to two miles before reaching a stretch where another stream flowed into Lodgepole Creek, creating a fairly thick border of trees and bushes, with grass for the horses as well. Perley pointed Buck's head toward the middle of it, rode up to the edge of the creek, and stopped.

"Won't find a spot much better'n this," he announced and stepped down from the saddle.

The women went to work right away on the nightly routine while Perley tended the horses. As he had before, he hobbled all the horses but Buck to ensure they stayed close, in case of horse thieves. The three Sioux hostiles who had been following them were no longer seen as a threat, so close to Cheyenne, but there was no sense in getting careless.

When Perley returned to the fire, he was carrying an armload of wood to help the women out. When he dropped it on the ground nearby, Stella said, "Thank you, kind sir. For that, you get a cup of fresh, hot coffee." She poured him a cup. "Anything else we can do special for you for escortin' me and Liz all the way to Cheyenne?"

"Reckon not," Perley said. "Biscuits seem special enough." He glanced at Liz when she seemed to find that humorous.

He had to admit that he might have felt like celebrating this last night, for it meant that he could soon deliver them to Cheyenne safely, and then he would be free to head for Colorado Territory to look for his grandpa. But there was something that had to be taken care of before he would feel like any celebration. Maybe, he thought, the biscuits might help soften the sharp pains he had been experiencing in his gut all afternoon in the saddle. Suspect, to him, was the slab of bacon he had brought from Ogallala, thinking it might have become rancid. He hadn't said anything about it to the women, since they hadn't complained, but he felt a definite storm building in his bowels, and he was afraid it was going to have to be dealt with pretty soon. Thankful for the fading light as the sun finally sank below the horizon, he felt he could rid his system of its burden.

"I need to take another look at the horses," he announced, set his cup down, and walked quickly toward the horses drinking at the edge of the creek.

"Don't be too long," Stella called after him. "My biscuits are gonna be ready pretty quick."

Without turning around, he acknowledged her with a simple wave of his arm. When he got to the horses, he kept walking and headed toward a row of thick laurel bushes. As he anticipated, his relief came immediately. Thankfully, there were plenty of leaves to serve his purpose. Feeling he was comfortable enough to enjoy Stella's biscuits then, he returned to the camp.

"Anything worryin' you about the horses?" Stella asked.

"No, not a thing," he answered quickly, embarrassed to think she might have suspected the real purpose for his sudden concern for the horses. "I just wanted to make sure they were all right."

Stella's biscuits were as good as she had boasted. Even the bacon tasted different to him than that they had cooked for breakfast. He supposed just that one slab had been rancid and the rest was all right. Whatever the reason, he felt no distress after finishing his supper. They sat by the fire and finished the coffee; then the women cleaned up the utensils.

"Anything else we can do for you, Perley?" Stella asked.

"No, ma'am, I reckon not," he replied. "I'm ready to get some sleep. We've got a little bit farther to go than I figured, so we'll get an early start." That said, he retired to his bedroll several yards from theirs, as was his custom.

"Well, if that ain't somethin'," Stella remarked to Liz. "I was sure he'd be wantin' a ride tonight. What the hell's wrong with him?"

"Like I told you," Liz said while she climbed into her blankets by the fire. "He ain't likely to think about bein' with a woman unless he sees one in church or somewhere and he thinks he wants to marry her."

"Dumb as a fence post," Stella said as she crawled under her blanket. "I'll be damn glad to get to Cheyenne tomorrow."

All was peaceful until late in the early hours of the morning, when Perley was awakened by the same evil that had cramped his bowels earlier. He lay there grimacing for a long while, hoping the demon would settle down and let him go back to sleep. When it became apparent that wasn't going to happen, Perley folded his blanket back and carefully got to his feet, pausing only for a quick look toward the women. When it appeared they were both sleeping, he grabbed his rifle and hurried to the bushes near the creek again.

Thinking she had heard a noise, Stella opened her eyes and listened. She then turned to look toward Perley's bedroll in time to see him heading into the bushes. She turned back on her side to go back to sleep, but started thinking about the shy young man who felt it necessary to hide deep in the bushes just to pee. A wicked grin formed upon her face as a mischievous thought occurred to her.

Being as quiet as she possibly could, she got up from her blanket and tiptoed away from the fire, which was now little more than glowing coals. Satisfied that Liz was fast asleep, she hurried toward the creek bank after Perley. Behind her, Liz raised her head, having awakened as well. A wicked grin, matching the one on Stella's face, parted her lips, and she thought, *She sure as hell hates to lose that dollar.* Then she lay her head down and went back to sleep.

Behind a large laurel bush, with his back toward a cottonwood tree, Perley did his business. On the other side of the bushes, he heard Buck whinny and was immediately concerned that one of the women was up. Fearing she might stumble into the same spot he had picked, he hurriedly grabbed his pants and pulled them up, with no time to button the flap on his underwear. Before he could button his trousers, he heard her call out playfully.

"Purrr-leeee," she said. "I know you're here."

Her voice seemed to come from only a few yards away from him. There was no time to button his trousers. He dropped to the ground, hoping she had not seen him, at the same time hearing the thud of the arrow when it struck the trunk of the cottonwood.

Not sure what he had heard until he looked behind him and saw the arrow sticking in the tree, he reacted then the only way he could. Grabbing his rifle, he rolled over and over on the ground, trying to spot his assailant. At the same time, he was concerned for the woman who had called out his name, but it was so dark there among the trees he couldn't determine where anybody was. And then, it came again.

"What's the matter, Perley," she called. "Are you bashful?"

Recognizing the voice as Stella's, he yelled, "Stella! Hide!"

As soon as he spoke, another arrow came whistling his way, to disappear harmlessly into the thick branches of the laurel. Holding his trousers up with one hand and his rifle in the other, Perley moved quickly to another tree. He crouched behind it, still trying to locate his attacker, reasonably certain that he was only one man.

He almost groaned aloud when he heard Stella call out again.

"You want me to hide?" she teased. "All right, I'll play your little game, but don't be too long."

"Stella, damn it, shut up and hide! There's an Indian in the bushes with us!"

Still convinced he was playing a little game with her, she grinned and started to reply. Before she could speak, she felt her head jerked violently back and the cold knife blade against her neck. In the next instant, she felt the bite of the blade and knew she was about to die. She dropped to the ground, never hearing the sound of the Winchester or the cry of death before Gray Wolf fell beside her.

It was only a matter of seconds before Stella blinked her eyes open, and the image she saw was that of Perley pulling up his pants and buttoning them. Confused at first, she was aware of a stinging sensation on the side of her neck, and she suddenly remembered what had happened just before she fainted. Her hand went immediately to the cut on her neck, and she gasped when she came away with blood on her fingers.

"It ain't bad," Perley assured her, "but it woulda been. He'd started to cut your throat, but I saw him just in time. The cut ain't no longer than an inch or so, and it ain't deep. We'll have to clean it up and put some grease or somethin' on it. Like I said, he just started to cut your throat. He didn't have time to finish."

"I swear, I thought it was you that grabbed me. Where did he come from?" Stella asked as he buckled his belt. "And why were your pants down?"

"I suspect he was one of those three Indians that have been trailin' us all along." He answered her first question and ignored the second, thinking she should be able to figure that out. "I don't know why he was by himself."

Then it occurred to him — where was Liz? At once concerned for her safety, he said, "Come on, we've gotta see if Liz is all right."

He helped Stella to her feet and they ran back to the camp, where they found Liz hunkered down behind her saddle, her Colt .44 in her hand.

When Stella saw her, she immediately wanted an explanation. "What the hell were you doin' back here when we were in the bushes with that wild Indian? Why didn't you come to help us? That damn Indian almost cut my throat."

Liz took a minute to holster her pistol and get on her feet. "I got ready to shoot the first son of a bitch that came after me once I heard that shot. I didn't see any use in jumpin' in the bushes just 'cause you two were runnin' around in the dark. I mighta got killed."

Stella shuddered when she thought about how close she had come to dying. "If it hadn't been for you, I'd be dead right now," she said to Perley.

"If you hadn't called me, I might be dead right now," Perley said, thinking of the arrow that struck the tree at about the same height as his belly would have been had he not dropped to the ground. "You kept callin' out to me, but in the dark back there I couldn't see you, and I was tryin' to get you to be quiet and hide. And I reckon that's the only reason both the Indian and me found you. I had to shoot fast, else he was fixin' to open up your throat. I was afraid I might hit you instead of him." He shrugged. "If I hadda hit you, I reckon it woulda beat gettin' your throat cut."

"Well, I guess that's one way of lookin' at

it," Stella replied sarcastically. "But I guess I still owe you my life. Is there any way I can repay you?"

"Huh," Liz grunted. "You don't ever give up, do ya? Why don't you just go ahead and give me that dollar? Ain't nobody gonna do nothin' for the rest of this night." She drew her .44 and checked to make sure there was a round in every cylinder. "I know I ain't gonna sleep no more tonight. There were three of those Indians, and I ain't sure the other two ain't sneakin' around this camp somewhere." She holstered her pistol. "Come on, I'll see if I can come up with something to bandage that cut on your neck."

"I think I'll stay awake," Perley said. "I don't know why, but I think that one came after us all by himself. He musta left his two friends, else we'da had arrows flyin' all around us. It ain't gonna be that long till sunup anyway — might as well bring this fire back to life."

As he had guessed, there was no further incident during the remaining hours of darkness. And when the early morning light began to dissolve the heavy shadows under the trees, he went back to the spot where Stella was attacked. The body of Gray Wolf was lying where it had fallen, the knife close beside it and his bow a few feet away.

Perley stood for a long moment, staring at the corpse of one who had come to kill him and the women. Hostile savage or not, he was a man, and Perley had taken his life. He had never killed anyone before, and the feeling of it was one he hoped he would never experience again. Being totally honest with himself, however, he could not say that he had had a choice. The Indian was in the process of slitting Stella's throat. "Well," Perley finally said, "I hope that's the last we see of those three."

He then pushed a few yards farther through the bushes and saw the arrow in the tree and, after another look, realized that Stella had indeed saved his life when she caused him to drop to the ground. Walking up to stand before the tree, he found that the arrow was even with his chest.

He went back to the previous site and knelt down to take a closer look at the body. The single round he had fired had struck the Indian in the side of his head. He tried to picture the shooting again and realized that he was lucky he had not hit Stella. It was so dark, the angle was not the best, and there was very little margin for error. He shook his head as if to clear the picture.

Then he thought of his brothers and the many shooting competitions they'd had between the three of them, both hunting and target shooting. Perley always won. He didn't know why — he was just a better shot, with a rifle or handgun.

His thoughts were interrupted then when he heard Liz calling him. He took another look at the body and wondered if he should bury it or not. It was only for a second, before he decided, *I'll leave it. No sense in cheating the wolves and the buzzards out of a meal.*

"Me and Stella decided we're gonna have breakfast this mornin' before we start out again. That all right with you? 'Cause if it ain't, we're wastin' bacon that's already in the pan and a full pot of fresh coffee."

"Don't make no difference to me," he replied, "if that's what you ladies want."

"We figured the danger's about over, since you shot that Injun last night," Stella said. "And if it ain't but about half a day's ride, there ain't no real hurry from here on in."

"And you've about starved us to death every day, waitin' for the horses to get tired before we can eat breakfast," Liz informed him.

"Oh," Perley muttered. "I reckon that's just a habit from drivin' cattle — start 'em early, then stop at noon to let 'em eat."

"So now we find out we're no better'n cattle," Liz said. "Whaddaya think about that, Stella?"

"I believe we've been insulted," Stella said. "He don't think we're ladies at all. We ought not let him eat with us."

He knew he was being teased. They were having a little fun at his expense, but he still could not help blushing. And the more he blushed, the more it encouraged them to keep it up. They were obviously feeling free of worry now that Cheyenne was so close. They kept it up for a little while longer before Liz said the bacon was going to burn black if she didn't take it off the fire. She served it up with some hardtack soaked in the grease, almost spilling Stella's when Stella placed a dollar in her hand. It caused them both to laugh, puzzling Perley.

They were not as close to Cheyenne as Perley had figured. Still, they caught sight of the buildings of the bustling town in the late afternoon. Perley was surprised by the size of the town and the number of buildings more than two stories high. Especially impressive were the Union Pacific Railroad depot and the magnificent Inter-Ocean Hotel, which they rode by on their way to the Cattleman's Saloon. The saloon was across the street from Dyer's Hotel, a two-story building with considerably less magnificence than the Inter-Ocean. According to Stella, who was bubbling with excitement to be back, the hotel was built by an Irishman named Timothy Dyer, and many of his customers frequented the Cattleman's.

Perley was still tying the horses at the hitching rail in front of the saloon when Stella, with Liz in tow, hurried inside to announce her return. He paused to take a look around him at the many people on the street and decided the town was too busy to suit him. *Good thing I ain't gonna be here that long,* he thought, then gave Buck a pat on his neck and stepped up onto the boardwalk.

Inside, the saloon was doing a brisk business for an afternoon, but he spotted Stella and Liz in an animated conversation with a short bald man sporting a black handlebar mustache. At about the same time, Stella spotted Perley and waved him on over.

"C.J.," Stella said when he walked up, "this is Perley Gates. He's the man who brought Liz and me back from Ogallala. Perley, this is C. J. Tubbs. He's the bartender here."

C.J. extended his hand while looking Perley up and down. "What was the name?"

Never surprised by the question, Perley shook his hand and replied, "Perley Gates." He noticed Stella's expectant grin, but C.J. made no comment about his name, prompting Stella to resume her conversation with the bartender.

"Where's Ed?" she asked. "Is he in the office?"

C.J. said that he was, so Stella said that she was going to take Liz back there to meet him. "Pour Perley a drink on me. We'll be back in a minute." She didn't wait for Perley's response as she grabbed Liz by the hand and led her to a door behind the bar.

"She's really somethin', ain't she?" C.J. commented as he poured Perley's drink. "I'm glad to see her back here. I thought she'd gone for good. How 'bout you? You fixin' to stay in Cheyenne for a while?"

"Nope," Perley answered. "I expect I'll be headin' out in the mornin'. All I agreed to do was bring Stella and Liz to Cheyenne; then I'm headin' south to Denver."

"Denver?" C.J. replied. "I'da figured you'd be headin' to Deadwood like most of the other strangers in town."

"Where's that?"

"Deadwood?" C.J. replied, finding it hard to believe there was anyone who didn't know. "Up in the. Black Hills where the gold strike is." He kept staring at Perley then, expecting him to react. When he didn't, C.J. went on to bring him up to date. "That's all most folks are talkin' about around here, goin' to the Black Hills to strike it rich. Folks are comin' from Denver to head up that way, too. If I was as young as you, I'd most likely join 'em. A feller came through town a little while back, headin' up there with a whole wagon train of people. Most of 'em was sportin' ladies. They've even set up a stagecoach line from Cheyenne to the Black Hills — the Deadwood Stage." He shook his head in wonder. "I can't believe you didn't even know about it."

"I've been outta touch," Perley said. "I came up from Texas with a herd of cattle. I only stayed in Ogallala one night, and nobody was talkin' about a gold rush — at least, not where I was. After that, I was on that trail between there and here."

C.J. shrugged. "Well, I expect you'll hear plenty about it now." Then, changing the subject abruptly, he asked, "Is Perley Gates your real name?"

Perley had wondered when he was going to get around to that. He very patiently told C.J. the story behind his name, which led to the reason he was going to Denver.

"So, you're lookin' for your grandpa, huh?"

"That's a fact," Perley replied. "But I reckon I'll have to drop off two horses at the stable. They belong to Liz and Stella, so I guess that's what they'll wanna do with 'em."

"There's two stables in town now," C.J. said. "The closest one to here is Tom Tuttle's." He pointed to a tall man at the end of the bar, talking to two other men. "That's Tom right there, the tall feller. You can tell him what you wanna do right now."

"Much obliged. I believe I will."

While Perley was making arrangements with Tom Tuttle to board the two horses the women rode in on, they were talking with Ed Freeman, the owner of the saloon.

"Well, I can't say as how I'm surprised to see you," Freeman remarked. "I told you you'd be comin' back here. What happened to that gambler you run off with? Is he back, too? 'Cause if he is, I've done told him he ain't welcome to run his game here."

"I was always plannin' to come back to the Cattleman's," Stella lied. "I thought you knew I was just goin' to Ogallala for a visit." She flashed a wide smile for him. "Charley ain't comin' back. I cut him loose. I don't know where he headed after he left Ogallala and I don't give a damn. Anyway, I talked Liz, here, into comin' back with me. She was one of the most popular girls workin' in the Cowboy's Rest, so I knew you'd be tickled if I brought her with me."

Freeman took a long look of appraisal at the sizable woman dressed in men's clothes before he responded to Stella. "What made her so popular? She looks like a mule skinner or a cowhand to me."

"You ain't seen me in my war paint," Liz said, speaking for herself now. "I clean up pretty good. I was robbed of all my clothes, and Stella and me had to run from Indians on the way here. We thought it best to try to make me look like a man from a distance."

Not certain he was hearing the true version of the story, Freeman commented, "You look like a man up close to me."

"When I get cleaned up and in some decent clothes, you'll see a helluva difference," Liz said. "I've had a lotta men pay good money to jump in bed with me, and I ain't ever had one jump outta the bed."

"She's tellin' you the truth," Stella said. "You'll see. Liz will sell a lot of whiskey for you."

"You're lucky you hit me at the right time," Freeman replied dryly. "Lottie Beale got married last month."

"You don't say," Stella responded, genuinely surprised. "That bashful farmer with one bad eye, I'll bet."

"That's the one," Freeman said.

"See, I knew you needed me and Liz. I'm glad we got here when we did so we can keep you from losin' any business."

"Ah, hell, all right." Freeman gave in, although he was still a little hesitant. "We'll see how it goes for a while, but damn it, you sure better not run off without so much as a 'kiss my ass' like you did before." He took another hard look at Liz. "And get her fixed up in some decent clothes so she at least looks like a woman. Ain't nobody using your old room upstairs, so I reckon the two of you can share it." They started to return to the barroom when he thought of something else. "You're gonna have to get along with Cora. She's been the queen around here ever since Lottie Beale got married."

"Oh, I'll set things straight with Cora," Stella said, and when they went out the door, she muttered low to Liz, "I'll kick her ass if she gets snotty with me."

"I thought you said he was a friend of yours," Liz said. She was still astonished by the story she had just heard. Stella had never mentioned a gambler named Charley, or how she happened to land in Ogallala.

"He was, and he will be again in a day or two," Stella replied confidently. "Let's go see how Perley's doin'."

They found Perley talking to Tom Tuttle and a couple of other men when they returned to the barroom. When they walked over to join the group, Perley said, "I was just talkin' to Mr. Tuttle, here, about boardin' your horses. I reckon that's what you wanna do."

Before they could answer, Tuttle interrupted. "You're Stella, ain't you?" She smiled and nodded. "I thought you looked familiar when you walked in a few minutes ago. You been away awhile. Least, I ain't seen you in here for a spell. Who's this fellow with you?"

Perley saw Liz wince and immediately felt her embarrassment. "That's Liz MacDonald," he was quick to respond. "She's just dressed up like a man. She don't look half that bad when she's dressed up like a woman." As soon as he said it, he knew it didn't sound right. "What I mean is —"

That was as far as he got before Liz interrupted. "I swear, Perley, you do have a way with words," she said, unable to keep from laughing. "I reckon the first place I need to go is to the store to get me some clothes. Then a good soakin' in a tub of hot water and a fresh coat of paint, and I'll show you my better self."

"Ma'am, I didn't mean no disrespect," Tuttle started to apologize.

"Never you mind," Liz said before he went any further. "I'm a whore and have been since I was fourteen. It ain't the first time I've been insulted. Now, you say Perley and you were talkin' about our horses?"

Before they left the bar, Liz had arranged a deal wherein Tuttle would buy the women's horses and saddles, despite the fact that Tuttle had not inspected either horse at that point. He agreed to meet Perley at the stable to take possession of the two horses as soon as he finished his drink with his two friends.

"I'll go ahead and bring the horses, soon as Liz and Stella get anything they've left in the saddlebags, and I'll wait for you down there," Perley said.

Liz and Stella walked out to the hitching rail with him, and he waited while they got the few things they had bought at Duck Bend, which wasn't much.

"Whaddaya gonna do after you take the horses to the stable?" Liz asked.

"I don't know," Perley answered. "Maybe

find somethin' to eat somewhere; then I'll make camp down along that creek close to town," he said, referring to Crow Creek. "Reckon I'll head out to Denver in the mornin'. If I'm lucky, maybe I'll cut my grandpa's trail somewhere down in Colorado Territory."

"I figure we owe you a good supper," Liz said and looked at Stella to receive her nod of agreement. "I know we owe you a helluva lot more than that for what you did for us. I don't know if we'da made it without you."

"That's mighty nice of you to say that," he replied. "But you don't owe me anything. I'm glad I happened along when I did."

"I'm gonna miss you, Perley Gates," Stella said, then caught herself before she got downright emotional. "You get through at the stables and come on back here. Liz and I will take you to supper at the diner next to Dyer's Hotel. There's a woman runs that place that's a helluva cook — might as well start you off to Denver with a solid meal in your belly. We'll either be in the saloon or upstairs, first room on the right, when you get back."

"All right, if you insist," Perley said. "I can't pass up a good supper."

CHAPTER 9

"Sorry to keep you waiting — Perley, was it?" Tom Tuttle said when he approached him standing at the hitching rail before the stable. Perley had separated the horses, with Buck and his packhorse at one end of the rail and the flea-bitten gray and three Indian ponies at the other. "I buy a lot of hay from those two fellows you saw me with, so they wanted to buy me a drink," Tuttle said.

"I ain't in a hurry," Perley said. "There's the two horses you bought, those two with the saddles on 'em. One of 'em's an Indian pony; the other one's the gray you see there. I was listenin' to the trade you were makin' with Liz, and I thought you were mighty generous with your offer. But I wouldn't be honest if I didn't tell you that gray ain't got many days left in him. The Indian pony's a pretty good horse, but you gave more than that gray's worth. So, if it's all the same to you, I'll throw in those other two Indian ponies, so you don't get skunked on the deal."

His offer astonished Tuttle. "Well, that's mighty decent of you. Did those two belong to the women, too?"

"Well, no, sir, those two belong to me. I was aimin' to sell 'em if I could, since I ain't got no use for 'em. But I think it would only be right to turn 'em over to you to make the deal a fair one."

Tuttle was more than a little confused. He wasn't sure he was hearing Perley correctly. "Are you connected to those women in any way? Married to one of 'em, or something?"

Perley chuckled. "No, sir. I just met 'em a few days ago, and they were stranded back this side of Ogallala — fellow they'd hired to take 'em here ran off with their pack-horse. So, I rode to Cheyenne with 'em. They're whores, but they're nice folks once you get to know 'em. You seemed like a reasonable fellow, so I didn't like to see you get skunked with a lame horse."

Tuttle looked as if he didn't know what to say. Perley continued. "And I'd like to give you a little business to boot. I told the women I'd let 'em buy my supper, so I'd like to leave my bay and my packhorse here till mornin'."

"Perley, that's the damnedest thing I've

ever heard, and I appreciate your honesty." He thought about it for a moment, then made an offer. "Tell you what, why don't I give you thirty dollars for the two extra horses, so you don't lose out on everything? And I won't charge you to board your other horses for the night — or you, either, if you wanna sleep with 'em. How's that?"

"That's fair enough," Perley said. "I 'preciate it. I hope you don't think Liz was tryin' to skunk you. Fact of the matter is, I don't think she knows enough about horses to tell if one is young or old or stout or frail."

"I think you're right," Tuttle said as he took a look in the gray's mouth. "I've got to be more careful when I do any tradin' with women." When Perley started to walk away, Tuttle said, "I lock the barn and the stable at seven o'clock."

"I'll be back before then," Perley assured him, then headed for the saloon.

When he got to the Cattleman's, he didn't see Liz or Stella anywhere in the room, so he walked up to the bar.

"Howdy, Perley," C.J. sang out. "Stella said to tell you she and the other woman are upstairs — top of the steps, first room on the left."

"Much obliged," Perley said and turned toward the stairs.

C.J. said first room on the left, but Perley was sure he remembered Stella saying first room on the right. He decided Stella most likely knew which room she had used when she lived there before, so when he reached the top, he went to the door on the right and rapped lightly. There was no response to his knocking. He waited a few seconds and rapped again — still no response. Obviously it was an empty room and C.J. was right, Stella's room must be on the left. Perley decided to look inside anyway, just to be sure, so he turned the knob and found the door unlocked. Since it was open, he walked on inside, thinking maybe it was Stella's room after all, and they had gone to the kitchen or maybe the outhouse. The room was dark, so just to make sure he wasn't catching them by surprise, he sang out cheerfully, "Everybody decent?" He was not prepared for the picture he saw when his eyes adjusted to the darkness in the room.

"What the hell?" the voice of an irate man erupted, obviously in the midst of a contract with the equally irate woman in the bed with him.

"Get the hell outta here!" Cora Burke yelled.

Another cow pie was the thought that flashed through Perley's mind, and in a matter of seconds, he found himself confronted by what he considered at that moment to be the biggest human being he had ever seen.

"Pardon the interruption, folks. My mistake, wrong room. Just carry on with your activities — I'll let myself out." He backed hurriedly toward the door, only to be followed by the enraged beast. "I don't blame you one bit for being irritated," Perley said in an attempt to calm the man. "I apologize one hundred percent, and I'll let you get back to your business."

Evidently, he had intruded at precisely the wrong moment, for the giant he could now see clearly, since the man had followed him into the hallway, showed no tendency to forgive. Cora's encouragement from inside the room didn't help the matter. "Kick his ass, Brady!" she yelled.

"There ain't really no need for that," Perley said, thinking to calm the brute. "I made a mistake and I said I'm sorry, so let's let that be the end of it and I'll be on my way."

Brady's response was an evil smile on his broad face.

"I don't wanna keep you out here in the hall without your clothes on," Perley continued. "You might catch pneumonia or something, with no more'n that little towel wrapped around you."

"I'm fixin' to break your back for you," Brady threatened, his voice a low growl. "Come bustin' in the room like that. I paid Cora for the whole night, and she ain't cheap."

"Kick his ass, Brady!" Cora repeated, her voice resembling the screech of a buzzard fighting over a corpse.

"She sounds charmin'," Perley couldn't resist commenting. "So, I'll let you get back to her now."

Behind him, he heard doors opening, as sounds of the altercation were transmitted down the hall. One of them was directly opposite the room he had mistakenly entered, and he heard a familiar voice.

"Perley! What's goin' on?"

"I walked in the wrong room and interrupted this fellow, and now he's wantin' to break my back, so he says," Perley answered while maneuvering warily, anticipating the big man's charge.

"He don't look like he's dressed for a fight," Liz said as she walked out to join Stella in the hallway. She took a moment to evaluate the situation, then stepped forward and grabbed the towel knotted around Brady's massive waist. With one quick jerk of the knot, she pulled the towel away, causing a chorus of snickering from the small audience that had come out into the hall to watch.

Shocked, the embarrassed brute tried to cover himself with his hands and fled back into the room to escape his humiliation. Liz popped him on his rear with the towel just as he disappeared through the doorway. The door slammed shut behind him.

"I'll leave the towel on your doorknob in case you wanna come out again," Liz yelled. Then she looked at Stella. "You ready? Let's get the hell outta here before he gets his clothes on."

"I'm ready," Stella replied, still giggling. She grabbed Perley by the elbow. "Sorry, Perley, I'm always mixin' up right with left. Come on, let's go eat supper."

He hurried down the stairs with the two women, running from a savage attack once again, just like their ride from Ogallala, only this time they were all laughing.

"What was all the fuss upstairs?" C.J. asked when they passed by the bar on their way out.

"Nothin' much," Stella answered, "just Cora and one of her gentlemen friends. If anybody wants us, we'll be at the dining room in the Inter-Ocean Hotel."

Once outside, they turned in the opposite

direction and headed to Katie's Diner, next to Dyer's Hotel.

"Say howdy to Katie Taylor and her cook, Myra Long," Stella said when they walked into the diner.

"I declare, gal, where in the world have you been?" Katie asked Stella. "I thought you musta found one of Myra's fingernails in the stew and started eatin' at that fancy dining room at the hotel."

"Nope," Stella answered. "I've been outta town for a spell. Got to missin' your cookin' so bad I had to come back to Cheyenne."

"I see you brought a couple of friends with you," Katie said. "And who's this handsome young feller?"

Stella introduced Perley and Liz. "I told 'em how good the cookin' is here, so don't go and make a liar outta me."

"We'll just let them decide that for themselves," Katie said. "I'm mighty pleased you dropped in," she said to Liz and Perley. "Everybody drinkin' coffee?" When she received three affirmative nods, she went to the coffeepot on the stove in the back of the room.

"I guess she doesn't mind servin' prostitutes," Liz commented when Katie was out of earshot, "or does she not know you're a workin' girl?" They were not welcome in the two diners in Ogallala.

"Hell, if it wasn't for the business she gets from whores, she wouldn't make it," Stella said. "She don't tolerate bad behavior, from whores or anybody else. She'll ask you to leave quick enough if you don't behave yourself. And if askin' ain't enough, Myra limbers up her shotgun."

Katie returned with their coffee and placed the cups around. "This young feller must be a big spender," she said. "He's buyin' your supper. Ain't many of your customers that'll spring for supper, too."

Stella laughed. "He ain't buyin' our supper — I'm buyin' his, and he ain't a customer. He's a friend, and a damn good one."

Katie raised her eyebrows at that. "Well, I beg your pardon, young man. I didn't know there was any such thing as a damn good man."

"Sounds like you've run into too many of the other kind," Perley said.

"You can say that for a fact," Katie replied. "Now, whatcha gonna have? I've got beef stew or bean soup, or a little of both, if you want it." Stew was the unanimous choice, so Katie yelled the order out to Myra in the kitchen.

The cooking was good, just as Stella had

promised, and had it not been for the four biscuits Perley polished off, he might have ordered seconds on the stew.

"It's a little better eatin' than we've had for the last four days, ain't it?" Stella commented. "I reckon this is the last time we'll break bread together, and I want you to know how much I appreciate you takin' your time to make sure me and Liz got here alive."

"That goes for me, too," Liz said. "You're a good man, Perley. I hope you find your grandpappy."

Perley was touched by their words, and more than a little embarrassed. He found himself feeling guilty again for having wished he had not been so unlucky as to have run into them on the South Platte. He decided at that moment that he was now glad that he had met the two women.

The feeling was not long-lasting, extending only past the fried apple pie, when the door of the diner was suddenly filled with the bulk of Brady Ennis. He said nothing for a long moment while he looked the room over, trying to recall what the man who had walked in on him looked like. His vision may not have been as sharp as it normally would be, due to the amount of whiskey he had imbibed during his search.

There were not that many people in the diner, so his gaze kept returning to the table where a man and two women sat. A slow smile began to form on the broad, hairy face as he settled on the two women and decided one of them, the one wearing men's clothes, was the one who had jerked the towel from him. So, that meant the man sitting at the table was the man who had walked into the room and caused all the trouble. Brady stood there, grinning with the anticipation of exacting his revenge and taking his time about it.

He ducked his head to keep from bumping it on the lintel and walked over to stand in front of the man and the two women, all of whom were staring at him in total shock. Even Liz was not prone to move.

"I've been lookin' for the three of you. You ran outta the Cattleman's before I had a chance to get my clothes on — been lookin' all up and down the street for you." His eyes locked on Perley's. "I promised to give you something."

"A broken back?" Perley guessed. "But there's no need to trouble yourself, I won't hold you to it." He gestured toward Liz and Stella. "We've forgotten all about it, so you might as well, too. Have yourself a slice of this pie and a cup of coffee. That'll make you feel better."

Brady, confused for a moment, couldn't believe what he was hearing. "Are you tryin' to make a fool outta me?"

"No, sir, I'm a little late for that job," Perley replied. "I'm just tryin' to keep you from makin' a bigger fool outta yourself. Everybody in the Cattleman's is laughin' at how you were runnin' around the hall upstairs buck naked. Pretty soon that's gonna be all over town. I'd think you wouldn't wanna hang around for that, but hell, I ain't sayin' I know what's best for you."

"What's it gonna be?" Brady demanded, his patience exhausted. "Knives? Guns? Bare hands? Are you gonna fight or not?"

"Well, given a choice and being a sensible man, I'd ordinarily say I'd rather not. But if you're tellin' me I've got to pick, then I pick guns for me and bare hands for you. And I think it's mighty damn sportin' of you to offer that choice. Now, when do you wanna have this contest? Next Thursday is good for me. How's your schedule?"

Confused and unable to believe the prattle coming from the man sitting at the table, Brady seemed stunned for a few long moments. Then his face and neck appeared to glow red beneath his beard as the frustration progressed to a state of uncontrolled rage, until it finally erupted like an explosion of dynamite and he dived across the table at Perley.

Stella and Liz screamed as the table collapsed under the weight of the brute, and they scrambled to escape the assault. Perley went backward, but unlike the women, he had counted on an insane attack, figuring that was most likely his only chance against the monster. While Brady was still in midair over the table, Perley had taken a firm grip on the handle of the heavy iron skillet that held half of a fried apple pie, which he learned later to be a favorite with Katie's customers. The heavy skillet sounded a dull thud when it bounced off Brady's skull on the first blow. The second seemed more like the clang of a bell. It was difficult to guess which one was the strike that knocked the beast senseless, to lie sprawled on the broken table.

The room was dead silent, as the few customers to have witnessed the attack were speechless. Katie and Myra, holding her shotgun, were just as stunned as they watched Perley knock Brady cold.

"Have you got any rope?" he asked Katie.

She shook her head.

"We've got a spool of clothesline," Myra volunteered.

"That'll do," Perley said, and she went immediately to fetch it.

Brady had not stirred when she returned with the clothesline. Perley took it from her, pulled Brady's arms behind his back, and tied his wrists. Then he tied his ankles, and while he worked, he asked a young man, one of the diners, to go and fetch the sheriff.

"Is he dead?" Liz wondered aloud.

"No, I don't think so," Perley replied, "but he's gonna have a helluva headache when he does come to."

"Well, I hope you tied him real good," Stella said, " 'cause he's gonna be madder'n hell when he does."

"I expect so," Perley agreed. He turned, talking to all the spectators in the place. "You all saw what happened. He came in here after me. I tried to talk him into sittin' down and havin' some pie and coffee, but he insisted on attackin' me. All I did was try to defend myself." He wanted to make sure they all saw the same thing, for when the sheriff got there.

"Ain't no doubt about that," Katie said. "I think everybody agrees on that."

In a little while, the young man returned with a deputy, the sheriff having already gone home for supper. The deputy, a no-nonsense individual named Bill Snipe, stood for a long moment over the prostrate body draped across the tabletop before he questioned Katie.

"What is that? Is that his brains spillin' outta his head?"

"No," Katie answered. "Them's fried apples."

"Oh," Snipe said. "Then he ain't dead."

To confirm it, Brady stirred as he began to come back from his sudden nap, growling drunkenly about killing someone. It was not hard to guess who started the trouble.

"Brady Ennis," Snipe said with a generous measure of disgust, "you ain't been in town two whole days yet and I've already had half a dozen complaints about you. I think a little time in jail is gonna be the cure for what ails you."

He untied Brady's ankles so he could walk, and with Perley's help, he got the huge man on his feet. Although groggy and unsteady when he stood up, Brady tried to resist when Snipe pushed him toward the door. Snipe drew his .44 and threatened him. "I ain't got time to fool with you, Ennis. I'm gonna fetch you another rap on the head if you don't start walkin'."

He held the pistol up, ready to deliver another blow to Brady's skull. It was enough to convince the huge man that he couldn't risk taking another one.

"Perley Gates," Brady mumbled as he stumbled out the door. "I ain't gonna forget that name."

"Perley Gates?" Bill Snipe echoed and looked at Perley. "Is that you?"

"Afraid so," Perley answered.

"You figurin' on bein' in town awhile?" Snipe asked.

"Nope, hadn't planned on it — figured I'd be leavin' in the mornin'."

"Good," Snipe said. " 'Cause I won't hold Brady more'n two days. That's about as long as we hold anybody for fightin' when nobody gets shot."

With Brady out the door, Perley turned to help the women clean up the mess Brady had caused. "I'm real sorry about the damage," he said to Katie as he rolled the tabletop out of their way. "Top's okay, but the legs are broke down pretty bad. I reckon I owe you for the cost of fixin' 'em. Sorry 'bout the pie, too. I'll pay for that, too. Shame to see it go to waste, though." He pointed to a fair-sized piece of it on the floor next to the wall. "There's a piece that could be salvaged."

Katie had to laugh. "Is that right? Well, how 'bout I serve it to you with another cup of coffee?" When he hesitated, not sure if she was joking or not, she said, "Don't worry about payin' for this mess. We'll clean it up, and I'll get Myra's husband to fix the table. He's handy with things like that."

"That's about all he's handy at," Myra said, causing the women to chuckle.

When the food and coffee were all cleaned up off the floor, Perley, Liz, and Stella walked back down the street to the Cattleman's. They paused at the door when Perley said he was going to say good night to them then.

"I reckon I'll go on back to the stable. I'm thinkin' I'll head out early in the mornin', so I'd best get some sleep."

"Well, I reckon this is good-bye, till you happen through this way again," Liz said. "I'll tell you one thing, Perley, there's always somethin' happenin' with you around. But speakin' for myself, I'm gonna miss you, and I wish you were gonna be around from now on."

On cue, Perley blushed.

"That goes for me, too," Stella said. "You take care of yourself — trouble seems to have a likin' for you."

He wished them good fortune and walked away. He had to admit that he had taken kind of a liking to them in the short time he had spent with them. But there was also the feeling that he had just lifted his foot out of a cow pie.

He got back to the stable to find Tom Tuttle waiting for him.

"I was just fixin' to lock up," Tuttle said. "Supper's waitin' at the house, and I thought you musta changed your mind about sleepin' in the barn."

"I got held up a little longer'n I figured on," Perley said. "What time will you open up in the mornin'?"

Tuttle said he'd be in at six for sure, maybe five-thirty, so Perley decided he'd get on the trail to Denver as soon as Tuttle showed up and worry about breakfast when his horses needed a rest. In his brief exposure to Cheyenne, he hadn't seen anything that would cause him to want to tarry there. To the contrary, the prospect of Brady Ennis getting out of jail was reason enough to make him eager to leave. He felt no fear of Brady, but it always suited him to avoid trouble if he possibly could.

After Tuttle left, Perley decided to help himself to Tuttle's oats, with a portion for both of his horses. He thought about whether or not to tell Tuttle about it in the morning. After making sure his packs were ready to load onto the sorrel in the morning, he decided to sleep in the stall with

Buck instead of in the barn hayloft as Tuttle had suggested. The big bay gelding probably needed the company.

The night was passed peacefully enough, and Perley was pleased to see Tuttle arrive on time. After telling Tuttle the saga of his grandfather, he saddled Buck, loaded the packhorse, and told Tuttle he owed him for two portions of oats.

"You don't owe me anything," Tuttle insisted. "I hope you find your grandpa alive and well."

"Much obliged," Perley said and stepped up into the saddle. "Follow the railroad straight south, right?"

"That's right," Tuttle replied. "The Denver Pacific Railway — runs straight south for about a hundred miles. You'll strike the South Platte about halfway there, and the railroad follows it right into Denver."

Perley touched his finger to his hat brim and turned Buck toward the railroad that the people of Denver had caused to be built when the Union Pacific ran their track through Cheyenne, one hundred miles to the north, instead of Denver.

CHAPTER 10

Riding alone once more, Perley was a whole lot more at ease, with nothing to set his mind on but finding his grandfather. Denver was where he aimed to start searching for him again, thinking that it was a good possibility the old man might indeed have had hopes of finding gold there. At least, that's what he kept telling his conscious mind. His inner thoughts were more in line with his brother John's thinking — that there wasn't a chance in hell that he would find any trace of his grandfather. Regardless of his success, however, one thing was for certain: the younger Perley Gates was going to see the Rocky Mountains.

At the end of the first day, Perley rode into a sizable town lying beside a river near the foothills of the Front Range of the Rockies. It appeared to be a quiet town, although thriving, judging by the appearance of the buildings he passed as he walked Buck down the main street.

"Excuse me, sir," he said when he saw a man coming out of a barbershop. "What river is this?"

"It's the Cache La Poudre River," the man answered. Then, guessing that Perley wasn't familiar with that, he added, "And if you're wondering where you are, you're in Fort Collins."

"Much obliged," Perley said, unfamiliar with town or river. He had hoped he might have struck the South Platte, but he knew now that it had to be farther south. At any rate, the railroad went to Denver, so it was impossible to get lost.

All day, he had been riding with the lofty peaks of the mountains to the west of him, now so close that he thought he could feel their lure. He imagined that his grandfather had felt the same call of the mysterious range. He decided that he would camp on the bank of the river that night, and in the morning, he would follow the river back up through the foothills in search of game. He was getting a little tired of salt pork. It was time to hunt for fresh meat. Following the pristine river back toward the mountains with his eyes, he figured there had to be deer or elk not far away. He was running low on supplies, too, a result of his taking

Liz and Stella to Cheyenne, so he decided to stock up here in town.

Realizing then that the man was waiting to see if he had any more questions, he apologized. "Sorry, I reckon I let my mind start wanderin'. Where's a good place to buy supplies, like coffee and flour and such?"

"Steiner's is as good as any," the man replied, then turned and pointed, "right down the street on the other side."

"Much obliged," Perley said again and turned Buck's head toward the building the man had pointed out.

He pulled his horses up beside a farm wagon tied at the rail and looked up and down the street before he went inside. Fort Collins seemed a far cry from a cattle town, or a railroad town like Cheyenne. The people he had seen so far looked to be farmers.

"Good evening, friend," a large, portly man with a full head of dark brown hair and a beard to match greeted him. "I'll be with you in a minute."

The man went on to finish filling a bag with seed, then totaled up the order for a customer standing at the counter. When the customer had left, he turned his attention to Perley. He studied Perley for a few seconds before asking, "What can I do for you? Don't recall seeing you in the store before. Just passin' through?"

"Yes, sir," Perley answered politely. "I'm on my way to Denver, and I'm runnin' short on some supplies — thought maybe I could buy 'em here." He called off a few things and the quantity he needed.

Satisfied with the sizable order and the cash it was paid with, the big man said, "My name's Louis Steiner. I appreciate you stopping in." He was curious about the polite young fellow, who looked like a cowhand, judging by the clothes he wore. "If you don't mind me asking, are you by any chance looking for a place to homestead? Because if you are, Fort Collins is the best place in the territory to claim a plot of land and raise a young family."

"No, sir," Perley replied. "I ain't lookin' for a place to homestead. My family's got a ranch in Texas. I'm lookin' for my grandpa." He went on to explain, and when he had finished, he asked, just to be sure, "You ain't seen an old fellow named Perley Gates come through here, have you?"

"No, sorry to say I haven't," Steiner said. "I believe that's a name I would have remembered. What makes you think he headed to Denver?"

"Nothin', really, except he seemed to be headin' that way when he left Ogallala, and folks said there was a lot of prospectin' on Cherry Creek there."

Steiner nodded while he considered that. "I expect it's too late to be lookin' for gold down there now. It's probably about mined out. Young fellow like you would do better claiming a lot around here, like the other young families. Build you a good farm and work to a solid future."

"Well, like I said," Perley replied, "I ain't huntin' for gold, I'm huntin' for Grandpa." He picked up the sacks containing his purchases. "Thanks again for your help. I expect I'd best get along if I'm gonna find something to eat before I camp for the night."

"Have you got a wife back there in Texas?"

"No, sir," Perley answered, "no wife."

"I expect you've probably had enough of suppers on the trail, haven't you?" Steiner asked.

"That's a fact if there ever was one," Perley answered. "But you get used to it, and it's better'n goin' hungry."

"Well, why don't you have supper with me and the missus tonight? My wife always fixes more'n we can eat, and she's always

239

happy to meet new folks comin' through town."

"Why, that's mighty kind of you," Perley said, more than a little surprised. "But I wouldn't wanna impose on you, and I wouldn't wanna surprise your wife with an extra mouth to feed."

"She'd be tickled to have you — she always is. We don't eat till after I close the store at five o'clock. I'll be looking for you at that time right here."

Perley was astonished. He wondered if Steiner treated all strangers to Fort Collins in the same way. "I can always use a home-cooked supper," he said after a moment's hesitation while he tried to think of a reason to refuse.

"Good," Steiner said. "I'll see you back here at five o'clock."

"Who was that, Louis?" Mary Steiner asked when she came in from the back.

"Just some young fellow passing through town," Louis answered. "Seemed pretty solid, the kind we need more of in Fort Collins."

She raised a suspicious eyebrow. "You didn't try to marry off one of our daughters again, did you?"

"Of course not," he huffed. "Why would you think such a thing? He's on his way to look for his grandfather. I just felt kinda sorry for him, so I invited him to supper — figured you wouldn't mind."

"Why, Louis Steiner," she scolded, "you could have asked me before you go inviting any old drifter to the supper table."

"I don't think he's a drifter, and he ain't old," her husband replied in self-defense. "I told you, he's trying to find his dear old grandpa."

"You should be ashamed of yourself," she railed. "Our five beautiful daughters are precious to me, and you're always trying to sell them off like they were sacks of potatoes in your store." She bit her lip to keep from speaking profanely. "You could have at least given me more time to fix extra food for some half-starved stranger. I've got to go home right now before Virginia puts the biscuits in the oven. We're gonna need more if we're gonna fill his belly."

She gathered up her shawl and headed toward the back door, leaving her husband to exhale forcefully in frustration and call after her, "Tell them to put on some decent clothes."

Five daughters, he thought, *in a territory where a man needs sons.* Five hungry mouths to feed: Virginia, his eldest at twenty-two, well past marrying age; Callie and Eunice, right at marrying age; Ethel, not far from it, coming up on her thirteenth birthday; leaving only Hope, eleven, and ugly as a mud fence. If God decided to burden him with five daughters, couldn't at least a couple of them have been a little more gentle on the eyes — and give him an opportunity to have two sons-in-law?

"Who is he, Mama?" Eunice asked as she prepared to set the table.

"I don't know," her mother replied. "Some young man who just happened to come into the store. Your father thought he was a bright young fellow and decided it would be a nice thing to do to invite him to supper, trying to get more folks to move to Fort Collins, I guess."

"Where do you wanna put him?" Eunice asked.

"Put him next to your father, so they can talk, I suppose. We'll set Virginia next to him, since she's the eldest. Then I don't guess it matters where the rest of you sit."

"Is he married?" Virginia asked as she walked into the dining room carrying a bowl of beans and another of potatoes.

"Your father didn't say, but it would be my guess that he's not," Mary said, knowing Louis's motive.

"Is he handsome?" Callie asked, causing her sisters to giggle.

"I don't know," Mary said. "I really didn't see him. He was going out the door when I walked into the store." She hesitated, but decided to do as her husband had suggested. "And have a care about yourselves. Brush your hair. You, too, Hope — you look like you've been rolling in the pigpen."

"You told me to slop the hogs," eleven-year-old Hope complained.

"I didn't tell you to get in the pen with 'em," Mary said. "Now, all of you, have a care for how you look. We've got company for supper and it's almost time. They'll be turning up any minute."

At about five minutes to five o'clock, Perley showed up at the store, still undecided if he should impose on Steiner and his wife. It didn't seem the polite thing to do to surprise the woman with an extra mouth to feed. But the store owner had been so insistent with his invitation, so Perley figured he and his wife probably welcomed the opportunity to possibly hear some news from other parts of the country. As soon as he thought it, he had to chuckle. There wasn't much news he could tell them, except maybe that there were two new whores at the Cattleman's in

Cheyenne. He stepped down from the saddle just as Steiner came outside and paused to lock the door.

"Well, I see you're right on time," Steiner said. "I thought you'd likely leave your horses in the stable."

"I picked me out a good spot to camp over by the river," Perley said, "but I thought I'd best bring my horses with me. Fort Collins looks like a mighty nice town, but I didn't wanna leave my packhorse down by the river."

"Right," Steiner replied. "I guess that's smart thinking, since you aren't staying at the hotel." He nodded to himself, thinking the young man showed common sense. "Well, come on, you can lead your horses. The house is on the street behind Main Street. I always walk it."

It was a short walk to the large white house with a wide porch across the front. Perley tied his horses to a corner post of the porch just as Mary came out to greet them. She waited for them to climb the steps before speaking, making an intense inspection of the young man her husband had deemed worthy of an invitation to sit at her table. "Welcome to our home," she said then.

"Thank you, ma'am," Perley replied, doing his best to be polite. "I have to apologize for droppin' in on you like this, without any notice a'tall."

"It's no trouble. We're glad to have you, and if I know my husband, he probably didn't give you much choice." She cast a sideways glance in Steiner's direction, which he acknowledged with an impish grin. She continued then. "Come on inside and let's eat while the food's still hot."

Perley followed her into the parlor, where he found a young girl standing near the dining room door. No more than ten or eleven, he figured, she stared openly at him. He nodded to her and she smiled back at him as she watched him walk past. So, they had a kid, he thought. He had somehow formed an impression that they had no children and that that was the reason they invited company. That impression was destroyed a moment later when he walked into the dining room, where he was met with three young women of various ages, standing around one end of a large table. Before any introductions were offered, another woman came from the kitchen with a large platter of biscuits. She smiled at him as she placed the biscuits in the middle of the table and stepped back to stand beside her sisters.

"Louis," his wife reproached, "are you going to introduce our guest?"

"Oh, of course," Steiner fumbled. "This is Mister . . ." he started before realizing he didn't know his guest's name. "Well, upon my soul, I don't believe I ever asked you your name."

"Perley Gates," he said.

"Perley Gates? I thought that was your grandfather's name."

"Yes, sir, it is. It's my name, too," Perley replied, aware of the amused expressions of astonishment on their faces. Eleven-year-old Hope could not suppress a giggle.

"Well, that's a most unusual name," Mary said, hastening to fill the void it had caused, "one I'm sure you're proud of."

"Not especially," Perley answered honestly, "but I reckon I've gotten used to it." He smiled at her. "Once you get past the name, I'm pretty much like everybody else."

"Well, we're glad to meet you, Mr. Gates," Mary said, with a frown in Hope's direction. She introduced each one of her daughters, starting with Virginia, and each one nodded in turn, still smiling broadly. "Let's sit down and eat — Mr. Gates, right here, next to Virginia," she directed, pulling out a chair for him.

Surprised to say the least, for he had hardly expected to have supper with so many women staring at him, Perley felt like a wild bear cub someone had rescued and was now watching to see his reactions to human beings. On the other hand, the food looked mighty good, so he reached for a biscuit just as Mary spoke again.

"Papa, I think we're ready. You can ask the blessing now."

Perley immediately jerked his hand back, causing Hope to giggle and the polite smiles on the faces of the other four daughters to turn into amused grins. Embarrassed, he was happy to bow his head while Steiner embarked on a lengthy blessing that offered thanks not only for the food on the table but that encompassed the fertile land that produced it.

While he listened, Perley was touched, but not so much by Steiner's words as he was by the toe that began to caress his knee. He peeked up at the daughter introduced as Callie, sitting directly across from him, but her head was bowed reverently, as was her sister's beside her.

At the sound of "Amen," Perley looked up quickly to find Callie smiling at him again, but with an expression that would indicate there was nothing going on under the table. He glanced at Virginia, seated beside him. She answered his glance with a smile, then promptly passed a bowl containing potatoes to him. There was no sign of mischief in her smile. That left only one other within easy reach of his knees, but surely it could not be Steiner's wife, so he decided it had to be Callie, she with the innocent expression on her face.

The rubbing on his leg increased to the point where he felt he had to do something to stop it. He shifted his legs around, and the poking stopped for a few seconds but started up again. Perley became extremely uncomfortable, and his brothers' words came to his mind again — *another cow pie.* He looked from Steiner to his wife. Neither seemed aware of the ill behavior of their daughter, and they appeared to be the kind of people who would not condone such carryings-on. He was not sure what he should do, but he had suddenly lost his appetite. Mary Steiner noticed it and spoke up.

"For a strong young man like yourself, you don't seem to be very hungry. I hope the food is to your liking," she said, looking truly concerned.

"Oh, yes, ma'am," he quickly replied. "It's a fine supper. I reckon I'm just wantin' to make it last a long time, so I'm eatin' it real slow. Oh!" he yelped involuntarily when he was sure he felt a foot thrust up between his legs. His sudden eruption caused everyone to look at him in astonishment.

Mary looked at once in Hope's direction. "Did you let that dog in the house again, young lady?" She didn't wait for Hope's answer. "Get him out of here. You know what I told you about letting Brutus in the house when we're eating."

Down at the end of the table, Hope displayed a pouty face but dutifully got up from her chair. Taking a piece of a pork chop from her plate, she lifted the tablecloth and called, "Come on, Brutus, you've got to go outside."

In a few seconds, a large hound, almost as tall as the table, came out from under it and followed Hope as she led it out the door.

"I hope you think we're a little more civilized than that, Mr. Gates," Mary said as Hope and the huge pooch left the room. "Hope lets that dog get away with practically everything he wants to do, but feeding him from the table is one thing I will not stand for."

"No, ma'am, not at all, ma'am," Perley responded, hoping the flush of embarrassment he felt in his face and neck was not obvious to see. As suddenly as it had left him, his appetite returned, and he began to eat as his hostess had expected him to.

"I believe you were hungry after all," Steiner commented. "Eunice, pass Perley the beans. The girls all help with the cooking. Virginia bakes the best biscuits in the Colorado Territory. I'm gonna lose her one day when the young men find out how good she can cook."

"I wouldn't be surprised," Perley said, thoroughly enjoying his supper now. "They're mighty good biscuits."

"Tell us about your home in Texas," Mary said.

"Not much to talk about," Perley replied. "It's just a cattle ranch about a half day's ride below the Red River." He went on to tell them about his brothers and his mother and the death of his father. "So that's the reason I'm tryin' to find my grandpa," he concluded.

"Sounds like yours is a hardworking family," Louis Steiner commented. "This part of the Colorado Territory is shaping up to be a real thriving community and a land of great promise for any young man to raise a family in. Most of the folks who have been coming in are farmers, but there's a real need for men who work cattle."

"Yes, sir," Perley said, "looks like a right nice town."

It had not sunk in at first, but Perley suddenly realized that all of Steiner's conversation seemed to end with a sales pitch for Fort Collins — that is, when he wasn't touting the homemaking abilities of his daughters. Happening to notice several occasions during the supper when Mary aimed deep frowns in her husband's direction, Perley began to believe that she was not in favor of Steiner's efforts to interest him in any of the girls. Perley could understand his host's situation, saddled with five daughters, most of them grown and none of them with husbands. *It's a shame they all seem to have inherited their looks from their father,* he thought. *If they'd gotten a little bit more from their ma, they'd have a better chance of finding husbands.*

After he finished a slice of apple pie that Steiner said his daughter Eunice had made, Perley thanked Mary and all her daughters for the fine meal. "It was mighty nice of you folks to invite me, and I'm pleased to make all your acquaintances. I reckon I'd best be on my way now. I have to take care of my horses and set up my camp. I'll be gettin' an early start in the mornin'. I've been a while with nothin' but salt pork, so I'm goin' up the river a ways to see if I can't find a deer. I saw plenty of signs of them by the river today."

"You could stay right here tonight," Steiner suggested. "Leave your horses in the backyard and eat a good breakfast in the morning."

The man doesn't give up easily, Perley thought. Mary had had enough, however, and said it for him.

"Oh, Louis, you can see Perley has things to take care of that he can do better in his own camp. So, let him go take care of his horses. Isn't that right, Perley?"

"Yes, ma'am, that's a fact, so I'll say thank you again and good night to you all."

With that, he took his leave, stepped up into the saddle, and turned Buck toward the river. Louis and Mary and all five daughters stood on the porch to watch him leave.

"Well, he wasn't as dumb as his name," Hope declared.

"No, he isn't dumb," her mother said, still perturbed by her husband's campaign to interest their guest in their daughters. "I think he's a fine young man — it's just too bad he's not looking for a wife."

Come on, he thought. *Come on down to the edge and get a drink. You know you're thirsty.* Crouching in a clump of berry bushes

252

beside what looked to be a common crossing for deer, Perley watched the four of them as they approached the river. An old buck with three does made his target selection easy. He would take the best shot presented to him.

He waited to let them drink, keeping his rifle sighted on one of the does in case they turned around instead of crossing the river. When they had satisfied their thirst, the old buck snorted a couple of times, then started across. Perley waited until the ladies followed, and when one young doe presented him with the perfect angle for a lung shot, he squeezed off the fatal round. She dropped immediately, while the other deer bolted up from the riverbank and disappeared into the fir trees on the slope beyond.

He hurried out of the bushes and ran to the fallen deer, anxious to end her suffering. When he approached, the deer began struggling in a frantic effort to get up, so to make it quick, he drew his .44 Colt and put a bullet in her head.

"I'm awful sorry I had to do that," he apologized. He always felt sorry for animals he killed for food, a weakness he was always careful to hide from his brothers, or anyone else, for that matter. "If I could live on nothin' but berries and such, like you do, I reckon I would."

The butchering of the deer was a different matter, however. He figured once the deer was dead, its spirit had gone on to wherever deer spirits went, leaving nothing but meat, and venison was a hell of a lot tastier than sowbelly. He decided to butcher his doe back at his camp, since it was not too far from town and he didn't want to leave his packhorse unattended there too long. With that in mind, he loaded the carcass onto Buck and started back down the river.

When within about fifty yards of the little clearing where he had made his camp, Perley suddenly reined Buck back. Something was wrong! He smelled smoke; then, looking up toward the tops of the trees, he saw faint traces of it drifting up from what had to be the spot where he had camped. He was sure he had put his fire out before going after the deer. Someone must have come upon his camp and his packhorse. He was stupid to have left the horse for the short time he was gone, only to have it stolen. *Well, we'll see about that,* he thought and urged Buck ahead slowly.

When about twenty yards closer, he halted Buck and dismounted. Leaving the bay gelding there in the trees, he made his way cautiously toward the clearing until abruptly stopping when he spotted a figure sitting beside his campfire. Glancing over toward the edge of the river, he saw his packhorse grazing, and he couldn't help wondering why the man hadn't taken the horse and fled — if that had been his goal.

Reckon we'll find out, Perley thought and pushed on through the trees, holding his rifle ready to fire. "Didn't know I was havin' company," he called out, in lieu of something better.

Startled, the figure by the fire jumped, then spun around to face him. Perley held his rifle ready, but there was no move by his guest to draw a weapon. And for a frozen moment, the two of them stood staring at each other in astonishment.

"What the . . ." Perley exclaimed. "What are you doin' here?" he finally managed, trying to recall who this was. "I can't place your name right now."

"I'm Ethel," Steiner's thirteen-year-old daughter said. "I thought I could find your camp, and when I saw the packhorse, I knew it was yours."

"Yeah — so what can I do for you?" Perley asked. "Did your folks send you to find me?"

"No, Mama and Papa are at the store, just

like every day," Ethel answered.

"What about your sisters? Did you tell them you were going to find my camp?" Perley asked, still baffled by the young girl's appearance.

"No, I don't have to tell them everything I'm gonna do."

Still baffled, Perley had to ask, "Well, is there somethin' you want from me?"

"I wanna go with you," she stated frankly. "I'll dry up and blow away if I have to stay here much longer. I can help you do the cooking and anything else you need. And you don't have to worry, I didn't tell anybody I was coming with you."

Perley found it hard to believe what he was hearing. "Ethel, you're mighty young to ride off with some man you don't even know. I wouldn't know what to do with you anyway. Besides, I'm gonna be on the trail for a long time, lookin' for my grandpa; then I'll be headin' back to my home in Texas. I don't think you'd enjoy that very much."

"I'd like to see Texas," Ethel said. "And I'm older than you think."

"No, you ain't," Perley replied abruptly. "You run off from home and you'll break your mama's heart. You need to wait till you're a couple of years older to think about takin' up with a man. You'll have plenty of time to meet the right one for you. Fort Collins is growin' every year. You'll have a lot to choose from."

She wasn't convinced. "I don't know about that. Virginia's twenty-two, and she's still waiting for somebody. I can't wait till I'm twenty-two."

"Take my word for it," he said in conclusion. "In the next couple of years, the men around here are gonna outnumber the women, so it's best you stay right here."

Considering that to be his final word on the matter, he now had another problem. "I'll take you back home, but it'll have to wait a little while. I've gotta skin and butcher a deer and smoke it before the meat goes bad. The weather's gettin' warmer now, and I'm afraid to wait too long to dry the meat. And it'd be a sin to kill an animal like a deer unless you used the meat." There was the matter of a missing girl at the Steiner house, however, which complicated things. "Are your folks gonna miss you if you're gone for a while?"

"Like I said, Papa and Mama are at the store. I go off all the time without telling my sisters. They don't care, anyway, so I can help you with the deer," Ethel offered quickly, although she could just as easily have gone home without escort, the same way she had arrived, but she still had hope of changing his mind.

"Maybe so," Perley allowed. "At least we can get it started."

He pressed his thumb and forefinger to his lips and whistled a short blast. In a few seconds, Buck came trotting out of the trees with the deer carcass on his back.

It was well past noon by the time Perley had butchered the deer and had it ready to smoke over a makeshift fire pit. Since neither of them had eaten anything that morning, he had Ethel make coffee and cut some strips of the fresh meat to cook over the fire. When they were done, the two sat down to eat, and that's what they were doing when Deputy Sheriff Martin Sumner rode into the clearing.

"Well, you ain't the smartest kidnapper I've ever seen," Sumner announced, surprising the two. With a double-barreled shotgun leveled at Perley, he carefully dismounted. "Are you all right, Ethel?" When Perley started to get up, Sumner warned him, "You set right where you are till I get some answers. I ain't got no patience for men like you, who take advantage of young girls."

"I think you're jumpin' to the wrong conclusion," Perley started to explain, but Sumner cut him short.

"You just keep your trap shut till I tell you to talk," Sumner ordered. Then he turned to Ethel. "Tell me what happened, Ethel. What are you doin' here?"

Frustrated by having been caught by the deputy, Ethel was about to confess that it was she who was at fault for being there. Then, thinking that the deputy might force Perley to marry her, she replied, "He had his way with me, Deputy Sumner. Snatched me right up off the street and brought me out here to his camp."

"What!" Perley exclaimed. "I did no such a thing! Ethel, tell the man the truth."

"I ain't gonna tell you again!" Sumner warned him and cocked both hammers on his shotgun.

"I did tell him the truth, darling," Ethel cried out dramatically. "You promised we'd get married. That's the only reason I let you have your way with me."

"That's a damn lie!" Perley exclaimed. "She showed up here when I came back from huntin'. She's makin' the whole thing up."

"Get on your feet," Sumner ordered. "Now, unbuckle that gun belt and let it drop." When Perley hesitated, Sumner threatened, "Mister, I ain't got no use for your kind. I just wish you'd give me a reason to blast a hole in your belly."

Perley could see he had no choice, so he did as he was told.

"Now," Sumner continued, "you're gonna saddle that horse and pack up those sacks on your packhorse. Then we're gonna ride back into town, and you can see how you like our jail while we decide what to do with you."

Perley made one more attempt to protest and received a blow to his head from the butt of Sumner's shotgun that sent him to the ground.

Once aboard Buck, Perley led Sumner and his packhorse out of the clearing, his handgun and his rifle in Sumner's possession, with the deputy's assurance that he was a crack rifle shot, in case Perley decided to run for it. Ethel rode behind the deputy, all the while afraid that her plan had backfired, but in too deep to confess.

When they completed the short trip back to town, Sumner guided Perley to the jail, where they were met in front of the two-story building by Sheriff Lloyd James.

"Good work, Martin," James greeted him. "I was fixin' to round up a posse to go after him. Where'd you find him?"

Sumner told him down by the river, smoking venison.

"He give you any trouble?" James asked.

"Not really," Summer replied. "I had to give him a tap on the head to let him know I warn't playin', that's all."

"There's been a misunderstandin', Sheriff," Perley said as he stepped down.

"I'm sure there has," James said. "Take him on inside and lock him up." He reached up and helped Ethel off Sumner's horse. "You all right, honey?" Afraid to open her mouth now, she just nodded. "You run on over to your daddy's store. They've been sick worrying about you. We'll take care of this feller."

Reluctant to look at Perley, she lowered her head and hurried down the street to the store. Watching her as she walked away, Sumner said, "The son of a bitch raped her."

"I did not touch her," Perley insisted.

The sheriff looked at him with a cold eye. "You're lucky we've got law and order in this town, so you'll get a chance to tell that to a judge. I'd just as soon hang you, if it was left up to me."

Perley could see that he didn't have a chance for justice without a confession from Ethel, and it appeared she was going to stick to her story. "What are you gonna do with my horses?"

"Don't worry about them," James said. "We'll take 'em down to the stable and take real good care of 'em. After your trial and your hangin', we'll most likely auction 'em off." He nodded toward his deputy. "Take him on in."

"You'd best lead that bay," Perley said. "He doesn't like anybody but me on his back."

"Is that a fact?" James replied and grinned at his deputy. "Hear that, Martin? After you put Mr. Pearly Gates in a cell, you'd best lead his horse down to the stable. You don't wanna get bucked off."

"Maybe I'd better," Sumner said while he pulled Perley's saddlebags off his horse. He pushed Perley inside, dropped the saddlebags on Sheriff James's desk, then marched Perley upstairs to a cell.

Perley sat frustrated on the one small cot in his cell, wondering how he was going to recover from stepping in this latest cow pie, when he heard Buck snort and neigh on the street in front of the jail. Buck's warning snorts were heard again, this time followed by a loud howl, then a dull thump. Perley didn't have to see it to know what had just happened. He shook his head slowly and muttered, "I warned you," while the sounds of Sumner's cursing carried to the second floor of the jail.

CHAPTER 11

While Perley was locked in a cell on the second floor of the jail, Ethel presented herself to her parents, who welcomed her tearfully.

"Where were you?" Mary Steiner cried when her daughter walked in the door. "Are you all right? We've been worried sick. We even went to the sheriff when Callie came to the store and told us you had disappeared."

"I'm sorry, Mama," Ethel cried. "Martin Sumner found me and brought me back to town." She was afraid to admit what she had done, thinking that her best bet was to stick to the story she had fabricated. "I didn't know he was gonna grab me."

"Who?" her father demanded. "Who grabbed you?"

"Perley Gates," Ethel whimpered.

"That son of a bitch!" Steiner roared. "I invited him into my home. He broke bread with my family!" He took Ethel by her shoulders, looking into her eyes. "What did he do to you?" When she refused to answer, he shook her violently. "What did he do to you?"

"He had his way with me," she lied. "I think he wants to marry me."

Her father was beside himself with anger, unable to talk for a full minute. He sputtered and fumed while Mary took their daughter in her arms and held her.

"You're safe now," she said, "home where you belong." She looked at her husband and confessed, "I've never been so wrong about a person in my life. I thought he was a decent young man."

Able to think rationally again, Steiner questioned Ethel then. "You said Martin Sumner brought you back. Did he arrest Perley Gates?" Ethel, still in her mother's embrace, nodded. "So, he's in jail?" She nodded again. "I'm going up there," Steiner told his wife. "You take her home."

"We can't both leave the store, Louis," Mary responded. "What are you going to do, anyway?" When he insisted that he had to go talk to the sheriff, she said, "All right, but wait till I take Ethel home, and you can go when I get back."

Although still fuming, he realized what

she said was true — he couldn't leave their store unattended.

Trapped in the web of lies she had created, Ethel went home with her mother, where she was welcomed with great relief by all her sisters. Mary told them what had happened to Ethel, and their reaction was total shock, just as it had been with their mother and father. When Mary left her in their care and went back to the store, they questioned her in depth about her abduction. She was inclined to be a little more explicit with the details of the incident than she had been with her mother, unable to resist an attempt to arouse envy. Instead of buying into her fantasy, however, they were inclined more toward skepticism, knowing their sister better than her mother did.

Virginia looked at Callie and winked, then addressed Ethel. "You seem like you're feeling much better now." When Ethel said that she was, Virginia said, "Good, 'cause we've got to take care of you, if he's done everything to you that you've said. We'll need to clean you up. I'd think that's the first thing you'd want."

"Yes," Ethel quickly agreed. "I wanna clean myself up after what I've been through. I'll do that now."

"No," Virginia said. "We'll take care of you. You've been through too much. Hope, go to the pump and get a basin of water. Bring a washcloth and a bar of soap."

"I don't need anybody to help me clean up," Ethel protested.

"No trouble at all," Callie said. "We'll do it, and that way we can see how much damage was done, and maybe we can clean you up to make sure you don't have a baby." She winked at Virginia.

"No, confound it," Ethel insisted. "I don't want anybody touching me. I'll take care of myself."

"I'll bet you made the whole thing up," Eunice said. "We'll know for sure when we get a look at your bottom."

"Ain't nobody getting a look at my bottom!" Ethel exclaimed. "Anybody tries will get a sock in the eye!"

"Is that so?" Eunice shot back. "I believe the four of us can hold you down."

"No, you won't!" Ethel cried and started to run from the room, but Callie caught her by the arm.

In a matter of seconds, her four sisters grabbed her and wrestled her to the floor, where her undergarments were discarded. The decision was easily unanimous — she had never been violated.

"How did you find him?" Virginia asked calmly when Ethel finally quit struggling.

Knowing her story had crumbled around her, Ethel didn't try to pursue it. "I walked up the river till I found where he camped."

"Why in the world did you make up that story?" Callie asked. "Didn't you know you would ruin that good man?"

"I thought the sheriff or the judge would make him marry me and I'd get out of this damn town."

"More likely they're getting ready to hang him," Eunice said. "We've got to go tell the sheriff the truth."

"No!" Ethel cried. "I don't want everybody in town knowing about it!"

"You can't let that man be punished for your foolishness," Virginia said. "Sheriff James is a thoughtful man. We can probably ask him to keep it quiet." She looked at her younger sister, waiting for her remorse, knowing that she was not without a sense of honor; she was merely foolish, as a thirteen-year-old can be.

Ethel hung her head in shame. Tears streamed down her cheeks as she surrendered to her conscience. "You're right. I can't let him be punished. He didn't do anything. He was going to bring me home." She looked up at her big sister. "Will you go with me to tell Papa and Mama?"

"I'll go with you," Virginia said. She felt compassion for her young sister, but she had already planned to accompany her to the store in case Ethel faltered in her promise to tell the truth.

Perley could hear Steiner's angry ranting downstairs in the sheriff's office, demanding swift justice instead of waiting for a trial for the man who kidnapped and violated his thirteen-year-old daughter. While Sheriff James fully understood the outrage the poor man was suffering, he was steadfast in his intention to carry out the letter of the law. When Steiner hinted that it might be easy to incite enough of his irate citizens to form a lynch mob, James made it abundantly clear that there would be no lynch mob in his town and that Steiner would likely wind up in jail with Perley if he was to try to put one together. Perley decided that the sheriff was a good, conscientious man and Fort Collins was fortunate to have him. However, he was still in jail awaiting trial.

Perley heard someone come into the office, and a moment later, a woman's voice carried upstairs to his cell. After that, there was a lot of talking by male and female voices, and he thought one of them sounded like Mary Steiner, no doubt come to demand justice for her daughter. Perley shook his head, wondering why he seemed to find himself in awkward situations more than most other people.

Things got quiet. Then he heard someone coming up the stairs to the cell room. A moment later, Deputy Sumner appeared in the doorway, holding a key on a ring. He walked straight to Perley's cell and unlocked the door, then motioned for him to come out.

"Lynchin'?" Perley asked, thinking maybe Sheriff James had caved in to pressure.

Sumner smothered a chuckle. "Nah, nothin' like that. Sheriff wants you downstairs."

When he got downstairs, Perley was startled to see not only Steiner and his wife but Ethel as well. James plopped his saddlebags, his rifle, and his .44 on the desk. With a wary suspicion, as if he was being set up for something, Perley looked from one face to another, from the sheepish expression on Steiner's wide countenance to the contrite smile on his wife's face. As for Ethel, he could not see her face, as she stared at the floor. After what seemed a long moment, the sheriff spoke.

"There's been a big misunderstandin' here. Looks like my deputy and I owe you an apology. Miss Ethel, here, has confessed that she let her imagination stampede and ended up causin' you a heap of trouble. But thank goodness, we got the straight of it before Mr. Steiner rounded up a lynchin' party."

"I swear, I'm sorry we doubted you, Perley," Steiner said.

"I think Ethel has something to say to you as well," Mary said, and she poked the humiliated young girl in the back with her forefinger.

"Yes, sir," Ethel managed to mumble, before her mother told her to speak up. "I'm sorry I caused you so much trouble, Perley."

Perley was amazed. It was one of the most bizarre situations he had ever found himself in. It was his first time in jail for anything, much less for abusing a child. "I reckon no real harm came of it," he said, unable to think of anything better. He found himself feeling sorry for the girl. He looked at the sheriff. "Am I free to go now?"

"Yes, sir," James said and apologized again for arresting him.

"How 'bout my horses? Where are they?"

"Down at the stable at the end of the street," the sheriff said. "Tell Orin I said to let you take 'em. There shouldn't be any charge after this short time, but if there is, tell him I'll take care of it." A mischievous smile parted his lips, and he couldn't resist adding, "Martin decided to ride that bay of yours down there but changed his mind and led him down to Orin's."

Deputy Sumner grinned sheepishly. "I think he mighta broke my tailbone when I landed on the seat of my pants. Maybe I oughta charge you for my doctor bill."

Perley chuckled. "You'll have to take that up with Buck. Maybe he'll give you a free ride to make up for that first one."

"No, thanks," Sumner said. "I don't need no more flyin' lessons."

"I reckon I'll be gettin' along now," Perley said and picked up his belongings from the sheriff's desk.

They all walked out to the street with him, and Steiner and his wife and daughter walked with him as far as the store.

"Don't be too hard on Ethel," Perley said in parting. "I'm sure she meant no real harm."

The family stood in front of the store and watched as he walked toward the lower end of the street with his long, loose gait.

"I'da gone with him if he woulda had me," Ethel remarked, already recovering some of her natural brass.

■ ■ ■ ■

Perley believed very much in the popular saying *The Lord moves in mysterious ways.* He thought about that as he walked down the street, a free man, after having thought he was heading toward a rope around his neck. Somehow, Ethel was persuaded to confess, against what he considered to have been pretty high odds. In reality, he was about to find the real miracle when he set foot in the stable and met Orin Jones.

"How do?" Orin greeted him, walking out of a stall with a pitchfork in his hand.

"Howdy," Perley returned. "I believe you've got a couple of horses that belong to me. Deputy Sumner brought 'em down here about an hour or so ago.

"That bay and the sorrel packhorse?" Orin replied. "Martin said the owner was gonna be in jail for a while. You didn't shoot nobody to get outta jail, did you?" He said it as a joke, but truthfully, he wasn't sure.

"Nope," Perley said. "It was a case of the wrong man. Sheriff James said he'd take care of any charges you had." He purposely refrained from telling Orin what the actual circumstances were, to keep from bringing shame to Ethel and her family.

Orin shrugged. "Well, I ain't really done nothin' for 'em yet. I was fixin' to feed 'em a portion of oats, but you got here before I did that."

"Well, go ahead and give 'em the oats," Perley said, "as long as the sheriff said he'd pay for 'em. I reckon he owes me at least that much for throwin' me in jail."

Orin chuckled and, extending his hand, said, "Why not, Mister . . . I didn't catch your name."

"Gates," Perley supplied and shook his hand. "Perley Gates, Mr. Jones."

"My stars!" Orin exclaimed. "If that ain't the dangedest coincidence I've ever seen. That's a mighty curious name — wouldn't figure you'd meet anybody by that name. I ain't sayin' there's anything wrong with it," he hastened to assure Perley. "It's just an unusual name, and to meet two men with it don't seem likely to happen, and within about three months' time, at that." Seeing the look of astonishment on Perley's face, he was moved to ask, "Have you got any kinfolk out this way?"

"My grandpa," Perley answered at once. "I was on my way to Denver to find him when I stopped here in Fort Collins."

"Well, you wouldn'ta found him in Denver. When he came through here, he was headin' to Cheyenne on his way to the Black Hills, like a heap of other folks lookin' to strike it rich."

Feeling like he could be knocked over with a feather, Perley was at a loss for a moment before he could think to ask questions. "How long was he here?" he finally asked.

"Not long," Orin replied. "I don't think he stopped anywhere else but my place. He wanted to sell me an extra horse he had with him, but we couldn't get together on a price, so he said he'd try to sell it in Cheyenne. If it'd been a good horse, I mighta give him somethin' for it, but it was damn nigh swayback."

He paused when Perley seemed to be thinking about something other than his conversation. "You say you're takin' your horses?"

Perley jerked his head back to the present. "Yeah," he said. "I'm takin' 'em."

When Orin went to get the grain bucket for the oats, Perley's mind went back to where it had flown a few moments before. He had to wonder about the coincidence that stopped him from going on to Denver and led him back to his grandfather's track. Maybe he was beholden to Ethel Steiner after all. Had she not pursued him and then concocted her outrageous story, he would have surely gone off in the wrong direction to have any chance to find his grandpa. *The Lord moves in mysterious ways, all right,* he thought.

When he got his packhorse loaded again and his saddle on Buck, he said so long to Orin Jones and thanked him for the information about his grandfather. Already having lost the time he had spent riding south from Cheyenne, he was anxious to head back in the other direction. It was well past noon by that time, however, so he knew he would not get to Cheyenne by the end of the day. It wouldn't matter if he set out immediately or waited until later, so he decided to ride back up the river to check on the condition of his camp.

When he reached the bend of the river, he rode through the fir trees hugging the bank, to the clearing where he had made his camp the night before. Nothing had been disturbed. The fires he had started to smoke the strips of venison had all burned out, but from all appearances, the dried-out meat looked to be perfectly fine, still staked out just as he had left it. To be sure, he tried some of the meat and found it to be usable. Another unlikely coincidence, he thought, and further evidence that he was supposed to find his grandpa. Encouraged by the way things had fallen into place for him, Perley went into his packs for some cloth to wrap the venison with, satisfied that he now had meat to last him awhile.

While working away to wrap his supply of venison, he suddenly had a feeling he was being watched. There had been no warning from his horses to alert him that someone was approaching, but he sensed that he was not alone. As a matter of precaution, he tried not to show any sign of awareness, while dropping his hand down to rest on the grip of his .44. As casually as he could manage, he turned to one side, far enough to look behind him.

At first, he saw nothing. Then the features of a face came into focus, watching him from the cover of the fir branches. He had company, all right, but he did not react at once. Instead, he rose slowly to his feet, walked to his packhorse, and loaded the meat he had wrapped. Then he turned toward his visitor and said, "I'll tell you what I'll do. I've packed enough of this deer meat to last me a good while, so I'm leavin' this last part of it here. And that oughta be enough for a good dinner for one coyote — enough for more, if you've got some friends with you. By the way, I 'preciate you not comin' along before I got back to save it."

Thinking it the least he could do, he climbed aboard Buck and led his packhorse back through the trees around the clearing. When he took one look back, he saw the coyote slink out of the trees and trot up to feast on the venison.

With no desire to linger any longer in Fort Collins, Perley rode straight through the town to strike the trail back to Cheyenne, over forty miles north. Following the trail along the Denver Pacific Railway, he rode about halfway before stopping to camp at a small creek he remembered from when he had traveled in the opposite direction.

He was ready to eat some of the venison by then, having had nothing since coffee and a strip of the freshly killed deer with Ethel Steiner earlier that day. The thought of that breakfast was enough to make him shake his head in disbelief for the day that had followed. Falling back into his usual disposition, however, his spirits were once again raised in anticipation of the adventure ahead. He was still of the opinion that something was leading him to find his grandfather. What that something was, he didn't question. He was just thankful for the extra help.

He started out early the next morning and

reached Cheyenne before noon. He headed straight for Tom Tuttle's stable, since Orin Jones had told him that his grandpa had stopped at his stable, hoping to sell a horse. There was a good chance that Grandpa had stopped at Tuttle's, and it frustrated Perley that he had not asked Tuttle about it when he was there before. Surely, though, if Grandpa had stopped there to sell his horse, Tuttle would have remembered the name as being the same as Perley's. He remembered then that there was another stable in town. He would question Tuttle, then check on the other stable if Tuttle hadn't seen his grandpa.

"I didn't expect to see you back in town this soon," Tuttle said in greeting him. "That's one helluva horse you're ridin', if he's already took you to Denver and back," he joked.

"If any horse could do it, I'd bet on Buck," Perley replied, with half a chuckle for Tuttle's humor. "No, we only got as far as Fort Collins before we found out my grandpa headed this way. Don't reckon you've seen him passin' through Cheyenne."

"If he did, he didn't stop here," Tuttle said. " 'Course, he mighta stopped at Jack Purcell's place, on the other end of town."

"Maybe," Perley said. "I figured I'd check

with him if you hadn't seen Grandpa." He stepped up into the saddle.

"You were right about that flea-bitten gray," Tuttle said. "I think his wind is broke, and I appreciate your honesty about him. I might have to put him down."

"I reckon so," Perley said. "He got Liz to Cheyenne all right, and I appreciated that."

He turned Buck and headed toward the other end of the main street. Tuttle's comment brought the two women to mind, and Perley hoped they were finding things to their liking in Cheyenne. *Maybe I'll stop by the Cattleman's Saloon before I head north,* he thought.

At first, Jack Purcell didn't remember anyone by the name of Perley Gates stopping by his stable. Perley told him that it would have been an old man and he most likely only stopped by shortly, trying to sell a horse. Purcell paused for a moment before the spark of remembrance struck his memory; then he recalled.

"A little bowlegged man, wearin' buckskins," he remembered.

"That sounds like him," Perley said.

"Stopped in here and wanted to sell me an old broken-down mare," Purcell said.

"That sounds like the horse," Perley said.

"I remember him," Purcell went on. "I

didn't talk to him long enough to learn his name, but it could be the fellow you're askin' about. I didn't have no use for that horse, so he wasn't here long."

"Did he say where he was headin'?" Perley asked.

"Said he was headin' north, up to the Black Hills to see what all the fuss was about. I felt kinda bad after he left for not givin' him somethin' for that broke-down horse. It was still cold weather when he was here, and he was leadin' a packhorse that didn't look like it was totin' much. What are you lookin' for him for?"

"He's my grandpa," Perley answered.

"Oh . . . Well, I hope you find him, young fellow."

"Obliged," Perley said and took his leave. He couldn't help wondering if his grandpa had made the same call on Tom Tuttle and, as with Purcell, didn't talk to him long enough for Tuttle to catch his name. It made no difference at this point anyway. He knew for sure that his grandpa had headed to the Black Hills. Whether he made it or not was for Perley to find out, and from Purcell's description of the old man, he might not have gotten that far.

It was getting along pretty late in the day by now, so Perley thought it would be to his liking to pay another visit to Katie's Diner, even though the last time he was there he had created quite a commotion. He tied his horses at the rail and walked into the little building close to Dyer's Hotel. Standing just inside the door, he looked for an empty seat at the long table in the center of the busy room. There were only two open, so he took the one closest to the kitchen. Nodding a polite hello to the customers on either side of him, he climbed over the bench and sat down. It was obviously apparent that he was way behind in the consumption of beef and potatoes, so he turned his plate right-side up and set out to catch up.

After a few moments, Katie walked in from the kitchen, carrying a large gray coffeepot. "Perley Gates!" she exclaimed upon seeing him. "When did you sneak in here?"

"I was hopin' I could eat and get out before you caught me," he teased, "but I had to wait for the coffee."

"Them that try to get away with that will have Myra and her shotgun on their tails," she said, laughing delightedly. "What are you doing back in town? I thought you were going to Denver."

"I got all the way to Fort Collins before I found out I was goin' the wrong way, so I turned around." He nodded toward the spot over by the wall where he, Liz, and Stella had sat before Brady Ennis joined the party uninvited. "I thought you said Myra's husband was handy at fixin' things."

"He's handy, he just ain't fast," Katie quipped as she stood poised with the coffeepot. "Stella and Liz know you're back in town?"

"Not yet," Perley said. "I thought I'd get me some supper first; then I'll stop in the Cattleman's and say hello."

"Well, your timing is pretty good — or pretty bad, depending on how you look at it — 'cause Bill Snipe was in for breakfast this morning, and he said the sheriff was gonna release Brady Ennis this afternoon."

"Maybe he's cooled down by now," Perley suggested. "He was just likkered up pretty good, and maybe he'd lost a lotta money, so he wasn't feelin' too friendly. He might be a nice fellow when he's sober."

Katie looked at Perley and shook her head. "Are you sure you ain't the one that got hit in the head with my iron skillet? You'd best make sure you don't run into him."

"I aim to," Perley said. "Now, how 'bout pourin' some of that coffee in my cup, before it gets too cold to drink?"

He was joking with Katie, but the truth of

the matter was, he hoped like hell he wouldn't have any contact with Brady Ennis. Maybe, he thought, it would be best to forget about stopping in to see Liz and Stella and just head on out to Deadwood. That would be the smartest thing to do, but they would find out he had been in town and didn't even stop to see them. That wouldn't be a very nice thing, because they might think he didn't want to associate with them since they were common whores. *I wouldn't want them to think that,* he thought.

As was his habit, he put concerns about a confrontation with Brady Ennis out of his mind and concentrated instead on the fine supper he was enjoying. When Katie told Myra that he was back, she came out to visit, so he got a later start to the Cattleman's than he had intended. He had not taken care of his horses, and since it was getting late, he decided it best for Buck and his packhorse to spend the night at the stable. *Hell,* he told himself, *I've already spent money on supper — I might as well spend a little more and make sure my horses have a good night.* He said good-bye to Katie and Myra and hurried down to the stable to catch Tuttle before he went home.

CHAPTER 12

"Well, look what the cat drug in," C. J. Tubbs sang out. "What you doin' back in town? I thought you was in Denver."

"My plans got changed," Perley replied as he walked up to the bar. "I'm headin' in the opposite direction now." He went on to explain the reason for turning around, but didn't get very far before he was discovered by Liz.

"Perley!" she exclaimed when she spotted him and immediately got up from the lap she was sitting on to join him at the bar. Ignoring the sputtering protests of the older man whose lap she was vacating, she beamed happily to see Perley.

"Don't let me interrupt your conversation with that fellow at the table," Perley said. "He looks like he ain't too happy about you leavin'."

Liz gave a little grunt of unconcern. "That's just ol' Gordon Broomfield. He's the postmaster, and pretty tight with a penny. Ain't that right, C.J.?" C.J. said that it was, and Liz continued. "He won't make no fuss over it, afraid his wife might hear about it. When I ain't got nothing else to do, I sometimes give him a little attention — makes him think about when he was a helluva lot younger."

"Well, that's mighty decent of you," Perley said. He took a deliberate step back and pretended to give her a good looking over. "I see you got some new clothes. You look like one of them actresses on the stage."

"Why, thank you, kind sir," she replied prettily and affected a little curtsy that looked quite dainty, considering what a big woman she was. "Now, what the hell are you doin' back here? Already miss me and Stella that much?"

"Yeah, that's the reason," he kidded. "I reckon I just got used to ridin' with you and her."

Once again, he started to explain why he ended up back in Cheyenne, only to be interrupted for the second time by the appearance of Stella, who was coming downstairs.

"Perley Gates!" Stella pronounced, delighted to see him, just as Liz had been. She came over to join them, making her way through a moderate crowd of patrons, with a smile for most of them, while dodging a few wayward paws. Arriving at the bar, she gave Perley a firm hug and asked, "What are you doing back here?"

On his third try, he managed to tell them what he had found out in Fort Collins, leaving out the part about being thrown in jail for allegedly kidnapping a thirteen-year-old girl. "I ain't sure how long Grandpa was in Denver, but he passed through Fort Collins on his way to the Black Hills. So that's where I'm goin'," he concluded.

"When are you leaving?" Stella asked.

"First thing in the mornin'," he answered.

"Well, we need to set down and have a drink for old times' sake," Liz insisted. When Perley claimed that he didn't want to take up their time and interfere with their prospects for earning a living, she smirked. "This is mostly the after-work crowd, men having a drink and a pinch or a poke before going home to their wives — like ol' Broomfield over there. So, we won't be making any money until later in the evening. Ain't that right, Stella?"

"Pretty much so," Stella agreed. "Besides, we can let Cora keep 'em happy. She's the queen of the old family men."

From the tone of her remark, Perley assumed that his two friends had not yet established a warm relationship with Cora.

"She had one customer that wasn't an old family man," C.J. reminded them. Perley knew right away who he was referring to before C.J. continued. "The word I heard was, the sheriff let Brady Ennis outta jail this afternoon. I wouldn't be surprised if he shows up here before the night's over. He was pretty sweet on Cora."

Both women looked at once toward Perley. Liz said what they were both thinking. "He might be looking for the fellow that served him up some fried apple pie at Katie's Diner."

Her remark brought a chuckle from all of them, even considering the possible consequences another meeting between Brady and Perley might create.

" 'Course, Brady couldn't have any idea you're back in town," Liz was quick to add. "I'm sure Bill Snipe told him you'd left."

"He might not even recognize you if he was to see you," Stella said. "He was pretty damn drunk when he walked into the diner. He might not remember any of us."

"Well, if I see him," Perley said, "I sure ain't gonna introduce myself. Let's sit down and have that drink you suggested. I'm sleepin' in the stable with my horses, and

Tuttle said he was gonna be there a little later tonight, so I've got time before he locks the place up."

They took the bottle and glasses C.J. produced and moved over to a table near the corner of the room.

When there was a lull at the bar, C.J. came over and stood by the table for a few minutes, in time to catch their conversation about their trip from Ogallala to Cheyenne. "Liz said you had some Injuns chasin' you," he commented.

"We sure did," Stella said, and she and Liz laughed. "Perley stole their horses while they were hiding in the trees, waiting to ambush us."

Perley shrugged, embarrassed. "I thought it was a good idea — thought it would slow 'em down. I swear, though, it didn't slow 'em down much, did it?"

"We got here with our scalps," Liz declared. She started to laugh again but cut it off shortly when someone at the front door made her eyes open wide. "Oh, hell," she gasped.

Perley followed her gaze, to settle on the imposing bulk filling the doorway. All conversation at the table stopped as each one in turn discovered the intimidating mass that was Brady Ennis.

Perley thought of the first time he saw Brady, in the darkened hallway upstairs. At the time, he appeared closer kin to a buffalo than to a man. Perley hoped he would never have to cross his path again, yet here he was. There was nothing to do but wait to see what Brady was going to do and hope he would be able to react in some fashion to keep from getting his back broken.

Brady paused at the door for a few moments, scanning the room. There was no doubt he was looking for someone, but his gaze skipped over the table where Perley and the two women sat, pausing for only a second before moving on. When he didn't see who he searched for, he turned and walked toward the bar. C.J. hurried over to meet him.

"What'll it be?" C.J. asked.

"Where's Cora?" Brady responded.

"Cora?" C.J. repeated, surprised. "She's up in her room, eatin' some supper. She oughta be down anytime, now."

"I'll go up there," Brady stated. Then, not waiting to see if C.J. had any objections, he turned and went directly for the stairs, ascending the steps two at a time.

Astonished, the three at the table could only speculate on why he had not erupted in a rage when he saw them.

"He doesn't recognize you," Stella declared. "He was so drunk that night he couldn't even recognize you now. He'd have to get up real close, I bet."

"I ain't got any plans to get up real close to him, I'll tell you that," Perley said.

"I expect he'll be up there for a while," Liz speculated, "so we might as well take the time to enjoy our drinks." She prepared to toss another shot down, but stopped when Cora appeared at the top of the stairs. "Oh, oh," Liz murmured. "Now, what's she up to?"

Cora paid them no mind and walked down the stairs to get a bottle from C.J. at the bar.

Liz laughed, "She had me worried there for a moment, but now I know Brady will be up there for the evening." She grinned at Perley. "Looks like you ain't gonna get the chance to rassle with a grizzly tonight after all."

That suited Perley just fine. He was frankly relieved to have escaped another meeting with the giant. "I wasn't figurin' on havin' more than a couple of drinks anyway," he informed them. "Gotta get up early in the mornin' and strike out on the Deadwood Stage road. Gonna check every stage stop between here and Deadwood. If Grandpa traveled up that road, somebody is sure to have seen him . . ."

He stopped talking when he realized no one was listening to what he was saying. Instead, both women seemed to have been hypnotized, staring at the front door again. He turned to see what had caught their attention just as Liz uttered one word: "Riker." Then she looked at Stella in total despair. "What in the hell is he doin' here?"

Stella was just as shocked. They had fled Ogallala to escape his vengeful wrath, certain that he would give up after a while and return to Kansas with the rest of the crew from there. As if having Brady Ennis released from jail wasn't enough, now they had the mad dog that was Riker in the house as well. And Riker had sworn to take his revenge on Liz.

The question that sprang to mind was, how did he know to come to Cheyenne, and specifically, this saloon? And the answer that followed immediately was Kenny Lamb, the scoundrel who had run off with their pack-horse.

"That son of a bitch," Liz fumed. "Kenny Lamb, he must have gone back to Ogallala and met up with Riker. He's just ornery enough to tell Riker where we were heading." She moved her chair a little more to the side, so she would have her back to him, hoping that maybe he would just glance around the room, then leave without looking closer.

Stella, still facing the door, watched the belligerent Kansas cowhand as he walked over to the bar. "I don't think he spotted you," she said. "He's gone over to talk to C.J."

Equally concerned, having had some history with Riker himself, Perley watched with Stella, his hat pushed down low on his forehead. He was trying to weigh his options, in the event Riker did spot Liz and recognized Perley as well. If they were lucky, since it looked as though he hadn't seen Liz, Riker might move on to look in another saloon. That possibility was immediately shot down, however, when they saw Riker talking to C.J. With no idea who he was, C.J. turned and pointed to their table.

"Oh, shit!" Stella exclaimed, her tone hushed and tense. "No, C.J., don't tell him."

But it was already done.

Doesn't look like there's much chance of talking my way out of this one, Perley thought as Riker made his way toward their table in the corner. The devilish smile of satisfaction on the man's broad face was not to be perceived as a friendly greeting. When he was close enough to get a better look, his smile widened as he recognized Perley as one of the Texas hands in the saloon in Ogallala.

"Well, well," Riker gloated, "if this ain't somethin'. It's like Christmas in summertime. I've been lookin' for you, bitch," he directed at Liz. "We've got some unfinished business to take care of." He shifted his smirk toward Perley then. "And to find you still hangin' around her — it's almost too much to ask for. You ain't got your two brothers here to keep you from takin' a whippin', have you?"

"No, they had to get back to the ranch," Perley answered. "I know they'll be sorry they missed you. Looks like that knot on the side of your head is healin' pretty good. Still a little swollen, though, and kinda yellowish, ain't it? I reckon, if you keep it clean and don't get into any kinda trouble, it'll heal up good as new."

Taken aback, Riker was dumbfounded by the seemingly senseless babble coming out of Perley's mouth. "You're a damn talker," he said, finally coming up with an insult. "If it hadn'ta been for this bitch sneakin' up behind me with that bottle, I'da shot you, and your brothers, too. But I reckon you'll have to do."

"I reckon she fetched you a pretty good lick with that bottle," Perley said. "But she kept you from shootin' one of us and havin' to go to prison for the rest of your life. I figure that's what she had in mind when she did it. As far as I'm concerned, I'm willin' to let bygones be bygones, and I reckon Liz, here, would say the same thing. So, whaddaya say, Riker? You ready to act like a human being? Shoot, we could all be friends."

There followed a full minute of dead silence, with Riker gawking in openmouthed disbelief. When he finally spoke again, he blurted, "Friends? You talk like a crazy man. You ain't no friend of mine, and I've had about enough of your talk. You're wearin' a gun. I'm callin' you out in the street, and we'll see if you can back up your foul mouth, you damn jackass."

"I reckon you know it's terrible bad luck to shoot a crazy man," Perley said. "Ain't no tellin' what'll happen to you. Don't make any sense to me. I think it's a bad idea all the way around, so I'll decline your invitation to see which one of us can kill the other one first. So, I reckon that ends this discussion and we can all go about our business."

"Mister, you're the craziest son of a bitch I've ever run across, but you ain't talkin' your way outta this." Riker looked around him, then back at Perley. "Everybody here heard me call you out, fair and square, to settle this thing. There ain't no gettin' around it. I aim to kill you, and if you run, I'll come after you and shoot you down like the yeller dog you are. So, what's it gonna be — take your chance facing me out in the street, or get it in the head sittin' here in that chair?"

"Riker," Perley said, dead serious now, "I'm tryin' to save your life. I don't wanna shoot you, or anybody else, but if we go out in the street, you're a dead man. You won't give me any choice."

Riker almost laughed but held his reaction to a wide grin. The confrontation was going the way he wanted it to, and he couldn't resist playing some mind games himself. "I bet you ain't ever shot a man, have you? I mean, killed a man facin' you and him trying to kill you. I have — more'n one. It ain't like killin' a dog, or a deer, 'cause they ain't tryin' to kill you. You ever done that?" When Perley didn't answer, he said, "I didn't think so." He drew his .44 and aimed it at Perley's head. "Get up outta that chair and face me right now, right here, or I swear, I'll shoot you where you set."

There was not a sound in the entire saloon

now, except for the scraping of customers' chairs as they cleared the floor. Liz, having sat speechless during the challenge, was now certain there was no way out for Perley. He had spoken a lot of nonsense to Riker, hoping to talk him out of it, she guessed, but none of it worked on the crude cowhand. She was familiar with Riker's reputation with a gun. Perley was not. She could hold her tongue no longer.

"Leave him alone, Riker. You've got no quarrel with Perley. Your quarrel is with me. I'm the one that hit you in the head with a bottle." She glared at him, her anger growing every second. "I wish to hell I had hit you harder."

Riker cut his eyes quickly toward her before returning to stare at Perley. "I'll take care of you later," he warned Liz, "and if you pick up that bottle, I'll shoot you down first." Back to Perley, he threatened, "In the chair, or on your feet like a man? I'm done jawin' with you."

There was no way out. He had hoped to confuse Riker to the point where he would get disgusted and forget about taking his vengeance. Perley should have known better, but he was now caught with no option other than to face the man.

"All right, Riker," he said and got up out

of his chair. "I'll face you, but let's take it to the street. Somebody's liable to get hurt in here."

"Oh, somebody's gonna get hurt, all right," Riker snarled. "But I ain't worried about no bystanders. We'll have it out right here. I ain't givin' you the chance to take off outside and hide someplace." He backed away from the table and positioned himself opposite the end of the bar, leaving a space of about fifteen paces between them.

"We don't have to do this, Riker," Perley said as he reluctantly took his position near the back wall.

"That's where you're wrong," Riker boasted. "Pearly Gates," he scorned. "Say hello to Saint Peter for me."

Then, not waiting for Perley to turn to face him squarely, he reached for his .44. Liz saw it, but in telling it later to C.J., she wasn't sure she really saw it. In a single moment's time, Perley's weapon was in his holster, then it was in his hand, cocked and aimed at Riker, who had not cleared leather. Stella saw it, too, but remembered it only as a blur.

Riker, dazed by the sight of the Colt .44 barrel staring straight into his eyes, was caught with his own handgun only halfway free of the holster.

"Don't," Perley commanded, and Riker knew he was done.

They stood frozen for a long second while Riker made up his mind.

"Take your hand off of it and walk on out of here," Perley ordered. "Go on back to Kansas, where you belong."

Riker swallowed hard. He knew he was a dead man if he tried to pull the weapon. Feeling the shame of his defeat, he released the .44 and let it drop back in the holster, turned around, and walked out the door. The silence in the saloon lasted for another thirty seconds, replaced then by a whispered wave of astonished comments.

Liz looked at Stella and uttered just one word: "Damn!" It was hard to believe that this was the same Perley Gates who had befriended them.

The women stared at each other, speechless, until Stella went over to stand beside Perley.

"You think he'll be back?" she asked.

"I don't know," he replied as he released the hammer on his pistol and returned it to his holster. "He might. It don't ever pay to trust a man like that, so I reckon it'd be a good idea to be careful, especially if you go outside the saloon. Sidewinder'll shoot you in the back if you turn it to him."

"You never said you were that fast with a gun," Stella said.

Perley shrugged. "You never asked."

"It never occurred to me," she admitted, thinking back over her brief history with the shy, easygoing Texas cowhand. She knew Liz felt the same way. Perley was a good man, and a good friend, but they had both given thanks for avoiding a confrontation between him and any of the reckless gunmen between Ogallala and Cheyenne.

Another thought came to her. In the excitement of the face-off between Riker and Perley, Stella had forgotten about the oversized animal upstairs with Cora. She wondered now if Brady had heard the excitement taking place in the saloon beneath him. She glanced quickly up toward the top of the stairs, expecting to see him, but there was no one. She remembered, then, having heard Cora comparing her sessions with the brute to mating with a buffalo. There were no gunshots, so evidently, they had been oblivious to the scene downstairs. *Perley's had enough to deal with,* Stella thought. *Best we finish our drinks and hustle him out of the Cattleman's before he's confronted with Brady Ennis.*

She took his elbow and led him back to the table, where Liz was still sitting, trying to combine the Perley she thought she knew with the Perley she had just witnessed. *Lightning* was the only word she could think of to describe the scene.

"I guess we'd better have that one last drink and let Perley get on his way," Stella said to Liz when they returned to the table. "He's gotta get an early start in the morning to go find his grandpa. Ain't that right, Perley?"

"Yes, ma'am," Perley answered. "I'm figurin' on gettin' a real early start, and I need to get down to the stables before Tuttle locks me out."

Still somewhat amazed by what she had just witnessed, Liz was not inclined to rush Perley off. But after Stella went through a series of contortions to her eyebrows and forehead in an effort to silently signal her, she finally understood and remembered the buffalo in Cora's room. "Right," she drawled. "It won't do to have your head aching in the morning. Me and Stella are gonna be getting busy here in the saloon in a little bit anyway."

They had one last drink, and both women urged him to visit them again if he was back that way. He promised that he surely would, then said so long to C.J. When he turned to go, first Stella, then Liz stepped up to give him a hug, causing him to grin, embarrassed.

"Take care of yourself, Perley," Liz said.

"I'll do my best," he said.

"Good luck finding your grandpa," Stella added, "alive and kicking."

He gave her a grin, turned, and walked to the door, where he paused. It was already getting dark by then, so he took a good look outside before leaving the doorway. Like he had told Stella, it was best to be careful after the standoff with Riker. He was sure the man wouldn't hesitate to shoot him in the back. Perley wasn't planning on giving him the chance, so he took a moment longer to look up and down the street before stepping out of the doorway and heading down the street to the stable. He felt lucky to have avoided Brady, and so far, it appeared that Riker had decided not to push his luck.

The really unfortunate result of the evening was that there were witnesses to the speed with which he drew his gun. He could not explain why he was so fast with his hands — he just was, like how some boys can run faster than all their friends. He probably wouldn't have even discovered his ability had he not always won in contests with his brothers when they were younger. His father had warned him against exhibiting that talent to strangers, lest he gain a reputation for himself. It was advice that he had accepted and was the reason he had been reluctant to duel with Riker. *At least I wasn't burdened with the guilt of having killed a man back there in the saloon,* he thought, *even if it was a lowdown bully like Riker.*

He remained on his guard, walking close in the shadows of the buildings along his way, until he reached the safety of the stable. The altercation at the saloon had delayed him beyond what he had planned, so he was relieved to see that the lock was not yet on the barn door. He pulled the door open and called, "Mr. Tuttle?"

"Yeah — Perley?" the call came back, and in a few seconds Tuttle came from the tack room, carrying a lantern. "I was about to give you up. Thought you mighta found you a bed with one of those women at the Cattleman's."

"Reckon not," Perley replied with a chuckle.

He paused for a moment before starting to speak again. In that moment's pause, he heard the metallic clicking of a hammer cocking. Without conscious thought, his survival instincts took over and he spun, drawing and shooting at almost the same time. The two shots sounded almost as one, but the bullet from Perley's .44 doubled Riker over, while Riker's bullet embedded itself in the barn wall.

Shocked speechless, Tom Tuttle dropped his lantern, causing a fire to start in the loose hay spilled on the barn floor. Perley yelled at him to stomp it out, otherwise the barn might have soon been enveloped in flames.

Perley turned back at once to make sure Riker was through. In severe pain, Riker could not move. He lay there, doubled up, groaning pitifully. Perley picked up the six-gun Riker had dropped and stuck it in the man's belt.

"I expect we'd best get the doctor and the sheriff," Perley said. He walked over and stomped out a few small flickers that Tuttle had missed.

"Right," Tuttle murmured, just then regaining his senses. "Bob Joyner's the night deputy. I'll go find him. Dr. Shaw usually stays in his office pretty late. You can probably catch him there. It's right next to the undertaker, between here and the Cattleman's."

"I just passed it," Perley said. "I'll get him." Before running out the door, he paused to speak to Riker. "I'm goin' after the doctor. Just lie still."

He and Tuttle both left on the run, leaving Riker curled up in pain. There was nothing more Perley could do for him, except put a bullet in his brain to stop his suffering, but he wasn't inclined to do that.

As Tuttle had speculated, Dr. Shaw was still in his office, having a shot of whiskey for his rheumatism. He was not happy to hear of the need for his services, but he dutifully picked up his bag, even though he didn't expect to do much good, after Perley told him Riker was gut-shot.

They got to the barn a few minutes after Tuttle came back with Deputy Joyner. While Doc examined the wounded man, Joyner questioned Perley. Tuttle had already told him that Perley was not at fault and had only defended himself.

"That feller lyin' there come up behind him and took a shot at him, but he missed, and Perley didn't. That's the whole story."

Joyner was willing to take Tuttle's word for it and told Perley he was free to go.

"Why the hell didn't you shoot him again and put him outta his suffering?" Doc complained to Perley. "There ain't nothing I can do to save him, with that bullet in his gut. Who is he? Has he got any friends or family around here?"

"No, sir," Perley said. "He was ridin' for

some ranch back in Kansas, and he followed a whore over here from Ogallala to kill her and kill me for helpin' her."

He went on to relate the circumstances that brought Riker tracking them to Cheyenne with the evil intention of murdering the two of them, while Tuttle nodded in agreement.

Deputy Joyner listened patiently until Perley finished, then, showing no emotion, walked over and shot Riker in the head.

"He's outta his pain now," Joyner declared. "I'll go get the undertaker."

Dumbfounded, Perley looked at Dr. Shaw. Doc shrugged and said, "Best thing for him. I'll need two dollars for examining him."

"You can get it when the sheriff comes in in the mornin'," Joyner said.

Chapter 13

Upon the advice of Tom Tuttle, Perley decided his best bet was to follow the stagecoach road to Deadwood. The Cheyenne station was right in front of the fancy Inter-Ocean Hotel, and he was fortunate to find a handsome Concord coach, pulled by a six-horse team, in front of the hotel that morning.

The driver, a man who gave his name only as Russ, was happy to advise Perley on the journey he was about to undertake. According to Russ, it was three hundred miles through the rugged mountains of the Black Hills in Dakota Territory to get to Deadwood. For a passenger on the stage, the trip took about fifty hours, with stops to change the horses about every ten miles. Perley figured it would take him about a week to make the trip on horseback, depending upon how rough the trail happened to be. Fort Laramie, one hundred miles from

Cheyenne, was a common crossing of trails from all directions, according to Russ. So, if Perley had not discovered any trace of his grandfather before reaching it, Russ thought he could surely find evidence of him there.

"Good luck to you, young feller," Russ said in parting. "Maybe I'll meet you somewhere along the way. The stage leaves Cheyenne every Monday and Thursday. It comes back from Deadwood every Tuesday and Saturday. You won't have no trouble followin' the road. There's been so many folks headin' up that way it'd be pretty nigh impossible to get lost."

"Much obliged," Perley said and stepped back to watch his departure. The big Concord coach, with a full load of passengers inside and four more on top, pulled away from the hotel with a crack of Russ's whip for encouragement, leaving Perley envious of the time it would make.

There were ranches contracted all along the way to change the horses, but again at Russ's suggestion, Perley planned to camp the first night at a place called Bear Springs, about forty miles away. "Don't fret yourself 'cause you can't keep up with that stage," he told Buck. "Those horses are gonna be through in about ten miles. You've gotta go all the way to Deadwood."

He pushed on, following a road marked with hoofprints and wagon tracks, some left by heavy freighters and oxen, over a rugged corridor of the high plains. The land looked to him to be barren of vegetation and water, yet every ten miles or so, he came upon a creek or a stream with a farm on its banks.

He didn't stop to inquire about his grandfather except for at one small farm, where he rested his horses and watered them in a little pond formed by a dam in the creek. The owner came out to pass the time of day with him, but he couldn't recall having seen Perley's grandfather. Perley expected as much. He still thought his best chance was at Fort Laramie, where his grandfather might have bought supplies, so he didn't waste time stopping at every stage change-over station. He ended the first day at Bear Springs, as he had intended.

Each day that followed was pretty much the same as that first day, until he rode over the Laramie River on the steel bridge into Fort Laramie late one afternoon. Having never seen such a bridge, he took a few minutes' time to stop and look the impressive structure over. Then he followed the road into the fort, stopping the first soldier he met to ask where the post trader's store was located.

"Ride straight across the parade ground," the soldier said and pointed to a two-story barracks. "That's the bachelor officers' quarters. Ride out that road that goes in front of it, toward the cavalry barracks. Before you get to it, you'll see a sizable building. That's the sutler's store."

"Much obliged," Perley said and gave Buck a nudge with his heels.

The store was easily found with the soldier's directions, so Perley pulled up to the hitching post and looped the reins over it. Inside, he saw a couple of men behind the counters and one sitting at a desk, shuffling some papers. Perley figured the man at the desk was most likely the sutler, so he walked over and spoke to him.

"Excuse me, sir. I don't mean to interrupt, but I was wonderin' if you could help me."

Gilbert Collins looked up from his desk at the rangy young man. "Well, we'll certainly try. Just tell one of the clerks over there what you need, and if we've got it, he'll get it for you."

"Yes, sir, I 'preciate that, but I was hopin' you mighta remembered seein' my grandpa if he came through here, maybe a couple of months ago."

"Your grandpa?" Collins blurted, astonished by the question. Being a gentle and courteous man, he refrained from answering unkindly. "Why, friend, I don't know. What's your grandpa's name?"

"Perley Gates," Perley answered.

Collins didn't say anything for a long moment. Then he put his papers down and gave Perley his full attention. "Young man, we get folks coming and going through here day in and day out — soldiers, trappers, settlers, Indians. We're not likely to remember any of their names, except maybe those of the men stationed here."

Perley was not surprised by his answer and started to thank him for his time, but Collins continued.

"But that's one name I found easy to remember, and I remember the man who wore it. I even gave him a bottle of rye whiskey at no charge. He and I talked for half the night, and he was gone the next morning." He couldn't help chuckling when he recalled it.

Perley was excited. He had actually struck his grandfather's trail, but before he could speak, Collins interrupted.

"Perley Gates," he pronounced, still chuckling. "What's your name, son?"

"Perley Gates," he answered.

Collins started to tell him he meant *his*

name, but realized then. "You're named after him?"

"Yes, sir." Perley was overjoyed to have found his grandpa's trail, but he was eager to ask for any additional information Collins could give him. He was rapidly coming to the conclusion that Grandpa had impressed the sutler.

Collins gave him further proof of this when he yelled to one of his clerks, "Hey, Jeff, you remember a fellow named Perley Gates?"

Jeff immediately smiled. "I sure do. Feisty little feller heading up to Deadwood. Said he was on his way to get rich."

Perley could feel his heart quicken. It was the confirmation he had needed, to give him faith that he was definitely on his grandfather's trail. "How long ago was he here?" Perley asked.

"Oh, let's see," Collins replied, stroking his chin while he tried to remember. "I don't rightly recall exactly, but seems to me it was still cold weather. In the spring, I guess."

Perley stayed to talk for a little while, asking any questions that he could think of that might help him, but Collins, although more than willing, couldn't tell him much.

Perley thanked him and rode out of the

fort to pick up the trail again before choosing a place to camp for the night. After another supper of coffee and venison, he passed a peaceful night and started out early the next morning.

A day and a half out of Fort Laramie, he was surprised to come upon a collection of rough buildings that appeared to be a small village. Thinking that this might be a place where his grandfather could have stopped, he guided Buck toward one of the larger structures, where he saw a man sitting in a rocking chair on the porch.

"Afternoon," he greeted the fellow. "Wonder if you could tell me what the name of this town is."

The man got up from his chair and walked to the edge of the porch. "This here is the Hat Creek Ranch and Stage Stop," he said. "Is that what you were lookin' for?"

"No, sir," Perley answered. "I ain't really lookin' for anyplace, just ridin' through. Wondered where I was. Wasn't expectin' to find a town here. I thought if it was a town, there might be a blacksmith. I think my packhorse has a loose shoe."

"Well, you're in luck. We've got a blacksmith just beyond that little shack with the flagpole. That's the post office," he said and pointed. "We didn't start out to be a town, but I reckon we turned into one. This here is the hotel. We've got a grocery, a bakery, stables — most anything you'd need." He seemed proud of their progress. "Where are you headed, young fellow? Deadwood, with all the other gold hunters?"

"Well, I'm headin' to Deadwood, all right," Perley answered. "But I don't know much about huntin' for gold. I'm goin' up there to try to find my grandpa, and he mighta gone up there for gold. I promised my mother I would so I could let him know that my pa has died."

"Is that a fact?" The man stepped down from the porch. "Come on, I'll walk down to the blacksmith shop with you." Perley dismounted and walked along beside him. "What's your name, young fellow?"

"Perley Gates."

"Perley Gates?" the man questioned, not sure he had heard correctly. "Well, that's an unusual name. And you're looking for your grandpa? What's his name?"

"Perley Gates."

"I shoulda guessed that. My name's John Bowman. I'm glad to meetcha, Perley."

They walked on down past the post office and telegraph office to the blacksmith shop, where Bowman introduced Perley to Ralph Baskin, the blacksmith.

"Perley, here, says his horse might have a loose shoe. I told him you didn't know nothin' about shoein' horses."

Baskin laughed, accustomed to Bowman's japing. "If you'da seen me tryin' to shoe that dark roan back there, you mighta thought that for sure."

"Why's that?" Bowman asked.

"The damn horse is crazy," Baskin said. "He likes to bite. I've shoed a lot of horses that wanted to bite me, and I took that right out of 'em quick enough, but that horse is a mean one. I went round and round with him till I said to hell with it. Look at this." He pulled his sleeve up to exhibit a nasty-looking bruised elbow. "He'da et me up if I'da let him."

"You'd better have Marge take a look at that." Bowman turned to Perley to explain. "Marge is the closest thing we've got to a doctor. She's Ralph's wife." Turning back to Baskin, he asked, "Whose horse is it?"

"One of those two fellers that have been hangin' around here for the last couple of days — say they're waitin' for somebody supposed to be on the stage. They look more like they're waitin' to hold up the stage. Anyway, he ain't gonna be too happy when he comes back for his horse and it ain't got new shoes." He shrugged, as if perplexed. "But that ain't doin' you much good, is it?" Baskin asked Perley. "I'll take a look at that loose shoe. Which horse?"

"The packhorse," Perley replied. "I expect you'd best check 'em all, but it's the left front that I noticed."

Baskin nodded and took the lead rope from Perley.

"If you don't mind, I'd like to take a look at that roan you're havin' trouble with," Perley said.

"Go right ahead, but you'd best watch him. He'll take a hunk outta you before you know what happened."

"I'll watch him," Perley said and walked to the back corner of a shed over Baskin's forge, where a black horse was tied to the corner post. Buck whinnied and the blue roan answered with a whinny; then Buck followed behind Perley. John Bowman watched the young stranger, curious as to what he was going to do.

The roan's nostrils flared, and he jerked his head back against the rope that held him.

"Settle down, boy," Perley cooed softly, and the horse settled down at once. Perley spoke a few more words of reassurance to the roan and then started to stroke its neck. Pretty soon, the horse was nuzzling Perley with its muzzle. Perley turned to find both

Bowman and Baskin watching him in open-mouthed wonder.

Bowman was the first to speak. "I thought you said that horse was mean."

"Look at my arm!" Baskin retorted. "What the hell did you say to that crazy horse?"

"It ain't what *I* said," Perley replied. "It's what Buck told him." He nodded toward the big bay. "Buck told him to behave himself, I reckon. I expect that whoever usually shoes this horse musta hurt him and he don't want any more of that treatment." He reached down and lifted the roan's hoof, and the horse made no attempt to resist. "Might be a good idea if you came over and introduced yourself again," he said to Baskin, "so he'll know you ain't gonna hurt him."

Perley had always had a knack for handling horses. He didn't know why, and neither did his brothers — he just did. It was another quirk about their younger brother. Although Perley had said it was Buck that told the roan to settle down, he had no notion if that was true. Horses can communicate with each other — he knew that to be a fact — so maybe Buck did let the horse know to be gentle.

Baskin, still in wide-eyed amazement, dropped the sorrel's hoof and came to join

317

Perley. Bowman was close behind. Somewhat cautiously, Baskin rubbed the roan's withers, then gently reached down and picked up its hoof.

The roan promptly bit him on his behind.

"Yow!" Baskin screamed in pain and scrambled out of the horse's reach. Finding it funny, Bowman couldn't help laughing.

Perley found it puzzling. He stepped back beside the horse and, after a few pats on its neck, reached down to pick up the hoof. Again, there was no reaction from the horse. After a minute or two, he released the hoof and turned to Baskin. "I reckon he just doesn't like you, Mr. Baskin." He glanced at Bowman, who was still snickering, "You wanna try him and see if he behaves?"

"No, indeed," Bowman said. "I don't need that devil to take a bite outta my bottom." He backed away a little farther. "Ralph, what are you gonna do? That horse ain't gonna let you shoe him."

Baskin was about to answer when an outburst came from the front of the shop.

"What the hell are you doin' around my horse?" an angry voice demanded.

They turned to see a flint-eyed, snake-thin man striding forcefully toward them. He wore a black derby hat that looked too small to contain the coarse black hair it was riding on, and he was packing two six-guns, with the handles facing out.

"We were just figurin' out how best to shoe him, Mr. Murdock," Baskin answered.

"You ain't finished with him yet?" Murdock exploded. "I told you I wanted him done by three o'clock, and it's close to four now. From back there at the store, it looked to me like you was workin' on that sorrel with the packsaddle. I need my horse and I need him now."

His demand was punctuated by the sound of the stagecoach pulling in from the north, on its way to Cheyenne. It seemed to make him even more agitated, to the point of outright aggression.

"I need a horse, damn it!"

"I'm sorry, Mr. Murdock," Baskin pleaded. "I tried to shoe him, but he bit me — twice, now."

"Damn you," Murdock cursed, while taking frequent glances over his shoulder at the stagecoach pulling into the station. Already, the team of six horses was being unhitched while the new team stood waiting. "I ain't got time for this! Take the saddle offa that bay and put my saddle on him, and hurry it up."

He looked at Perley. "That your horse?" Perley nodded. "Well, he's mine now —

we're swappin' horses. You got any objections?" He dropped his hand to rest on the grip of one of his pistols.

There was little doubt in Perley's mind that Murdock was involved in some plan that had to do with the stagecoach just arrived — robbery, more than likely. The man already had his hand on his .44., so Perley saw no sense in challenging him when he had Buck to rely on. "No, sir, I ain't got any objections."

He turned and pulled his saddle off his horse and stood back while Baskin picked up Murdock's saddle and put it on Buck. Since Perley was the only one wearing a gun, Murdock pulled the .44 and held it on him while he climbed up into the saddle.

"Now, I'll ask you to draw that weapon out real slow with your left hand and drop it on the ground," Murdock said. When Perley did so, Murdock smirked. "You ain't as dumb as you look." He then wheeled Buck hard and raced toward the hotel at a gallop.

"He's fixin' to rob the stage!" Bowman exclaimed. "And the cavalry patrol left this morning for Rawhide Buttes."

"I reckon he musta known that," Perley said as he cleaned the dirt from his handgun. "We'd best be ready for him when he comes back."

Surprised by Perley's casual attitude, considering Murdock had just stolen his horse, Bowman asked, "Why do you think he's coming back here?"

" 'Cause he most likely wasn't plannin' on makin' his getaway on foot," Perley answered. He turned to Baskin. "I figure you must have a weapon here somewhere." Baskin said that he did. "Well, you might wanna get it." Back to Bowman again, he said, "You can use my rifle." He drew the Winchester from his saddle sling and handed it to the obviously befuddled man. "It's gonna wanna shoot a hair to the left, so you might wanna set your sight a hair to the right."

"We need to do something to warn them up at the stables!" Bowman exclaimed.

"Give 'em three quick shots with that rifle," Perley said.

He would have done it himself, but he thought it'd be a good idea to see if Bowman knew how to shoot it. When the man cocked and fired three shots into the air, Perley said, "Maybe that'll let 'em know something's goin' on. How many men has this fellow got with him?"

"There's just the two of 'em," Baskin answered, "him and another feller he calls Curly. I can't believe they're figurin' on holdin' up the stage with just the two of 'em. Hell, there's four men that work right there at the . . ."

He stopped speaking when Buck suddenly appeared from behind the post office, carrying an empty saddle.

"Attaboy, Buck," Perley said when the big bay walked up to him. He gave him a few affectionate pats, then pulled Murdock's saddle off and replaced it with his own. "I figure we'd best get ready to say hello to Mr. Murdock any second now. At least, that's what I think, but you might have a better idea."

"Hell, no." Bowman spoke for both of them. "What do you want us to do?"

"Find yourself some cover," Perley said, "and we'll try to get the jump on him from three different directions."

Both of them hurried to take cover in the niches Perley pointed out, never questioning the directions from the young stranger. In a matter of thirty seconds, they were set up in ambush.

A few minutes more saw Murdock come running into the shop, frantically looking for the bay. When he saw Buck at the back of the forge, he went directly to him, too desperate to question the disappearance of the three men who had been there. He and his partner's half-cocked plan to take the strongbox while the horses were being changed had come apart when the warning shots were fired. Murdock had been flat on his back when he heard the three shots, having just been thrown from the horse he had stolen. When he looked toward the stagecoach, he saw four men on top of Curly, so there was nothing for him to do but run.

In his panic to escape the angry ranch hands and the stagecoach guard, he didn't notice a different saddle on the bay. He was within six feet of the horse when Perley, Bowman, and Baskin all popped up from their hiding places, with three weapons aimed at him.

At that point, Bowman took charge of the arrest. "Throw your hands up or we'll shoot you down!" he commanded.

Murdock hesitated, raising his hands less than shoulder-high beside him. He looked from face to face, studying the three men he had buffaloed so easily just minutes before. He couldn't see a killer's face on any of the three. "All right," he said, calm now after he had weighed his chances. "Here's what we're gonna do. I'm gonna step up on that crazy horse and ride outta here, and nobody gets shot."

"That horse is gonna throw you again,"

Perley said confidently.

"If he does, I'll put a bullet in his head," Murdock replied, getting edgy again when sounds of men coming toward them reached his ears.

"You're not going anywhere," Bowman said. "You're under arrest for trying to hold up the stage."

"And horse stealin'," Perley added.

Murdock glanced again at the men confronting him. He decided he liked his odds, so he turned and faced Bowman. "The hell I am," he swore and went for his gun, only to drop it a split second later when a bullet from Perley's .44 smashed his wrist and he let out a yowl of pain.

Bowman stood there, frozen by the threat upon his life.

Perley walked over from the water barrel he had taken cover behind and relieved Murdock of his other pistol. "Now we'll walk on back to the street — maybe do something to fix that wrist," he said. "I don't know if there's a doctor here or not, but maybe you oughta wrap your bandana around it to slow that bleedin' down."

"That was a helluva shot," Baskin said, finding his voice again after a short period. "I mighta shot, too, but in my hurry to get my rifle, I forgot the cartridges. If you hadda missed, I mighta hit him in the head with it, though." He nodded slowly. "That was one helluva shot," he repeated and shook his head, still thinking about it. " 'Course, you mighta been aimin' at his chest, I reckon."

"Mighta been," Perley said. He saw no need to explain that when he saw Murdock draw his pistol, he visualized Murdock's moving hand, much as he had the striking rattlesnake back in Paris. And it was the hand he was trying to kill.

They were met in the lane that served as a street by a sizable gathering of people, including most of the stage passengers, who had gone inside the hotel dining room. Willis Adams, the ranch foreman, took their prisoner into custody and had a couple of his men march him and his partner to a smokehouse for safekeeping until the cavalry patrol returned from Rawhide Buttes.

"That was about the dumbest attempt to hold up a stage that I've ever heard of," Adams remarked after Murdock and Curly were locked in the smokehouse. "Right in the middle of the station, where any number of men could have shot 'em, instead of out along the road somewhere. Who shot that one in the wrist?"

"This young man right here," John Bowman spoke up. "Perley Gates is his name, and he saved my life, because that fellow, that Murdock fellow, was fixin' to shoot me."

"Well, good work, Perley," Adams said and stepped up to shake his hand. "I haven't seen you around here before. You passin' through? Ain't by any chance lookin' for a job, are you?"

Perley said that he wasn't, then went on to explain why he was on his way to Deadwood.

"Well," Adams continued, "I expect Bill Daley and Slim Cotton will want to thank you for your help. They're the driver and guard for the stage company."

Perley shook hands with each of them, and Adams said, "After you find your grandpa, if you need work, I can always use a man like you."

"Thank you, sir," Perley said, "but I expect I'll go back to Texas."

"Well, I'll tell you where you're gonna eat supper tonight," Bowman said. "At the hotel, with my wife and daughter and myself."

"I wouldn't wanna cause any extra bother for your wife, Mr. Bowman. I've got plenty of supplies to cook my supper."

"Nonsense," Bowman insisted. "She'd be mad at me if I didn't invite you to supper.

If you don't accept my invitation, I'll have Willis, here, lock you up with those two for insulting my wife."

Perley grinned. "In that case, I reckon I'll accept the invitation, but I'll need to take care of my horses."

"You can leave 'em in the stable," Adams offered. "We'll give 'em water and oats, and you can pick 'em up in the mornin' whenever you're ready to leave."

"Much obliged," Perley said. "You mind if I sleep in the stable with 'em?"

"Better than that," Bowman said before Adams could reply. "You'll be stayin' in the hotel tonight as my guest."

A spectator to the conversation to that point, Ralph Baskin spoke up. "And I'll shoe your packhorse first thing in the mornin' — no charge."

"Well, you can't beat that," Perley said, overwhelmed by the outpouring of generosity on everybody's part. "I'm much obliged to all of you, but I'm able to pay my share."

"No such a thing," Bowman replied. "I'm sure you can, but you hadn't planned to, so just accept our gratitude for helping us out. Now, you go on and take your horses to the stable, and bring your saddlebags and whatever you need to stay overnight. Then come on back to the hotel, and I'll fix you up with a room for the night. After that, we'll go to supper."

"I 'preciate it," Perley said and walked back to the blacksmith shop with Baskin to get his horses.

Behind them, Bowman and Adams watched them walk away.

"It's too bad that young man isn't looking for a job," Bowman remarked. "You could definitely use a man like him. He knows horses. I saw a demonstration of that when he calmed that ornery horse Murdock was riding. Probably knows cattle, too, since he said home was a cattle ranch in Texas. But more than that, he's the best I've ever seen with a gun, and when it counts. I swear, Willis, I thought I was a dead man. That son of a bitch drew on me — had his gun already out — and Perley shot it outta his hand before he could pull the trigger. No, sir, there's a lot more to Perley Gates than meets the eye. He just happens to have that innocent look about him."

Adams shrugged. "You heard me offer him a job, but he didn't seem to be interested in it. He might have a wife and young'uns back in Texas. Did you ask him?" Bowman shook his head, so Adams shrugged again. "Why don't you and Lucille and Martha work on him tonight? Maybe you can convince him there's opportunities for young men out here."

They stood there a few moments longer until Perley and Baskin disappeared around the corner of the forge.

"Well," Adams concluded, "I've gotta get back to work before my men think it's a holiday." He started toward the barn, then stopped and turned around. "Perley Gates — that's a helluva name, ain't it? Wonder how many barroom fights that's started?" He turned back again, not waiting for Bowman's answer.

Perley couldn't help feeling a bit guilty when he showed up at the hotel a little while later, carrying his rifle and saddlebags. There was no one at the small desk in the foyer, but he saw a bell on the desk, so he rang it a couple of times.

A gray-haired man came from the hallway and, upon seeing him, asked, "Are you Mr. Gates?" Perley confessed that he was, and the man said, "Welcome. Mr. Bowman said to show you to your room — if you'll just follow me."

He turned and led Perley back down the hall. Stopping at the last door before another one leading outside, he said, "This room is close to the washroom, if you're wanting to clean up — just outside that door and about five yards away. If the door's open, feel free to use it. Mr. Bowman said he'd meet you in the dining room at six o'clock."

"Much obliged," Perley said, already enjoying the regal treatment he was receiving, something he was not at all accustomed to.

It was after five o'clock, confirmed by his railroad pocket watch, but there was still time to take advantage of the washroom, so he got his clean shirt, underwear, and socks out of his saddlebags, as well as his shaving mug and razor, and went at once to the washroom. He had not planned to change into clean clothes for another couple of days, but considering the occasion, he felt it was called for. The door to the washroom was open, with a sign on it that read IN USE, so he went inside and closed it behind him.

After a good scrubbing, he toweled off and emptied his bathwater into a large square hole in the floor beside the tub that seemed to be a good place to get rid of it. Then he pumped a bucket of water and placed it on the small iron stove where he had found it, assuming that the next bather would fill the tub from the pump, then warm the water with that on the stove, just as he had. Clean-shaven and freshly scrubbed, he felt ready to dine with Bowman and his wife.

The dining room was a cozy room with a stone fireplace at one end, not surprising to Perley, since it was a small hotel. There was a long table in the center, which occupied a large portion of the room, with two smaller tables with four chairs each, close to the fireplace. There were only three people at the long table, since most of the diners had been there at five when the dining room opened for supper.

Seated at one of the small tables, he saw John Bowman and two women. Upon spotting Perley, Bowman waved to signal him. Remembering his hat then, Perley removed it and proceeded to join them.

"Perley," Bowman began, "we're glad to have you join us. This is my wife, Lucille, and my daughter, Martha."

"Ma'am . . . ma'am," Perley responded, nodding to each of the women in turn before he pulled the chair out and sat down.

"Ladies," Bowman announced, "this is Mr. Perley Gates."

Perley detected the faint trace of a grin on the young lady's face, although she struggled to hide it.

Lucille Bowman, however, maintained a passive reception to his name. "We're so glad you could join us, Mr. Gates. My husband tells me we owe you our thanks for saving his life."

Perley flushed a soft shade of crimson. "Why, no, ma'am," he stuttered. "I just helped your husband and Mr. Baskin a little bit."

"You're too modest, Mr. Gates," she replied. "John told us all about it."

He was saved from having to reply when a woman came in from the kitchen carrying a tray with four serving bowls on it and placed them on the table. Perley realized then that Mrs. Bowman had not cooked supper for him as he had at first assumed. He felt stupid for not having guessed that Bowman was the owner of the hotel. The next few minutes were busy with the passing of the bowls of potatoes, beans, corn, and a platter of pork chops, along with fresh, hot cornbread. Except for the meal at Steiner's house, it was a great deal more food than he had been accustomed to eating since leaving the Triple-G almost three months ago. It surpassed anything offered at the occasional diner he had happened upon on his journey to find his grandfather.

Perley cautioned himself at once to control his urge to dive right in, lest they think him uncivilized. Resisting the desire to pick up the pork chop with his fingers and gnaw the meat away, he tried to cut it away using his knife and fork like the ladies did.

Then Mrs. Bowman suggested, "Tell us about your family in Texas."

"Not much to tell," he said. "My pa just died, but my ma's alive, and my sister and two brothers live on the ranch." He nodded toward Martha. "I've got a sister-in-law named Martha. She's my brother John's wife. My older brother Rubin's wife is named Lou Ann."

"But you're not married?" Lucille said.

"No, ma'am."

Martha was the first to notice his discomfort. "I think Perley would like to enjoy this fine supper Grace has prepared for us," she announced. "Let's dig in and eat before we let it get cold."

"Martha's right," her mother said. "Let's let the man eat." She had found out what she wanted to know anyway.

They had finished the meal and the apple pie when John Bowman started talking about his plans for Hat Creek Ranch and the opportunities that would surely be available there for any enterprising young man. Perley suddenly felt a chill down his spine when he recalled a similar pitch about Fort Collins, Colorado.

He immediately glanced at Martha, but

could see no resemblance to thirteen-year-old Ethel Steiner. He could not guess Martha's age, but knew it was considerably older than thirteen. He told himself that he was in a panic over nothing. Martha Bowman was a handsome young woman. She would have no problem finding a husband, unlike poor homely Ethel, so he put the notion out of his head. When he took another glance at Martha, her look of boredom told him he might as well. She surprised him, however, when she interrupted her father.

"You're probably boring Perley to death, talking about Hat Creek," Martha said. "Perley, why don't you pick up your coffee and we'll go out on the porch where it's cool, so Grace and her girl can clean off the table. She's too polite to tell us to get out of the dining room, so she can get through sometime tonight."

"Of course — you're right," her mother said. "You two young folks go out and enjoy the porch. It's time we old folks went upstairs."

It was obvious by his expression that her husband was not finished with his plans for the future of Hat Creek, but he managed a gracious smile and a warm good-night.

Perley thanked them for their hospitality, then followed Martha to the porch, coffee cup in hand. She led him to one side and a pair of rocking chairs, laughing at his efforts to sit down without spilling his coffee.

They talked about the weather and the summer season for a few minutes, before Martha asked, "Is there a girl waiting for you back in Texas, Perley?"

The question surprised him, but he could read nothing in her face but idle curiosity. "No, no girl," he answered. "There was one I thought I was interested in, but it turned out I wasn't. I reckon right now I ain't got time to think about a girl." He told her about his feelings of responsibility for finding his grandfather, to fulfill a task that his mother thought important.

"Do you think it's important?" Martha asked. " 'Cause if you don't, you sure have ridden a long way from Texas looking for a grandfather you've never seen before."

"Oh, yes, ma'am," Perley was quick to reply. "I surely do think it's important. My father wanted to bring his father back into the Gates family, and I aim to find my grandpa to tell him that."

She studied his face while he spoke of his father and the Triple-G Ranch in Texas, and decided that the shy, innocent man was a disarming façade for a much deeper man within.

There's more to Perley Gates than meets the eye, she told herself, *and I'm sure he's not even aware of it himself. Maybe it's because of that silly name he's wearing.*

"I expect I'd best turn in now," Perley said when darkness began to descend upon the Hat Creek Valley. "I'll have to be on my way in the mornin'. I've really enjoyed talkin' with you, but I don't wanna overstay my welcome. I'll take my cup back to the kitchen."

"Give it to me. I'll take it back for you," she said.

"Thank you, ma'am," he said and handed her the cup.

"When are you going to stop calling me ma'am?"

"Right now, I expect."

She laughed. "Good. I was beginning to think I must look like an old lady."

"No, ma'am," he said before he caught himself. "I mean, no, Martha, you don't look like an old lady — not by a lot." Feeling the ice was broken now, he ventured to ask, "How come you ain't married? Are all the men around this place blind or just plain stupid?"

"Now you're starting to ask the questions that my father asks," she replied with a laugh. "The truth is, the right man hasn't come along yet, and I'll die an old maid before I marry the wrong one." She got up from her chair.

Feeling that to be a signal that the visit was over, he jumped up, too. "I enjoyed meetin' you, Martha, and I hope the right man comes along pretty soon."

"I'm in no hurry," she said. "I enjoyed meeting you, too, Perley. I hope we'll see you again when you're back this way, and good luck with your search for your grandfather."

"Thank you, ma'am," he said, moving quickly to hold the door for her. He was baffled by the little impatient smile she gave him, unaware that he had called her ma'am again.

Eager to try out the hotel bed, he went to the outhouse, then went straight to his room. Never one to have trouble going to sleep, he lay awake for what seemed a long time, thinking about his conversation with Martha Bowman. *Some young fellow will be lucky to throw a rope on that little lady,* he thought before drifting off.

CHAPTER 14

The hotel bed proved to be a comfortable one. In his small room on the first floor, he could hear the sounds of breakfast preparations in the kitchen, and he was immediately gripped by near panic when he saw the time. He had not planned to sleep so late, and he nearly fell on his face in an effort to get into his trousers and boots. Sleeping late was akin to pure laziness, in his opinion, and he was anxious lest someone catch him abed at this late hour. With that in mind, he was intent upon getting his clothes on, grabbing his rifle and his saddlebags, and vacating the room before anyone saw him.

He should have already been to the stable to pick up his horses and take them to Baskin's blacksmith shop. *Baskin is probably wondering where the hell I am,* he thought as he slowly turned the doorknob and eased the door open a crack. Peeking through the opening, he could see down the hall, and he was immediately relieved to see it empty. So, he pushed the door open and stepped out into the hallway, being extra careful not to let his rifle bump on the doorjamb.

He wasn't aware of her presence until he closed the door and turned to go out the washroom door.

"Good morning, Perley," she greeted him sweetly.

Startled, he almost dropped his rifle as he blurted "Martha!" before he could catch himself.

"I didn't mean to startle you," she quickly apologized. Fully aware that she had caught him by surprise and he was obviously embarrassed to have been caught, she graced him with a wide smile. "Did you sleep all right?"

"Well, I reckon I did," he answered, "seein' as how I slept half the mornin' away." In the warmth of her smile, he could see that she was not judging him, and he realized that he was being silly by letting himself get so worked up over his sense of pride.

"I was wondering why Papa stuck you in that room with the hard mattress on that old bed. When he told me what room you were in, I was afraid you wouldn't sleep at all."

"It sure beat sleepin' on the ground, like I've been doin' for a couple of months, so like I said, I slept so good I almost didn't wake up till suppertime." He grinned sheepishly.

"That's what Papa said when I complained about that room," she said. "You probably needed a good night's sleep." She made a pretty little frown and teased, "You weren't trying to sneak out without saying good-bye, were you?"

He couldn't believe how nice she was, but he still felt like a clod in her presence. "No, ma'am," he said, even though that had been his intention. "I just wanted to get outta the room in case you needed it for a payin' customer. And I needed to take my horses over to Mr. Baskin's first thing, but I guess I just slept through 'first thing,' didn't I?"

She laughed again. "There's not but a couple of people staying in the hotel right now, so you shouldn't worry about that. Since you're not going to be able to start out before daylight now," she teased, "why don't you wait until you've had breakfast?" When he seemed short of an answer, she pressed, "Are you in such a big hurry to get to Deadwood that you can't wait until after you've had a good breakfast?"

"I don't know," he answered after a few

moments' hesitation and coming up with no real reason to hurry. "I reckon it really doesn't make a whole lotta difference how soon I get there, if we're talkin' about a day or two."

"Good, then why don't you do this? Go down to the stable and take your horses to Mr. Baskin, and he can shoe them while you're having breakfast back here."

"I would enjoy one more meal at your table," he said, grinning. "That's just what I'll do."

She walked with him to the front door before turning around to head for the kitchen to tell Grace that Perley would be back for breakfast and she wanted to make sure he got one that he would remember.

When Perley pulled up to the blacksmith shop, Ralph Baskin was working on a wagon-wheel rim, but he put it aside when he saw Perley.

"I thought maybe you'd changed your mind," Baskin said.

"Nope," Perley said. "I meant to get here earlier, but I got tied up with some things at the hotel. I got to thinkin' about that loose shoe on the sorrel. I know you offered to fix it for me for nothin', and I appreciate that. But while you're at it, I think you might as well check the bay's shoes, too. He oughta be due before long, so you might as well do the job now. Of course, I'd pay you for that job. Whaddaya say, can you do that this mornin'?"

"Sure," Baskin replied, glad to get the business. "It might take me a couple of hours, though."

"That'll be fine," Perley said. "I ain't had my breakfast, so I'll go do that while you're workin' on my horses."

He started walking back to the hotel, having a little talk with himself on the way, afraid that he might be letting a pretty girl get in the way of finding his grandfather. He didn't presume that Martha had any interest in him other than just being hospitable because she thought he saved her father's life. She was just being friendly, and he could always use a new friend. He told himself that it was all right to enjoy a friendly conversation with a young lady.

His thoughts flew to Lucy Tate, back in the Paris Diner, and the way her conversation was always flirty, causing his imagination to lead him to wrong conclusions. Martha was more like Becky Morris — friendly, but not flirty. He tried to summon an image of Becky but kept coming up with one that looked like Martha.

When he walked into the dining room, he headed for the long table in the center but was intercepted by Martha and led to the same small table as the night before.

"I'll be back with some coffee," she said, "and Grace will have your breakfast ready in a couple of minutes."

When she returned, she was holding two cups, and she sat down at the table with him, much to his delight.

"Are your folks comin' down to eat?" Perley asked.

"Why?" she responded. "Are you ready for another speech from Papa about how big the Hat Creek Ranch is gonna be?" Before he could answer, she said, "Papa's already at work in his office. He eats when the kitchen opens, and Mama won't eat anything till noon, so you're stuck with me for company."

That suited Perley just fine.

The breakfast was as good as Martha told him it would be, and the conversation was light and enjoyable. It might have gone on longer than it did, but it was Martha who was the first to suggest it was time to get on with the day.

"I know you're anxious to get started," she said. "But I've enjoyed getting to know you, Perley Gates. I hope you'll come back to see us sometime, and I hope you find your grandpa soon." She got up and extended her hand.

He jumped up and shook her hand. "Thank you for the visit. I feel like I made a friend."

"Why, of course you have," she said.

Unable to think of anything else to say, he blurted, "Who do I pay for my breakfast?"

"Pshaw," she replied in mock irritation. "You're my guest, for goodness' sakes."

"Thank you, Martha, I mean ma'am," he said, grinning.

She answered with a grin of her own. "You take care of yourself, Perley Gates," she said, then watched him until he went out the door.

He had been right when he said he had made a friend. She couldn't help thinking that she might have been inclined to become more than a friend, but Perley Gates was one of a kind. He struck her as incredibly innocent and, consequently, vulnerable to blundering into dangerous situations, just as he had there in Hat Creek when Murdock drew on her father. Next time, he might not be so lucky — *and I don't look good in a black dress and veil.*

Close enough now to feel the spirit of the

mysterious mountains the Indians called Paha Sapa, Perley was impatient to ride up into the dark pine-covered hillsides before him. He imagined that his grandfather must have felt much the same attraction when he first approached the Black Hills. It would have to wait until morning, however, because his horses were tired after a long day on the rugged trail, and the wide stream he was about to cross might offer the best choice to make his camp. Looking left and right, Perley decided to follow it upstream, since there appeared to be a heavier covering of trees farther up the slope. He had been cautioned by Ralph Baskin to be aware of the outlaws that preyed on those who traveled the Cheyenne-to-Deadwood road, so with that in mind, he always tried to make his camp inconspicuous. After following the stream for what he figured to be a quarter of a mile, he decided that he should have gone downstream, but then, up ahead, he saw the clearing.

Probably caused by a fire many years ago, the results of which left an open area of about an acre now covered by thick grass, it offered an ideal place to make camp. He pulled his saddle and packs from his two horses and left the animals free to drink and graze while he gathered sticks and limbs to build a fire.

When he had enough wood, he took his little coffeepot to the edge of the stream to fill it with the cold, clear water. He had failed to notice, until he lifted the pot from the water and glanced upstream, that there were remains of an old sluice box a couple dozen yards farther up. Curious, he set his pot down and walked up the bank to take a look at it.

The only part of the sluice box left was a section that appeared to have been fashioned from a wagon box. *Wonder if they found any pay dirt?* He looked around, trying to imagine a couple of miners hovering over their pans, searching for their fortunes.

Leaving the bank, he found the remains of the prospectors' camp and decided they had picked a better spot than he had. They were obviously camped there for a while, and had set up a tent or a large canvas, judging by the marks left in the ground. And there was a small fire pit made of rocks taken from the creek. *Ready-made,* he thought, and went back to move his saddle and packs to the new location. Then he returned to pick up the firewood he had gathered and brought it back as well. *Better protection, too,* he decided, because of a section of the bank that rose about four feet behind the fire pit. It would make a good rampart in case of an Indian attack.

From the looks of the camp, it had been abandoned for a long time. The prospectors who panned for gold here might have been run off, or killed, by Oglala Sioux. It wasn't that long ago that all this mountain range belonged to the Sioux. Nowadays, however, there was more danger from outlaws.

Once his fire was going, he set his coffeepot on a couple of crossed limbs to boil and fashioned a spit to roast some of his venison. When it was done, he poured himself a cup of coffee and sat on the edge of the embankment to eat his supper.

He had not finished his first cup when he heard Buck whinny. Long accustomed to paying attention to Buck's communications, Perley became at once alert. When the sorrel nickered as well and Buck snorted, it was enough to cause him to slowly put his cup down and pick up his rifle, being careful not to move too suddenly. He had a feeling that he had company, and if he did, he didn't want to let on that he was aware of it.

Once he had his rifle in hand, he slid down behind the raised portion of the bank and scanned the trees in front of him, searching for some sign of movement. In a few minutes, he heard the source of Buck's concern.

"I ain't lookin' to cause you no trouble," a voice called out. Perley quickly scanned the line of trees but could not determine where the voice came from. "You ain't got no call to be worried about me," it came again.

The voice sounded almost childlike, or maybe it came from a woman — Perley wasn't sure. "If I ain't got nothin' to worry about, how come you're hidin'?"

" 'Cause you might shoot me if I come out."

"What would I do that for?" Perley called back.

" 'Cause you might be one of them friends of Mott Mason."

"I don't know anybody named Mott Mason. What are you doin' out here in the mountains?"

"Hidin' from Mott Mason."

I reckon I should have figured that out, Perley thought. *I've got a feeling I'm fixing to step in another cow pie.* "Are you hungry?" he asked, thinking that might be what instigated this discussion with the pine trees.

"Yes, sir, I sure am. I could smell that coffee cookin' way back up the hill, and I ain't had nothin' to eat but a frog I caught in the stream yesterday." There was a pause of a few seconds, then, "What's that you're cookin' on the fire?"

"That's deer meat," Perley answered, "and I've got a gracious plenty of it." He waited, but there was no reply from the pines. "You're gonna have to come on outta your hidin' place if you want any. I ain't gonna throw good venison into the bushes, so whadda you gonna do?"

The pause continued, but finally there came the question, "Are you gonna shoot me if I come out?"

"Not if you behave yourself. I don't generally shoot women and children, if I can help it." He was convinced by this time that the voice belonged to one or the other. *Why me?* he had to ask himself. It seemed that God arranged for every woman in trouble to cross his path, and in places where most people would meet no one. It was inconceivable to think he might be facing another lost soul. He put his rifle aside, however, went to his packs, found his extra coffee cup, and held it up for her to see. "I've got an extra cup and plenty of coffee."

That proved to be more than she could resist, and after a minute or two, she stepped out of a pine thicket, then walked slowly toward him with both hands up in the air.

A woman, he thought, then changed his

mind. It was a girl, but it was hard to tell how old, for she looked to be in pretty rough shape. "You can put your hands down," he said. "You ain't under arrest." He poured her cup full and held it out to her.

He couldn't help thinking it was like trying to get a wild dog to take food out of his hand. She reached out very cautiously, as if expecting him to jerk it away. When it began to look like she was never going to take the cup, he set it on the ground and backed away from it. Again, like a wild animal, she quickly reached down to grab the cup, spilling some of it before she took a step back and started sipping the hot coffee.

"Here," he said and held the improvised spit out to her, and she quickly pulled a strip of roasted venison from it. "Slow down, or you're gonna choke on it," he cautioned, but she continued to eat as fast as she could. "How long has it been since you've had anything to eat, besides frogs?"

She shook her head while still chewing feverishly. "I don't know," she managed. "About a week, I reckon."

"Well, take it easy. It ain't goin' anywhere," he said. "And you can stop bein' scared — I ain't gonna hurt you." He let her eat in peace for a while, until she eventually seemed to calm down, before he asked her more questions.

"Where'd you come from?"

"Omaha," she answered.

"Omaha?" he responded with surprise. "What, on a wagon train or somethin'?" When she seemed confused, he realized why. "I don't mean where were you born. I mean just now, back up that hill. Have you got a camp up above here? Is there anybody else up there?"

"No, ain't nobody but me, and I ain't got no camp."

Perley was just before losing all his patience with the young girl. Finally, he threw his hands up in frustration. "Well, what in the hell are you doin' here?"

"I told you — hidin' from Mott Mason," she said.

"Who's Mott Mason?" Perley asked, then stopped her before she could answer. "Wait, what's your name?" He wanted to know if her name was also Mason and he might be stepping into a family squabble.

"Lena Rooney," she answered, hesitated, then asked, "What's yours?"

"Perley Gates."

She gave him a suspicious look, thinking he was japing her. "Pearly Gates?" Then she realized he was serious. "Damn, you've got a crazier name than me," she declared. "Why'd they name you Pearly Gates?"

"My pa's family name is Gates. I've got two brothers and a sister, so they named me Perley so folks could tell which Gates I was."

He didn't want to go into the whole story about his grandfather at this point. First, he wanted to find out who Lena Rooney was and how he happened to be so lucky as to have her cross his trail. He couldn't help thinking about Ethel Steiner and the trouble she had caused him. Lena Rooney seemed about the same age, and she was evidently running wild in these mountains. What was he to do with her? "Who's Mott Mason?" he asked again.

Instead of answering his question, she asked, "Is deer meat and coffee all you've got to eat?"

"It's all I've got to eat tonight," he replied. "I didn't plan on havin' a guest for supper or I'da fixed some beans and pan biscuits." He couldn't resist a bit of sarcasm. "I'm travelin' to Deadwood. All I wanted was somethin' to keep the sides of my stomach from rubbin' together."

"Oh, I ain't complainin'," she hastened to say. "I was just wonderin', that's all. You say you're goin' to Deadwood? Can I go with you? I'm handy as can be. I can cook for you and do chores."

"Cow pie," he blurted before he thought to stop it.

"What?" she asked, not sure she had heard him correctly.

"Nothin'," he replied. "I don't know if you can go with me or not, at least till I find out a lot more about how you happen to be runnin' around out here in the woods. Besides, you don't know anything about me. You might not wanna travel with me at all."

"It'd be better'n travelin' with Mott Mason," she said. "I can guarantee you that."

His patience left him. "Damn it, Lena Rooney, who is Mott Mason and why are you hidin' from him?"

"He's a mean son of a bitch," she replied, then finally went on to tell Perley her story. "My daddy sold me to Mott Mason for a milk cow and thirty-five dollars. I've got two brothers, but Mott didn't want no boys, and Daddy was glad to get rid of me anyway. He said he could get milk and butter from a cow, and I didn't give him anything but an extra mouth to feed."

"Why did this Mason fellow wanna buy you?" Perley asked. "Did he take you for a wife?"

"Hell, no," Lena protested. "He was wantin' to make a whore outta me! He already had two women ridin' with him. They're older'n me and had experience whorin', and he was on his way to Custer City. He was fixin' to teach me how to please men. I told him I didn't want to please no men. He said I didn't have no choice, that I was his property, bought and paid for, and I'd do what he told me to. I told him in a pig's eye I would, so he whupped me good with his belt and said if I ever tried to run away, he'd track me down and beat me to death. I promised I wouldn't try to run, but I was just waitin' for the right chance, and that came along when that horse of his couldn't pull the wagon up a steep trail that was supposed to lead to the wagon road to Custer City. He made us all get outta the wagon and get behind it and push, so I pushed as hard as I could, until my feet went out from under me on some loose gravel and I landed right on my face." She made a pouty face for him then. "Do you think they'da stopped and helped me up? Well, you'd be wrong. They just left me a-layin' there, my dress tore and blood runnin' outta my nose, and they kept goin'."

"Is that when you ran off?" Perley asked.

"I figured I wouldn't likely get a better

chance, with ol' Mott up ahead, leadin' the horse. So, I just rolled over to the side of the trail and gave him about five minutes to miss me. He was too busy tryin' to get the horse up that trail, and Belle and Lucy didn't give a damn if I was all right or not, so I got up and took off across the side of the mountain."

"How long ago was that?" Perley wanted to know.

She paused to recall. "I swear, I ain't sure. I ran around that mountain till almost dark. Then I found me a place to hide in a gully. I fell asleep after a while, and when I woke up, it was daylight, so I took off again, between that mountain and another'n, tryin' to head north. That night, I piled up a bunch of leaves and slept under 'em. I know I walked two more days before I started up this stream."

Perley handed her another strip of venison when it was done, which she took eagerly, tearing into it like a hungry wolf. A few minutes before, she had said she hadn't eaten in a week, causing him to be a little skeptical, since she didn't appear to be as weak as she would have been if her story was true. He asked, "Did you really eat a frog?"

She screwed her face up like she had eaten

a sour pickle. "A little bit of one. I was so hungry I thought I could eat the whole thing, but his legs were still kickin' when I tried to chew him up, and I spit him out."

What the hell am I going to do with her? This was the question Perley now asked himself. "You said you were tryin' to head north. Where were you thinkin' about goin'?"

"Deadwood," she answered, and when he asked why, she said, " 'cause Mott Mason is goin' to Custer City. And Deadwood is where most people are headin' now, so I figure I've got a chance to find myself somethin' I can do there to survive — washin' dishes, cleanin' up, washin' clothes — somethin'."

She could read it in his face that he was trying to decide what to do with her. After a long moment when he said nothing, she pressed, "That's the reason I wanna go to Deadwood with you. I don't know how to get there by myself, and I won't cause you no trouble. Like I said, I'll do for you and help you out all I can, and when we get to Deadwood, I'll just say thank you and goodbye, all right?" She studied his face intently, hoping that when she said she would *do* for him, he wouldn't take that to mean the same thing Mott Mason expected of her.

The thought of Mott caused a feeling of nausea momentarily. At least with Perley, it would not be as disgusting. "So whaddaya say, Perley? Can I go with you?"

"I reckon," he answered right away. He had no choice. He couldn't leave her to find her own way. She had no means to even stay alive unless he took care of her. "I oughta tell you, though, I've never been to Deadwood, so I'm just followin' the stagecoach road, and it passes through Custer City before it goes to Deadwood. So, I reckon we'll have to go around Custer, if that's where this fellow Mason is headin'." He took a long look at her and shook his head. "Too bad you didn't run off with some more clothes with you. That dress looks like it's just holdin' together. I've got a coat in my packs. You can put that on, and I've got an extra blanket I figured I might need if I was still here when cold weather hits. We can make you up a bedroll with that."

She was suddenly all smiles. "I won't be no trouble, Perley. You won't be sorry."

I already am, he thought, wondering how he happened to attract one stray after another, starting with Liz and Stella, then Ethel Steiner, now Lena Rooney. He wasn't sure how far he was from Custer City. He had told her he would ride around it, but he didn't want to do that. It might be the very place he could strike his grandpa's trail. *I reckon I'll have to hide her someplace while I go into town,* he told himself.

"Well, let's get you a bed fixed up," he said and went to his packs to find the extra blanket. "If you wanna help, you can rinse out the coffeepot and cups."

Without waiting for him to suggest it, she busied herself collecting firewood to keep the fire going while he went to check on his horses. He hobbled the sorrel's front legs, then spent some time checking Buck to see how the new shoes were working out.

"What's his name?" Lena asked when she walked up to Perley and the bay gelding.

"His name's Buck," Perley answered.

She gave that a moment's thought, then asked, "What's the other one's name."

"Packhorse," Perley answered with a chuckle, since the sorrel didn't have a name. He had cut him out of the remuda at Ogallala, never thinking about naming him. "You can think up a name for him while we're ridin' to Deadwood."

"I'll think on it," she said.

"Well, I'm turnin' in," Perley announced. "You need some help with that blanket?"

"Nope, I'm just gonna roll up in it." That's just what she did, while Perley walked downstream to find a place to take care of business in private.

Still a little concerned about her own safety, even as nice as Perley seemed, she lay there, stone still and stiff as a board, awaiting his return. If he had any ideas about crawling into that blanket with her, now was the time, and she listened as he approached from the creek bank. She could hear his footsteps as he walked through the low bushes under the pines. Then, after what seemed a short period with no sound at all, she turned her head slowly in his direction. He was settled in his bedroll, and by all appearances, already on his way to sleep. *Thank you, Lord,* she said in a silent prayer of gratitude. *You sent me a decent man.* She turned over on her side and went to sleep.

She awoke the following morning to the aroma of coffee bubbling in the pot. After a moment of confusion while she remembered where she was, she suddenly sat straight up. "Oh, shit!" she exclaimed. "I shoulda been up before now."

"What for?" Perley asked.

"To cook our breakfast," she said. "I shoulda been up before you."

"I think you needed the sleep. You looked

like you hadn't had any decent sleep for a while, so I didn't think you'd mind if I went ahead and started it."

"Well, I'll take over," she declared, scrambling out of the blanket. "Just give me a minute to visit those bushes over near the clearin'. I'll be right back." She took off without waiting for his reply.

"Take your time — ain't no hurry," he said, even though she was already out of earshot. "I reckon I oughta be used to travelin' with women by now." He turned his attention back to the bacon in the frying pan.

Squatting in a thick row of serviceberry bushes close to the grassy clearing and a considerable distance from the fire, Lena was busy getting rid of some of the coffee she had consumed the night before. About to thank her lucky stars for having been sent a Good Samaritan in her time of need, she froze when she heard the bushes parting behind her. At once frightened and angry at the same time, she turned to defend herself, only to find the big bay gelding gazing at her in idle curiosity.

Unable to contain it, she let out a whoop, and laughed at her immediate presumption. Finishing up her business, she grasped the nosy horse's bridle and stroked his neck and face. Then, for the hell of it, she jumped up on his back and, taking the reins, turned him toward the campfire and rode back, to pull up before a startled Perley.

Still sitting astride the big horse, Lena was puzzled by the look of amazement on Perley's face. "What is it?" she asked.

"Nothin'," he answered, not sure himself. Unable to resist finding out for certain, he had to ask, "You done much ridin' before?"

"I used to ride my pa's horses all the time when he had the farm," she said.

"How 'bout ridin' Buck down there and lead the sorrel back up here near the fire, so I can saddle 'em?"

"All right," she said and wheeled Buck around. In a few minutes, she returned, leading the packhorse. When she saw the same strange expression on Perley's face, she asked, "Is everything all right? Did I do somethin' wrong?"

"Nope," he answered as she slid off the horse's back. "It's just that you're the first person I've ever seen come offa Buck of their own accord. Buck don't let anybody ride him but me." He paused and scratched his head. "And now, I reckon, you."

His declaration pleased her, and she immediately took over the cooking. "Have you got any flour?"

"In the packs," he replied, pointing to one, still puzzling over the fact that Buck didn't buck her off.

"You go saddle up, and I'll see what you've got to cook with. We'll have us a good breakfast before we get started to Deadwood."

He did as she instructed, not realizing that she had taken charge of things in short order. He was yet to learn that it was her nature to tend to do things as she thought they should be done. One thing he found out right away, however, was her ability to cook, which almost made him glad she had crossed his path. This, even though he had no idea what he would do with her when they reached Deadwood.

It was not until they had finished eating and Lena had washed the cups and pan that she asked why he was going to Deadwood. So, he told her about his grandfather, whose name he shared, and his quest to find the old man. She listened with rapt attention.

"So, you ain't goin' to Deadwood lookin' to hunt gold like everybody else?" she asked when he had finished. "And your grandpa don't even know about you?"

"That's right," Perley answered.

She was impressed. "I reckon you're pretty

proud to be wearin' your grandpa's name, then."

"Well," he hesitated, "I reckon I ain't ashamed of it, but sometimes it's caused me a little trouble."

CHAPTER 15

With Lena riding behind him, holding the packhorse's lead rope, Perley guided Buck back down the stream and returned to the Cheyenne-Deadwood Stage road. They would travel about fifteen miles, following the sometimes treacherous road, before Perley decided the horses were working too hard on the mountain trail. When they came to a parklike campground that looked to be a change-up station for the stage line, he let the horses rest.

There was grass on the hillside and a strong creek for water. A man who had been standing on the porch of the large log house, watching them approach, stepped down to meet them.

"Good day to ya," he said, as he continued to study Perley and the young girl behind him.

"Howdy," Perley replied. "Mind if we water our horses outta your creek there and let 'em rest awhile?"

"Don't mind at all," the man said. "We don't own the creek anyway, and if you wanna graze your horses, you can turn 'em out in my pasture, there." He talked to Perley, but he continued to study the bedraggled-looking girl behind him. "How 'bout you and your lady friend, there? My missus can cook you up some dinner for twenty-five cents apiece."

"I was figurin' on cookin' my own dinner," Perley said and turned to give Lena a look. "But maybe it'd be a nice thing to treat you to a good hot dinner. Whaddaya say, Lena?"

"That'd be real nice," Lena replied, "as long as you ain't expectin' me to come up with a quarter."

"I reckon we'll buy some dinner, then," Perley said to the man.

"Good," he said. "My name's John Potter. I'll tell my wife to fix up a couple of plates. Just come right on in the house after you take care of your horses. The young lady can come on in while you're doin' that."

"Much obliged," Perley said while Lena climbed down. Then he rode Buck over by the creek to leave him and the packhorse to drink.

Once inside the house, Potter turned at

once to face Lena. "Are you all right, young lady?"

Surprised by the question, Lena hesitated, thinking the man might be touched in the head. Then she remembered that she must look a sight, and she couldn't help laughing. "I will be after I eat — if your wife can cook halfway decent." She realized that Potter might be thinking Perley had abducted her and treated her badly. "I fell out of a wagon back yonder in the mountains, and if Perley hadn't come along, I'd still be wanderin' around in the woods."

Potter looked relieved. He had summoned his courage to step in and do the right thing if the situation was, in fact, what it first appeared to be. He was now happy to take Lena's word that she was not being abused. "Come on in the kitchen," he said, then called his wife. "Sarah, we've got two travelers that wanna buy some dinner."

When they walked into the kitchen, Sarah was standing there waiting. Like her husband, her initial reaction to Lena was to gasp in alarm.

"Child," she cried, "what happened to you?"

Lena told them of her sale to the cruel Mott Mason and of her accident while pushing his wagon up a steep trail.

"You poor child!" Sarah Potter wailed. "Then, who is the man who brought you here?"

"Like I told your husband," Lena said, "he found me after I'd been wanderin' around lost. He said he'd take me to Deadwood." She hung her head to affect a convincing appearance of disgrace. "I know I look a sight, but I ain't got no clothes. Mott Mason rode off with every stitch I had."

Sarah shook her head, overcome with compassion for the unfortunate young girl. "Well, thank the Lord for guiding you to us. I can clean you up a little, and I'm sure I've got an old dress that would at least give you something better than that ragged one you're wearing."

"That's mighty kind of you, Mrs. Potter, but I know Perley's in a hurry to get to Deadwood. He's tryin' to find his old grandpa, and I wouldn't wanna hold him up. He coulda left me in the mountains like Mott Mason did, but he said he'd take me to Deadwood, so I don't wanna make no fuss."

"Well, he can just wait till we take care of you," the resolute woman said. "You can't go a step farther till we fix you up. And that'll start with a good meal. You're too late to eat with the hired hands, but I can rustle up some ham and eggs in a jiffy." Hands on hips, she turned to face the door when she heard Perley walking across the porch.

Somewhat startled because of the frowning faces he was met with from John and Sarah Potter, Perley felt as if he had walked into a courtroom and he was on trial. In contrast, Lena's face was lit up with a satisfied smile that reached from ear to ear. He was about to ask what Lena had told them, but Sarah Potter didn't give him the chance before she began telling him what was going to happen.

"Welcome to our home, young man," she started. "You're doing the right thing, taking this girl to Deadwood, and you should be applauded for that. She says you're in a big hurry to get there, but she needs some attention before she'll be ready to go on. So, you'll just have to cool your heels for a little while till she's ready." When she was met with a look of pure astonishment on Perley's part, she added, "To make up for it, there won't be any charge for your dinner — or hers." She stared sternly at him, waiting for his response as if she anticipated some disagreement from him.

He didn't reply right away, glancing again

at Lena, who was still smiling. It was easy to guess that she had painted a picture for them, and he wasn't sure if he had been depicted as the villain or not. "Whatever Lena thinks is best," he said.

"Oh," Sarah blurted in surprise, obviously expecting an argument. Then, not sure he realized what she meant, she went on. "She needs a good bath and something decent to put on, not just food."

"I reckon you're right about that," he agreed. "But I didn't think she'd appreciate it if I tried to give her a bath."

Lena couldn't help laughing outright at that. It served to alleviate the tension John Potter had begun to build up when his wife started to lay down the law to the young stranger. He realized that Perley was joking and nodded his approval, when Perley continued.

"I don't normally carry a spare dress in my packs, but I did let her use my coat till we got to a place where we might buy one." He gave Lena a wink and concluded, "If it's gonna take too long before you get her ready to ride, I can just leave her here with you folks, and I'll go along about my business."

"No, no," Sarah quickly replied. "It won't take us that long. I've got several old dresses that I can't wear anymore. At least one of them oughta be just right for her. We won't delay you any more than necessary to take a nip and tuck in it, and you'll be on your way. To look for your grandpa, was that it?"

"Yes, ma'am," Perley replied.

Feeling comfortable now and enjoying his wife's retreat, Potter laughed and asked, "What's your name, young feller?"

"Perley Gates," he answered. Seeing the reaction in Potter's face, and accustomed to it, he went on to explain that he was named for his grandfather.

More interested in Perley then, Potter asked if his grandpa knew he was coming to find him, so Perley told them the whole story behind his trip, all the way from Texas, to search for his grandfather.

"And he ain't ever seen you?" Potter asked when Perley had finished. "And he don't even know his grandson is named after him?"

"That's a fact," Perley said. "And now that my pa's dead, my ma thought Grandpa oughta know about it."

Potter shook his head, thinking about it. "That's a powerful long way, just to tell that old man you're his grandson."

"My ma thinks it's important," Perley declared, "and that's enough reason for me."

Potter's wife nodded approvingly after that remark, deciding that she liked Perley even more. She finished slicing strips from a salt-cured ham to fry with some eggs and serve with cold biscuits and hot coffee. "You folks sit down and eat, and I'll heat some water for a bath after you're done," she announced.

While they ate the ham and eggs Sarah Potter had prepared, Lena watched Perley for a few long minutes before she asked, "Are you thinkin' about stoppin' in Custer City?" She wanted to remind him that Custer City was where Mott Mason was heading and Perley had told her they would go around that town.

Understanding her fears, Perley nevertheless knew he had to find out if his grandpa had stopped there. "I know what I told you, but you can see that it's important that I make sure we're still on Grandpa's trail. We'll find you a good place to hide, and I'll go into town by myself. Shouldn't take long — then I'll be right back and we'll go to Deadwood. All right?"

"I reckon," she said without much enthusiasm. When she had finished eating, Sarah marched her off to the washroom.

Perley almost didn't recognize Lena when

Sarah brought her back. She was dressed in a plain cotton dress, but Sarah had washed and combed her hair, so that she looked like a proper young lady. Were it not for the sassy expression upon her face, Perley might have mistaken her for someone else.

"Dang," he teased. "Maybe I shoulda brought a carriage." She made a face, but said nothing. "Are you ready to ride, ma'am?"

"I reckon I am," she replied, "if you think you can quit gawkin' long enough to get started."

"How far is Custer City from here?" Perley asked Potter and was told it was a distance of about fifteen miles. "That'll put us there by suppertime." He glanced at Lena. "I'll find a good place to leave you and the sorrel while I take a quick look around."

He climbed up into the saddle, then reached down to give Lena a hand as she climbed up. "Much obliged to both of you for your hospitality," he said and wheeled Buck away from the porch.

John and Sarah Potter remained on the porch, watching them until they forded the creek and returned to the stage road.

"I hope that young man has sense enough to take that girl someplace where she'll be all right," Sarah remarked.

"He strikes me as being cut outta the right kind of cloth," John said. "I'm more worried about what he could do to protect her if they was to run into that Mason feller she talked about. He's wearin' a Colt .44. I wonder if he knows how to use it, if he was forced to — looks more like he oughta be totin' a Bible instead." He started down the steps. "We oughta be gettin' a stagecoach in here before long. I'd best go see if the boys are ready to change that team of horses."

Later that afternoon, the outer buildings of Custer City came into view as they approached a valley with mountains on both sides. There was no need for comment — Perley could feel Lena tense up, so he sought to put her at ease right away. He pulled Buck back to a stop while he took a look at the town ahead of them. After a few moments, he pointed toward the hills to the west.

"We'll head toward those hills and find some water and grass for the horses. It looks like that might be a creek or a stream cuttin' down through that stand of pines."

As he had assumed, they found a stream flowing down from the mountain where he had pointed, and, not surprising, the remains of an old mining claim, now abandoned.

"Good a place as any," Perley decided, so they unloaded the packhorse and gathered some wood for a fire. "I reckon you'll be all right here till I get back. I'll leave you my rifle, just in case."

"You goin' to town right away?" Lena asked. "Before you eat?"

"I reckon so. I want to catch the blacksmith or liveryman before they go to supper."

She nodded, then said, "I guess you'll be stoppin' in at a saloon before you come back to eat."

"Well, I hadn't planned to," he replied.

"How do I know you'll come back? You might be thinkin' it'd be a whole lot easier for you if you didn't have to bother with me."

He was really quite surprised to hear her sudden return to the fears she had when they first met. Perley couldn't help wondering if she had lost her cocksure attitude at Potter's place. Maybe it got washed off in the bathwater. It occurred to him that she had probably never had a good relationship with any man. Her father sold her for a cow and a little money to boot, and the man who bought her treated her like a slut. Perley guessed it was only natural that she would paint all men with the same brush, especially since she was no more than thirteen or fourteen.

"Well, you can be pretty sure I aim to come back, 'cause I'm leavin' my packhorse, my rifle, and all my supplies with you."

"Oh, that's right — I forgot about that." Her usual saucy attitude returned at once. "Well, you'd best not take too long, or I'll cook supper for myself and leave you to cook your own meal."

"I'll get back as soon as I can," he assured her. "I aim to take you to Deadwood." He could feel her watching him as he rode off toward town.

He came to the stable first, but no one there recalled ever having seen his grandfather, so he rode up the street to the blacksmith shop, to find the smithy hard at work on an axle. He stopped when Perley pulled up.

"Yes, sir, can I help you, sir?"

"I'm tryin' to catch up with my grandpa," Perley said. "I was wonderin' if he mighta stopped by your place."

"It's hard to say," Jim Coker replied. "What does he look like?"

"Little old fellow," Perley said. "His name's Perley Gates."

A wide smile broke out on Coker's face. "Perley Gates — I remember that name. Funny little old man ridin' a paint horse. He might be the reason Lem Wooten sold this forge to me for a right good price. That was about a month ago."

"Do you know where he is?" Perley asked.

"No. He came lookin' for Lem and musta told him somethin' that built a fire under Lem's behind. As soon as I gave Lem the money, they didn't wait around for a second. Got on their horses and rode straight outta town." He pointed toward the north end of town.

It had to be his grandpa! Perley still didn't know for sure where the two of them were heading when they left Custer, but it was logical to assume it was Deadwood. He thanked Coker for his help, immediately turned Buck around, and headed back toward his camp.

He was eager to get on the road to Deadwood, but the horses had already gone thirty miles that day. That was not too many, even though much of it was rough going, but it would be better to start out fresh in the morning. Besides, Lena most likely had already begun cooking supper, maybe even making biscuits if she was in the right mood.

When he rode over the low ridge next to the stream, he was surprised to see no one where he thought he had made his camp. There was no fire, no horse, and no Lena. At first, he thought he must be too far along the ridge. He looked right and left, searching for signs of smoke in either direction. There were none, and he knew he was not mistaken. This was where his camp was supposed to be.

She ran off on me! It hit him totally by surprise. He would have bet against it.

"Damn it!" he blurted aloud. "She's got my rifle and my horse — and everything I need to cook with."

John and Rubin are right, he thought. Once again, he was reminded of his brothers' fondness for japing him about his tendency to step in a cow pie more often than most. *Well, she ain't gonna get away with it,* he swore to himself. *I shoulda left her back there in the mountains where I found her.*

Determined to track her, he stepped down from the saddle and started searching the ground beside the stream for tracks that might show him which way she had gone. There were tracks, clearly defined by the sorrel's new shoes, where he had left him by the stream. Perley suddenly stopped when he saw the clear tracks of a wagon —

fresh tracks that were not there when he left the sorrel before. He was sure he would have seen them. He followed the wagon tracks until they crossed over the low mound at the end of the ridge.

Standing there, he looked in the direction the tracks led. It was apparent they were heading toward the stage road to Deadwood. He felt certain then that she had not run off, she had been taken. Somehow, this Mott Mason had found her, for Perley knew that was what had to have happened. Angry at her only seconds before, he was now angry with himself for not being there to try to protect her.

He wasted no more time wondering how Mason had happened to find her. It was extremely unlikely that anyone had seen them when they rode west of the town and picked a place to camp. Mason had either just happened to look for a place to rest his horse in the same spot Perley had, or he had somehow been able to track them. The fact of the matter was that somehow Mason had found her, so Perley's only option now was to catch them as quickly as he could. And that wouldn't be hard to do, since they were driving a wagon and would have to think about stopping for the night pretty soon.

Following the deep wagon tracks across the valley, Perley soon came to the stage road, north of Custer City, and the angle at which the tracks intercepted the road indicated that Mason intended to continue north. Conscious of Buck's hooves pounding out the miles on the well-traveled road, Perley was thankful that the big bay had gone only about thirty miles so far that day.

He didn't anticipate the wagon making more than ten miles before darkness, so he started looking for likely camping spots almost immediately. There were many streams cutting across the narrow valley, most of them too small for him to consider following them up the slopes. Still, he paused at each one and looked for signs of smoke that might indicate a camp up in the trees.

"You want me to untie her from the back of the wagon now?" Belle Tatum asked.

"Hell, yeah," Mott Mason blurted. "She ain't gonna set around and watch the rest of us work."

He walked around to the tailgate with Belle, prepared to set out some rules. Addressing Lena, he asked, "Did you enjoy your walk from Custer? We was all glad to have you come back to the family after your little vacation, wasn't we, ladies?" He glanced at the two women sullenly watching him, receiving no more than blank stares in response.

Back to Lena then, he said, "Trouble with folks takin' vacations is, they has to pay for them when they come back. Now, it woulda been a little easier on you if you'da come back on your own, instead of me havin' to find you — mighta even let you ride in the wagon. Looks to me like you still ain't got it in your head that I own you, bought and paid for, and I don't let nobody cheat me outta my money. And I gave a damn good milk cow to boot." He paused to chuckle at the thought. " 'Course, it don't make no difference if I stole the damn cow from that sodbuster down the road from your pappy's farm."

Maintaining a tight-mouthed silence to that point, Lena felt compelled to say, "People ain't for sale. If you had any sense a'tall, you mighta heard there was a war about that not too long ago."

Her comment earned her a hard backhand that knocked her to the ground. Lucy Drover took her arm and helped her up, frowning at her in an effort to warn her not to rebel. Lucy, like Belle, felt compassion for the young girl, but they were in no position to help her. Both approaching middle age, they were with Mason voluntarily. Whores since they were Lena's age, they had run out of choices to survive. Mason was likely their last chance.

With a determined look of defiance, Lena steadied herself on her feet again.

"You just ain't gonna learn, are you?" Mason slurred. "You gonna act like a little girl, then I reckon I'll have to treat you like one. Bend over and lean on that tailgate. Lucy, you and Belle hold her hands down. Little young'uns act up, then they gotta get a spankin'."

He took his belt off, pulled up Lena's skirt, and proceeded to whip her until she dropped to her knees.

"Now," he said, "get yourself together and collect some wood for a fire." He started to go unhitch the horse but stopped to give her a final warning. "You try to run off again and I'll shoot you down. It won't be no spankin' next time."

Lena did as she was told and helped Belle and Lucy cook some of the smoked venison from Perley's packs. Before he ate his supper, Mason uncorked the last bottle of the whiskey he had bought in Custer City. He leaned back against the front wagon wheel and leered at the runaway returned.

"You got any whiskey in them other packs?" When she answered no, he asked, "Where the hell did you get that horse? You ain't never said yet."

"I stole it," she said, thinking it better than telling him who it belonged to. "Took it from a mining claim back yonder in the mountains." She felt bad about costing Perley his horse and rifle. She didn't want to take the chance that Mott might go after everything else Perley owned. Mott was evil to the core, and she was afraid he would be too much for Perley to handle.

"Stole it, huh?" Mason grunted. "Good. Maybe you're startin' to learn how this world operates. It's about time I started teachin' you how to be a good whore, how to please a man, so he'll keep comin' back for more. You'll be as good as Belle and Lucy, and you ain't old and wrinkled like they are."

There was no reaction apparent from either of the older women, but Lena could imagine they felt the same disgust that sickened her. He had talked before about "bedding" her, as if it was some kind of ritual that he alone knew about. The dread of it was the primary reason she decided to risk escaping when they were trying to push the wagon up that rocky trail. Now he was talking again about bedding her, and the thought of the vile man approaching her was enough to make her wish she was dead. Her only hope was that he would continue to empty his whiskey bottle, because he almost always passed out. If he did, she was going to run again.

As the evening wore away, it began to look as if Lena's hopes might be realized, for Mason grew more and more obnoxious, and his slurred ramblings became an even mix of personal boasts and threats of violence. Unfortunately for Lena, when Mason's eyelids started drooping, he realized he was losing control. He had enough presence of mind to tie her hands and feet together and secure her to the wagon wheel.

"Now, by God," he announced, "anybody untyin' her will answer to me in the mornin'."

Helpless to do anything else, Lena lay close to the wagon wheel and tried to find a comfortable position, what with her hands and feet tied behind her. Belle and Lucy rolled up in their blankets to sleep, afraid to offer any comfort to the young girl.

In a short time, Mason started snoring, dead to the world. All Lena's efforts to settle into a comfortable position failed, and she resigned herself to lying awake all night.

Soon, a nasal chorus of snoring dominated the chirping of the crickets in the nearby stream. After a long, miserable while, she succumbed to fatigue and drifted off to sleep.

It was not to last long, however, for she was suddenly awakened by a hand clamped tightly over her mouth. Knowing that it was Mott, come to fulfill his threat to bed her, Lena struggled to resist him.

"Be quiet." The whispered command did not come from her drunken captor. Her heart threatened to leap from her chest! She knew the voice! When he felt her relax, he removed his hand from her mouth, cut the rope holding her to the wheel, then quickly went to work on the rope binding her hands and feet. When she was free, she immediately threw her arms around his neck, causing him to almost step into the coals of the fire.

"We got to get outta here," he protested, unlocking her arms from his neck. "Where's my rifle?"

"Beside the wagon seat," she whispered.

He turned her around and pointed toward a clump of pine trees farther down the stream. "Go and wait for me in those trees. I'll be right behind you."

"What about your packhorse?" she whispered.

"He's already in that bunch of trees. Pack's on him, ready to go, so get goin'."

She paused for a moment before leaving him. "Don't shoot the women. They couldn't do nothin' to help me." She assumed he asked for his rifle because he intended to shoot them all.

"I ain't gonna shoot anybody," he said. "Now, get goin'. I just ain't leavin' my rifle."

She needed no further encouragement and immediately started creeping out of the camp, passing within several feet of the snoring drunk, resisting the urge to jam the empty bottle down his throat.

Almost as if he sensed it, Mason grunted and turned over, coming awake momentarily, at least enough to mumble drunkenly, "What the hell's goin' on?"

Standing by the front of the wagon, Perley raised his rifle, ready to react to Mason's next move.

Lena had the presence of mind to reassure Mason. "Nothin's goin' on. You're drunk — go back to sleep."

Mason grunted and turned back on his side, causing Lena to giggle softly. She looked back at Perley, who was signaling frantically for her to get going, and waved in acknowledgment. Then she picked up Mason's boots and ran toward the trees Perley had pointed out. He was close on her heels, and when they reached the stand of trees, Lena paused to throw Mason's boots into the water.

"Come on!" Perley urged. "We need to get outta here."

She continued to giggle as she watched the stream sweep the boots along, until Perley took her by the arm and pulled her toward the horses. Up behind him, she put her arms around his waist and held him tight, a broad smile painted on her face. There could not have been a rescue more dramatic, in her mind, and surely never one so downright entertaining. She pictured the surly ogre when he woke up in the morning to discover her gone, and the packhorse, too. She buried her face in Perley's back in an effort to stifle her giggles as he guided Buck through the dark stand of trees.

CHAPTER 16

After leaving Mott Mason's camp, Perley rode back to the Cheyenne-Deadwood Stage road and headed north, planning to ride through the night in order to keep well ahead of Mason. It was the only way he knew to find Deadwood, and the road was defined enough to follow in the dark of night. As far as Lena was concerned, she was in high spirits after her rescue, too high to be able to sleep, in fact. So, he held Buck to a steady pace until he decided it time to rest the big horse.

Having fully expected Lena to be terrified, Perley was astonished to find her almost giddy with thoughts of Mason's surprise when he awakened in the morning, and the rage he would go into when he couldn't find his boots. She became concerned for only a brief moment, when she said, "I hope the son of a bitch don't take it out on Belle and Lucy." That moment was a short one, however, before her exuberance returned and she was chuckling over the incident again.

Part of her excitement was due to her perception of the rescue, which Perley would have no knowledge of. In Lena's world, before Perley came along, she was deemed to have no value, among her family or others who knew her. Now, for the first time, someone had risked his life to rescue her. And that had to mean he thought she was important enough to save. She had considered the fact that Perley might have followed them just to recover his packhorse and other property. But he had already recovered the horse and hidden it in the trees before he came to get her. He could have simply ridden away, but he didn't — he came back for her. She knew she was mighty lucky to have crossed paths with Perley Gates. As she thought it, she couldn't help adding, *even with a name like that.* She had no idea if Perley was man enough to go up against a brute like Mott Mason, but she knew he was not afraid to come after her, and that pleased her.

"This looks like as good a spot as any," he said when they approached a wide stream that cut a channel across the wagon road. "We'll rest the horses here for a while, so you can start a fire and make some coffee if you want to."

He crossed the stream and rode up the bank a short distance before reining Buck to a stop and helping Lena down. "I ain't expectin' your friend to catch up with us with that one-horse wagon, but we'll keep movin' tonight, just in case he's got wings on it."

Without knowing if anyone in Mason's camp had alerted him to the missing girl before daylight, Perley could not say how far ahead they were. When he had retrieved his Winchester from beside the wagon seat, he had seen the two women sleeping in the wagon bed. At least, they appeared to be asleep, and they sounded no alarm, so he was inclined to believe he had all the lead he needed. Although not sure if Mason would come after Lena, Perley had to assume that he was intent upon continuing to Deadwood, so Perley decided he'd best keep an eye on his back trail. In an effort to maintain his lead, he was back in the saddle when he felt Buck and the sorrel were rested, even though it was still in the early hours of the morning.

The first rays of the sun found them approaching what appeared to be a small settlement — a mining town, by the look of it. By this time, they were both feeling the effects of a night on horseback without sleep. So, when Perley spotted a large tent with a sign that said EATS hanging on the tent pole, he decided it would benefit them both to see what was being served for breakfast.

There were no horses tied out front of the tent, so Perley figured he and Lena were too early, but there was smoke coming from a stovepipe sticking up through the top of the tent. They dismounted and tried the makeshift wooden door.

Inside, they found a rather large woman, wearing an apron and seated at the end of the one long table in the center of the tent. She was drinking a cup of coffee, and looked up in surprise to see them.

"Well, good morning, folks. Are you two lost?"

"I reckon you could say that," Perley replied. There was a coffeepot sitting on one corner of a large iron stove at the rear of the tent. He motioned toward it and asked, "Any chance we could buy a cup of coffee from you?"

She raised an eyebrow at that. "Why, sure you can. Are you looking for breakfast?" She got up to fetch a couple of cups.

"Yes, ma'am," Perley said. "Saw your sign out front."

"You'll have to forgive me if I'm acting kinda strange. I ain't seen a customer in a couple of days. Since you folks are strangers, you probably didn't notice that almost all the tents and shacks on both sides of the creek are empty. It wasn't long ago you'da had to stand in line outside my tent. Now the strike is in Deadwood, and I'm fixing to leave, myself. But I can rustle you up some breakfast, just as long as it's pancakes you're craving. I'm out of everything but some side meat and mixings for pancakes." She shrugged as if helpless. "So what'll it be?"

"I think I'll take pancakes," Perley said with a grin. "How 'bout you, Lena?"

"That sounds good to me," she replied. "I think I'll have pancakes, too."

The woman responded with a big laugh. "Good, sit yourselves down and I'll rustle you up some of the finest pancakes on French Creek." She went at once to get the coffeepot. "My name's Mamie Dance," she said. "Welcome to my diner. You folks might be the last two customers I serve before I close up and head to Deadwood Gulch."

"We'd be honored. Ain't that right, Lena? Did you say that creek is French Creek?"

Mamie nodded.

"Ain't French Creek where they made the first big strike?"

"That's a fact," Mamie said.

"And now it's played out?" Perley asked.

"Pretty much. There ain't but a few left, and most of them are fixing to go." She put some more wood in her stove and placed an iron skillet on top to heat up. "Lucky I got some lard left," she muttered. "Honey," she said to Lena, "see that jug on the sideboard? That's pure maple syrup. You can set it on the table, if you wanna."

In a short while, Mamie served up two stacks of flapjacks, as she called them, and sat down to talk while they ate.

"You folks never been in Hill City before, have you? That's what they call the little town that sprung up here. You on your way to Deadwood, too?"

"Reckon so," Perley answered. "I guess we might as well join everybody else there." He decided not to mention the fact that they were in a hurry since there might be somebody right behind them with evil intentions.

"If all your customers are gone, how come you're still here?" Lena asked.

Mamie shrugged, as if hesitant to answer. "Well, I would be gone already, but I've gotta stay for a while 'cause I'm taking care of somebody who's pretty bad off, and I can't go and leave him. Without somebody to take care of him, he'd die for sure, and I reckon I can't have that on my conscience."

"That's too bad," Lena said. "Have you got a place to go in Deadwood? You know somebody there?"

"Oh, I sure do," Mamie responded. "I've got a dandy place in Deadwood, where I'm gonna be cooking. It's my son-in-law's hotel."

Seeming to be interested, Lena asked another question. "But you gotta stay here to take care of somebody? Somebody in your family sick?"

"No, he ain't family — just a poor fellow down on his luck. He wouldn't be at my place if he had anywhere else to go. He ain't no kin of mine, but I ain't got the heart to leave him to die."

"What's ailin' him?" Perley asked, interested now as well.

"Gunshot," Mamie answered.

"Gunshot?" Perley responded. "How'd he get shot?"

"According to what he says, him and his partner were going down French Creek to an old mining claim to get some gold that was hid there, but after they got there, they were jumped by outlaws. He said the men came up on 'em one night while they were

393

asleep. They never had a chance. Those horrible men walked into their camp while they were sleeping and just started blazing away. Shot both of 'em, stole their horses and everything else they had, then left 'em for dead. He said his partner *was* dead, and he played dead till the two killers were gone."

"That is mighty hard luck, all right," Perley said, slowly shaking his head. "How'd he end up with you?"

"He said he just started walking toward Hill City and almost made it before he just gave out. I found him lying in the mud behind my shack when I went to the outhouse one morning. I thought he was dead, but he opened his eyes when I poked him on the shoulder."

"Where is he now?" Lena asked, since he was not in the tent.

"In my shack, behind the tent," Mamie said. "I made him as comfortable as I could. I didn't know what else to do for him, and I had to keep my eye on my business. With so many folks abandoning this place, there's people going through empty shacks, taking anything they find, and I didn't want anybody hauling my stove off somewhere." She gave them a helpless look. "I just look at him every night to see if he died yet — ain't much else I can do for him. Try to feed him a little something, but I ain't got any red meat or beans left to give him any strength."

"If he's still alive," Perley said, "I've got some deer meat, and beans, too, on my packhorse. I'd be glad to let you have some, and maybe you can build his blood back up to make him strong." He knew he could not do otherwise, even with the knowledge that Mott Mason might be on his heels.

Lena must have been thinking the same thing, for she gazed at him intently, seeming to hang on his every word. Perley looked back at her and nodded his head.

"I'll go with you and we'll see if there's anything I can do," he said to Mamie. "Anyway, I'll leave you some deer meat to cook up, 'cause I reckon you could use a little yourself."

"Mister, I'm mighty glad you came along!" Mamie exclaimed. "Let me put the padlock on my door, and we'll go see how my patient is doing."

"Might be a good idea to lead the horses around back, too," Perley told Lena, still thinking of Mott Mason and hoping that he had a big enough hangover to discourage him from following them.

Mamie brought them behind the tent to a small board shack. There was a shed and corral behind it that served as a shelter for one mule. Perley tied the horses to the corner post of the tiny porch, and he and Lena followed Mamie inside.

The wounded man lay on a pallet of quilts near the fireplace. Dead or alive, it was hard to tell, so Perley knelt down close to him and placed his hand on his shoulder. The man opened his eyes and tried to draw away.

"Easy, there, old-timer," Perley said softly, for he could see that the man was up there in years. His gray hair and whiskers were evidence of many winters. "I ain't gonna hurt you. I wanna take a look at your wounds. Maybe I can help." He rolled the man gently over so he could inspect his wounds. "One in the chest and looks like another'n in his back." Perley looked up at Mamie, and she nodded her agreement. "What's his name?"

"He said his name was Pearly," Mamie answered. "I don't know what his last name is."

Perley didn't speak for a long moment. In fact, he couldn't speak. He felt as if the blood was rushing away from his brain. Puzzled by his apparent state of shock, Mamie looked from him to Lena, only to see the same look of amazement in her eyes.

"Gates," Perley finally blurted. "His name

is Perley Gates, same as mine."

This, in turn, shocked Mamie, leaving her to stand with her mouth open but no words to come out.

"He's my grandpa, and he's the only reason I came out here to these mountains."

Feeling a panic settling into his brain, Perley knew that everything depended upon saving his grandfather. He could not believe that fate would be so unkind as to let him find his kin, then take him away before the old man knew who Perley was.

Lena, a stunned spectator to that point, stepped in then. She placed her hand on the old man's forehead.

"Why, hell, he's burnin' up with fever. We need to cool him down. No wonder he's actin' outta his head." She turned to Perley, then to Mamie. Since neither one of them seemed to know what to do, she took over. "Perley, if you'll take that bucket over there and go to the creek for some cool water, we'll use it to cool him down. Mamie, have you got some rags we can use?"

While both Perley and Mamie jumped to do her bidding, she pulled the quilts away from the old man and unbuttoned his shirt. Next, she pulled his boots off and removed a pair of socks that looked like they had had a birthday on his feet. Inside one of the socks, there was a flap of deerskin wrapped around his foot, leading Lena to believe he must have sprained it. When Perley returned with the bucket of water, Lena cleaned away the dried blood from the bullet holes.

"They're all red and puffy-lookin'," she said. "He needs a doctor."

Since there was none available, they decided to do what they could to bring his temperature down, then see if he had the constitution to survive the gunshots.

Perley and Lena continued to apply cool rags to the old man's forehead, feet, and chest for several hours, until Perley turned the job over to Mamie while he went to take care of his horses. He apologized to Buck for not removing his saddle until then and walked both horses down to the creek to drink.

While he stood on the bank, watching them, his thoughts strayed from his grandfather for a few moments and drifted back to Mott Mason. Whether Mason was bent on tracking him down, or was just following the stage road to Deadwood, he would no doubt pass Mamie's tent, just as Perley had. But with the lock on the door, Mason should have no reason to stop there. He should drive straight through, depending upon what time of day or night he reached

Hill City. And that was the one thing Perley couldn't accurately predict, but he decided he would have to be damn unlucky if Mason stopped to camp in the town.

Returning his thoughts to his grandfather, he would graze his horses on what little grass was left on the bank of the creek and he would sleep with them that night. Lena could stay inside the shack with Mamie and his grandpa, and Perley would see if there was any improvement in the morning.

When he went back inside to tell them, he was pleased to find Lena confident that the old man was finally showing signs of cooling down.

"We'll get his fever down," she said. "He opened his eyes a little while ago, and I swear, I thought he was gonna say something."

Mamie smiled and added, "I believe Lena's got a real gift for healing. He might come around after all, and I sure wouldn'ta believed it this morning when I left him." She paused, a serious expression on her face. "If you came all the way from Texas to find him, I just know the Lord wouldn't let you come this close and not let your grandpa know you."

It was early the next morning when Perley

came inside, after sleeping near his horses all night. He found Lena dozing in a rocking chair near the fireplace and Mamie asleep in her bed. He thought to make a fire in the fireplace to fix some coffee, but decided to take a look at his grandfather first. The old man looked peaceful enough — so much so, in fact, that Perley thought he might be dead.

A few seconds later, he was startled when the old man's eyes suddenly snapped open and he demanded, "Who the hell are you?"

When Perley seemed too surprised to answer, Lena, having been awakened by the old man's outburst, answered for him.

"He's your grandson!" She got up out of the rocking chair and came over to place her hand on his forehead. "That fever's gone."

"Grandson?" the old man echoed. "I ain't got no grandson."

"Maybe you ain't," Perley said. "What's your name?"

"Perley Gates," the old man replied defiantly. "What's your'n?"

Perley smiled. "Perley Gates, same as yours — so, like it or not, I'm your grandson, and I've had a devil of a time chasin' you over half the country."

"What for?" the old man asked.

"So I could tell you you've got a grandson and I was named after you," Perley insisted.

There followed a pause while the old man strained to think over the possibility. Finally, he put it all together.

"You're Nathaniel's boy?" His head was swimming again, and this time not from the fever. When he had left Texas after his wife died, Nathaniel was a baby.

"That's right," Perley replied, "one of 'em. Nathaniel had three boys — Rubin, John, and me. He had a girl, too. Her name is Esther. Your daughter-in-law's name is Rachel — that's my mother — and she sent me to find you to tell you that your son died when he took sick after gettin' bucked off a horse."

It was almost too much to swallow for the old man. "My son . . . that baby . . . is dead?"

"Yes," Perley said. "So, Grandpa, Mama sent me to tell you that, and to let you know that he thought enough of you to name me after you."

The old man mulled that over for a long moment, before suddenly cocking his eyes suspiciously at the young man, giving him this response: "Well, young feller, I've got to admit, that's one helluva story, but I have some bad news for you. That big cache of gold dust hid under a rock in French Creek turned out to be a corker of a tale, too. There weren't no gold, and it cost the life of my partner and damn-near killed me to find that out." He smirked at Perley and asked, "Am I still your grandpa?"

Perley didn't answer right away. He paused while he fished for something in his vest pocket. In a moment, he held a velvet pouch in his hand and offered it to the old man. "Has it been too long for you to remember this?"

His grandpa took the small blue velvet pouch from him, and his fingers began to tremble slightly as he pulled the silver locket from inside, fumbling as he opened it.

"Mama said that's the locket you gave my grandmother when you asked her to marry you," Perley said softly, as tears began to form in the old man's eyes.

"Marcy, darlin'," the old man mumbled softly as the tears found their way down the wrinkled face. "I couldn't stay there after you were gone."

"Well, do you think you can eat somethin' now?" Lena sang out, wiping a tear from her eye. She was afraid if she didn't break the mood, she might end up bawling, and she didn't think that would be good for her image. "It's past time to start some breakfast, and we've got deer meat and beans on the menu."

"And I'll bake some biscuits," Mamie volunteered. In the drama of the previous moments, no one had noticed when she sat up in bed and dried her eyes with a corner of the sheet.

The mood changed after that first tearful meeting of grandfather and grandson to one of celebration. It was considerably more positive when it became apparent that, although the old man's wounds were grave, they evidently had not hit any internal organs. He was eating for the first time since Mamie found him behind her outhouse, and that was a positive sign. Since there was no surgeon available, however, he would be carrying the slugs in the muscles of his chest and back permanently.

Most of that morning was spent with Perley bringing his grandfather up to date on the family and the Triple-G Ranch in Lamar County, Texas. The old man was fascinated to hear about the successful cattle operation his son had created and was eager to return to Texas when his grandson proposed it.

"You sure I'd be welcome?" the old man asked. "After all, I ran out on your great-grandma and left her with a young'un to raise."

"You'll be welcome," Perley assured him. "They wouldn't have sent me way out here to find you if you weren't welcome. And now, it looks like you're gonna make it back from that ambush, so I'm thinkin' we'll just stay here till you're well enough to ride."

There was one more thing Perley had to think about. He had promised Lena he would see her safely to Deadwood, and he intended to keep that promise. He couldn't leave her stranded on her own, like she was when he first found her. Maybe he could persuade Mamie to stay on in Hill City a little longer, at least until he had time to take Lena to Deadwood. By then, his grandpa might be able to ride and they could start for home.

Things would be a great deal better if the outlaws that jumped the old man and his partner hadn't stolen his horse.

"I'm sure gonna miss that horse," Perley's grandfather lamented. "As fine a horse as I've ever rode," he went on. "He was an Injun pony, a paint. His hindquarters were solid brown, all the way to his hooves. Made him look like he was wearin' a pair of pants. I traded a fine horse for that pony. I was ridin' a big ol' black Morgan that a U.S. deputy marshal gave me for helpin' him capture an outlaw hidin' out in the San Bois

Mountains. Wasn't nothin' wrong with the Morgan, but that paint just suited my style."

Perley still had supplies Mamie could use for cooking, but he needed to go hunting. They could use some more meat, and his grandfather said the deer were coming back to the creek since the miners moved out, so Perley decided to take care of that need later toward evening, when the deer would be feeding.

When he told Mamie what he wanted to do, she agreed to stay on, since he was going to supply them with food, but she preferred to go to Deadwood with him when he took Lena there. She had been apprehensive about packing everything she planned to carry on her mule and making the trip by herself. Perley could hardly blame her for that, so it looked like they were all going to have to wait until his grandfather was well enough to ride. The group would go to Deadwood together, then Perley and his grandfather could turn around and head for Texas, which now seemed ten thousand miles away. Perley's planning kept coming back to the one problem he hadn't figured out. He needed another horse.

Later that afternoon, when his grandfather felt like talking again, Perley asked him about the men who shot him.

"They hit us when we was asleep," his grandpa said.

"So, you didn't see 'em, or even how many there were?"

"Oh, I know how many there were," Grandpa replied. "I'm pretty sure there was two of 'em, and I got a pretty good idea which two they were."

Perley asked how he knew that if he was asleep when they shot him, and Grandpa told him, "There's two fellers that moved in on a claim about a hundred yards downstream from where we was pannin'. They said the feller who was workin' it left for Deadwood, but that feller told us he wasn't gonna leave his claim. We knew our claim was played out, but we worked it for a few days to keep anybody snoopin' around from finding out we was really workin' to get that gold that was supposed to be hid under a big rock in the side of the bank. Anyway, them two fellers kept comin' around to see if we was makin' any money. They didn't look like they done any minin', except maybe in somebody else's pockets. Like I said, I didn't get a look at 'em that night, but I'd bet anything they're the ones who jumped us and left us for dead. I had to play dead, so I never moved a muscle the whole time they was goin' through my pockets. If one of 'em hadda felt my pulse, they'da known I weren't dead. My heart was beatin' about a hundred miles an hour when they dragged me and my partner away from the fire. They rolled me over the edge of a gully and dropped his body on top of me. I laid there for a helluva long time under his body till I decided it was safe enough to crawl away from that gully."

"How did you come to partner up with the man with you?" Perley asked. "Was his name Lem Wooten?"

"How'd you know that?" Grandpa responded.

Perley told him he had found out in Custer City that his grandpa had left town with Wooten.

"Well, that's a fact, but I didn't know him before that. When I first started up that creek, I came upon a feller layin' in the middle of the trail, shot full of holes and lookin' like he'd been scalped. He was still alive, but not by much. I dragged him outta the road and tried to see if I could do anythin' for him, but he was too far gone. He said some outlaws jumped him and took everythin' he had except his trousers and his boots. He said he was tryin' to get back to his brother's place in Custer City. Hell, it musta been only four or five miles to Custer. I told him I'd take him there, but he didn't look to me like he'd make it another mile. I stayed with him that night, but the next mornin' he knew he was fixin' to die. He told me to pull his boot off, so I did, and there was a piece of doeskin wrapped around his foot. It had a map drawn on it to show where a gold treasure was buried. Only problem was, it didn't say where in the world it was located. He said to take it to his brother in Custer City, where he had a blacksmith shop, and that he knew where the claim was. I figure he wanted to make sure his brother got his share of that gold. He died a few hours after that, and I went on back to Custer to find Lem Wooten."

"But you never found that treasure?" Perley asked.

"Oh, we found it," Grandpa snorted. "I was lyin' when I told you there weren't no gold. The trouble was, we were afraid to dig it out from under that rock. Those two fellers got wind of it somehow, and they were stickin' pretty close to us. They musta knowed Lem's brother had struck it rich. I wonder if they're still lookin' for that gold."

His comment hit Perley as something he hadn't considered. *I wonder if they* are *still there looking for that treasure.* He decided right away that it was worth a look. Maybe the men who shot his grandpa and murdered Lem Wooten might still be at that mining claim. Perley was going hunting anyway, so he might find more than deer down French Creek. "Tell me how to find that claim you crawled here from."

"It's on that flap of deerskin you found wrapped around my foot," he said. "That'll take you to the claim, but there's somethin' more you have to know to find that buried gold. When we figure it's safe, we'll go there and dig that gold outta there." He grinned at Perley and winked.

With the help of the map, Perley had very little trouble finding the spot where his grandfather and Lem Wooten were attacked. The old man had given him ample signs to look for to make sure he was at the right claim. When he figured he was getting close to it, he became more cautious, and rode a few hundred yards closer before dismounting and leading Buck through the pines that skirted the rapidly flowing creek.

Even though his directions were detailed, Perley was still wary of the possibility of sneaking up on the wrong claim. Another fifty yards or so and he spotted smoke up ahead, so he left his horse there, and with his rifle in hand, he began to advance cautiously through the pine trees. *I hope to hell I know what I'm doing,* he thought, for he wasn't sure what he was actually going to do. He inched his way closer until he could see two men sitting by the fire, drinking coffee.

Still uncertain if they were the right two men, Perley hesitated to confront them, until he saw the horses tied to a rope stretched between two trees near the water beyond them. There was no mistaking one of the horses — the paint that looked like it was wearing a pair of brown trousers. The men had not even taken the saddle off. Perley noticed then that four of the six horses he saw tied to the rope were saddled. Maybe the men were getting ready to give up on their search for gold, or maybe they never cared enough to pull the saddles off.

Back to what he should do. He couldn't decide. The men were thieves and murderers, but he didn't like the role of judge, jury, and executioner. He was still trying to decide what to do when he took a step to the side without looking down to see the rotten pine limb beneath his foot. When his weight came down on the dried limb, it cracked loudly, causing both men to startle at once.

With no choice left to him, Perley walked out of the trees, his rifle trained on them. "All right," he warned, "don't make any move that's gonna get yourselves shot."

Stunned, both men stood and stared for a moment, before realizing Perley was alone — then one of them reached for his pistol. There was little time to aim and no time to think. Perley's reflexes took charge, sending a rifle slug into the man's right shoulder, spinning him around. His partner threw both hands up when Perley ejected the spent shell and brought the Winchester to bear on him.

"Unbuckle your gun belt and let it drop," Perley commanded. He glanced back at the man he had shot and warned him, "If you pick up that pistol again, the next shot is goin' in your chest. Back away from it."

The wounded man did as he was told and stepped away, his face twisted in pain from the shoulder wound, his arm hanging useless and bloody. His partner, having obeyed Perley's order to drop his gun belt, found his voice when Perley didn't shoot them both down.

"Whaddaya want from us, mister? There ain't no gold here. It played out long ago."

"I ain't after gold," Perley replied. "You two tried to murder my grandpa, and you murdered his partner and stole their horses. You've gotta pay for that."

"Now, hold on there, mister. You got the wrong two men. Me and Sam, there, just happened to come along and find this old claim, just this mornin'. You didn't have no call to put a bullet in his shoulder."

"Is that a fact?" Perley asked. "You don't know what happened to the two fellows who were workin' this claim? How 'bout those horses — you find them here, too?"

"No," the man replied. "We brung them with us. We're in the horse-tradin' business. We was on our way to Deadwood Gulch to sell some of these horses."

"Can't help but notice they're totin' four saddles and you ain't got but two fannies to set in 'em," Perley said. "That paint there belongs to my grandpa, and I can't let you get away with that. You shot him and left him for dead."

The outlaw was beginning to realize that Perley wasn't cold-blooded enough to execute him and his partner. If he was, he wouldn't have placed his shot in Sam's shoulder.

"Listen, mister, there's been a big mistake here — just hear me out. I ain't no outlaw. My name's Jed Riley, and my partner is Sam Ingram. The fact of the matter is, we bought these horses from two fellers yesterday. We didn't know they was stolen. I don't blame you for bein' mad, and we'd be willin' to stand before a judge if there's one in that town upstream."

All the while he talked, Riley shuffled casually to the side, until he had forced Perley to turn slightly to keep an eye on him. Aware that his partner was trying to create an angle too great to allow Perley to watch both of them, Sam moved slowly toward the six-gun he had dropped. Riley, seeing that Sam was thinking like him, kept talking, trying to hold Perley's attention.

"What would it take to make you see we ain't out to hurt nobody?"

"For one thing," Perley replied, "maybe your partner can stop right where he is. 'Cause if he doesn't, I'm gonna have to put the next shot where it'll hurt."

"You know what I'm thinkin' now?" Riley asked, figuring the odds against him. "I'm thinkin' you ain't fast enough to cover both of us. If you fire that rifle at Sam, I'll guarantee you I'll put a bullet in you before you can crank another cartridge into the chamber and turn back around to shoot at me. If you shoot at me instead of Sam, he's gonna put a bullet in your back. Ain't that right, Sam?"

"That's right, Jed," Sam replied. "I ain't hurt that bad. I can reach my gun before he can eject that shell."

"That makes it kinda different, don't it, friend?" Riley chided, noticing his partner still inching toward the .44 on the ground. "You still think you're fast enough to get both of us?"

"I do," Perley answered honestly.

"Well, mister, you're a special kind of stupid," Riley jeered, and suddenly went for the .44 on his hip.

Perley squeezed the trigger, dropped the rifle, and drew his Colt before Sam could pick up his pistol and cock it.

Caught with his pistol not cocked, staring at the Colt aimed at him and Perley patiently awaiting his next move, Sam Ingram looked death in the eye. Riley was bent double, lying on his side. After a moment, Ingram tossed his gun on the ground.

"I reckon you've kilt both of us," he said.

Perley gazed at the thief and murderer, suddenly rendered pitiful. He felt disgust for the episode just finished.

"I reckon you both deserve to die, but you ain't worth carryin' on my conscience. You've got a bullet in your shoulder and your partner's gut-shot. I don't know if he'll make it. You can make out the best way you can. If I see you again, I'll finish the job."

He pressed his fingers to his lips and whistled. In a few seconds, the big bay emerged from the trees and loped toward him.

"Sit down over on the other side of the fire," he ordered, and Sam did as he was told, leaving his partner to lie where he fell. Perley picked up the dropped weapons and took them to the horses tied to the rope. While watching the two wounded men closely, he untied the rope between the trees and used it as a lead rope. He climbed into the saddle and started to lead the horses out of the camp, pausing only a moment to respond to Sam's desperate plea.

"You just gonna leave us here without no horses or weapons to hunt with?" Sam cried.

"I reckon I could shoot you and put you out of your misery, but that would be too easy on you. If there was a lawman hereabouts, I'd turn you over to him, but there ain't one, so I'm gonna leave your horses up the creek a ways, but I'm takin' that paint and two others. You can manage any way you can."

"We're both wounded," Sam protested. "You might as well shoot us dead."

"I reckon it'll be up to you to see how bad you wanna live." He nudged Buck and rode

415

out of the camp.

When he was about half a mile up the creek, Perley took the paint and the best two of the other three saddled horses, then left the remaining horses to graze on the creek bank. He was not sure whether what he was doing was right or not, but he didn't have it in him to execute the two outlaws. It would be difficult for them, but he felt he was giving them a chance to make it to their horses and possibly survive. Why? He couldn't explain. He just didn't like the idea of shooting the pair when he had them helpless before him.

Sam Ingram watched helplessly until Perley disappeared into the trees. Then he went over to check on his partner, still lying doubled up on his side.

"You gonna make it, partner?" Sam asked.

"I don't know," Jed gasped painfully. "I'm shot pretty bad. You're gonna have to help me." He coughed up a little blood when he tried to say more.

"I will, partner," Sam said. "I'll take care of you." He drew his skinning knife, grabbed Jed by his hair, and yanked his head back. One hard swipe with the knife laid Jed's throat open.

When he was done, Sam stood over him and said, "If it was me 'stead of you, you'da done the same thing. He said he was gonna leave our horses up this creek. I don't know if he will or not. I can walk outta here, but not if I have to carry you. We wouldn't make it if I had to come back and try to take care of you. I've gotta take care of myself. That's just the hand we was dealt."

CHAPTER 17

It would be a couple of days before his grandpa was able to ride, and that was probably still too soon, in Perley's opinion. But the old man insisted he could stay on his horse, especially since Perley had recovered his paint Indian pony.

"That horse fits me like a rockin' chair," his grandfather claimed. "He'll rock me to sleep. You don't have to worry 'bout me."

Lena was now riding a saddled horse also, one that had belonged to Lem Wooten, as verified by Perley's grandfather.

"That's Lem's horse and saddle, all right," Grandpa said.

When Perley had taken it, he had no way of knowing if the horse was Lem's or one of the outlaws'. He just took the best-looking horses. He also had two more — his own packhorse plus one that he brought back to replace his grandpa's packhorse. He offered to let Mamie ride one of them, but she preferred to ride her mule.

"Me and horses ain't ever got along too good," she claimed. "Me and that mule understand each other, so I'll ride easier on him."

Perley had taken advantage of the time spent waiting for his grandpa to recover by using it to hunt, and he found that Grandpa had been right when he said the deer were coming back to the creek. So, there would be plenty of smoked venison loaded on the packhorses when they started out for Deadwood.

On the day before they left, Perley returned to the mining claim where he had shot the two outlaws. He found Jed Riley's body still there, but the horses and his partner were gone. Perley lingered over the body for a moment, wondering if Riley would have made it had his throat not been cut. There was no way to know if his partner would be in search of Perley or not, but Perley's gut feeling was that he would not.

The next morning, Perley led his little party out to strike the stage road to Deadwood, behind him one recovering old man, an optimistic widow, and a confident young girl. There had been a bit of reluctance on Mamie's part when it came to abandoning her stove and her tables and chairs, but they had no means to transport them. She consoled herself with the knowledge that she would have everything she needed at her son-in-law's hotel. Perley's major desire at this point was to take his grandfather home to Texas, but a secondary obligation was to escort Lena and Mamie to Deadwood. He felt it was typical of so many of his endeavors, riding north when he should be heading south.

It was late in the afternoon when they descended a steep hill, on a winding road that led them down into Deadwood Gulch, a narrow gulch about ten miles long. Perley's first reaction to the settlement that had sprung up in the gulch was to compare it to an insane asylum. The narrow street was filled with people and animals, including horses, mules, and oxen. There were tents and shacks built along the banks of Deadwood Creek, as well as places of business. In fact, it seemed that every other building was a saloon or gambling house.

Deadwood itself was farther ahead and was not the only town occupying the gulch, so they rode along the winding creek road through a couple of other towns until reaching Deadwood, where Mamie took command of their party and led them to the

Gaines Hotel, between two saloons.

"This is it!" she proclaimed. "This is my son-in-law's place." Eager to surprise him, she pulled her mule up to a stop and slid off its back. "Come on, folks, and I'll introduce you to my daughter and her husband."

She and Lena hurried inside the hotel, but grandfather and grandson both took a wary look around them, wondering if their possessions were safe on a street teeming with every kind of villain imaginable.

Perley was already wondering about where they would stay the night. From what he could see, there was no place near the creek where he could camp. "We might have to ride back out of this gulch and find someplace to make camp back up in the hills."

"That'd suit me just fine," his grandpa replied. "This place is so crowded I bet they have to come out and stir it with a stick once in a while so folks can go about their business."

"Well, let's go inside and make sure Mamie and Lena are gonna be all right." Perley wasn't really concerned about Mamie as much as he was for Lena. All she had requested of him in the beginning was that he take her to Deadwood, but he couldn't help feeling some responsibility for her

421

beyond that. He need not have worried, however, for when he and his grandpa went inside, they found Mamie and Lena talking excitedly in a happy reunion between Mamie and her daughter, Julia.

"Come meet my daughter," Mamie invited when the two men walked into the tiny lobby. "Julia, this is Perley Gates and Perley Gates," she announced with a chuckle. "They were kind enough to see us safely here. Boys, this is Julia. She says that she and Ron, that's her husband, have been waitin' for me to get 'em a dinin' room up and runnin'. I told her I'm rarin' to get started." She turned to give Lena a wide smile. "Told her I've brought my help with me."

This immediately caught Perley's attention, and he turned to see Lena smiling at him. She nodded, and he knew she was happy with the arrangement, so there was nothing else for him to worry about.

"Well, I'm right pleased to meet you, ma'am," he said to Julia. "This looks like a nice little hotel you've got here. I reckon my grandpa and I will be headin' back to Texas first thing in the mornin'. We'd best go see about findin' someplace to keep our horses overnight. Maybe you can direct us to a good stable."

"There are two good stables in town," Julia said, "but you can keep your horses in our barn, where my husband keeps his. We have a few stalls for our guests, and there's no one using any of them right now. My husband should be back anytime now, and I know he'll insist on helping you with your horses. And I've got a room for you and your grandfather, so you won't have to go somewhere else looking for one."

"Much obliged," Perley said. He looked at his grandpa and grinned. "That would be mighty nice of you." Like his grandpa, he had expected to sleep in the stall with his horse. "We wouldn't wanna trouble your husband none. We'll just take the horses to your barn."

Things couldn't have worked out much better. Mamie's daughter seemed genuinely pleased to see her mother, and Lena appeared to be happy with her new role. Perley and his grandfather could go home now, with nothing in their way but a long ride to Texas. Perley was eager to get started. Morning couldn't come quickly enough.

The hotel's stable was a small affair, half of it built into the side of the steep hill behind the hotel. The barn was almost filled with hay bales, since there was no piece of ground with grass for the horses to graze.

Perley was in the process of forking some hay into the stalls when a slight man with a neat mustache and short dark hair came into the barn.

"Glad to meet you, gentlemen. I'm Ron Gaines. Julia said you were getting settled all right. I want to thank you for seeing my mother-in-law safely here."

"Weren't no trouble a'tall," Grandpa spoke up. "She didn't put up no fuss to amount to anythin'."

Ron laughed. "I'm glad to hear it, but she can be a handful if she sets her mind to it."

Perley shook Ron's hand when it was extended to him. Upon meeting Julia, he had been impressed that a young couple could start a business as demanding as the hotel. He could see now that Ron was quite a bit older than his wife, already showing a bit of gray in his sideburns. "We're obliged for your hospitality," he said to Ron. "It won't hurt us to bed down out here with our horses, if you can sell our room tonight."

"I wouldn't hear of it," Ron insisted. "You'll be my guests." He smiled at them both. "We'll see if the women can rustle up something fit to eat. See if there's any hope they can open a dining room for our guests."

Mamie wasted little time in taking over her

daughter's kitchen, with absolutely no resistance from Julia, who was never the cook her mother was. However, she joyfully assisted in the preparation of their supper, with Lena's help. It was a meal enjoyed by all partakers, especially Ron, for he was already beaming when he thought of the dining-room business he was bound to steal from the other hotels.

After supper, Lena helped Grandpa clean up his wounds and apply clean bandages. There was still some bleeding around the wound in his back, enough so that Lena asked Perley to wait another day before starting out for Texas.

"It's not gonna hurt you to wait one more day, to make sure that wound ain't gonna start bleedin' like hell. I ain't so sure he's feelin' as well as he claims he is. A ride like that might be pretty hard on that old man — and him with nobody to take care of him but you."

Perley conceded, but complained about the insult. He figured there were some supplies they were short on, so he might as well replace them tomorrow. With that settled, they retired to their rooms for the night.

Morning brought another occasion for a big breakfast, as Mamie was intent upon showing her son-in-law what a good investment she was.

"I could get used to this pretty quick," Grandpa commented. "I might decide to stay here, instead of ridin' all the way back to Texas."

"You sure ain't gonna get any breakfast like this on the ride back, if I'm doin' the cookin'," Perley said, "so don't go gettin' used to it. Dr. Lena said that wound ain't bleedin' as bad this mornin', and if it doesn't get any worse today, they're gonna kick us outta the hotel tomorrow."

"Speakin' of Dr. Lena," Mamie said as she sat down with them to have a cup of coffee. "I'm gonna have to take that girl shoppin' for some clothes. She can't spend the rest of her life in that one dress."

"I reckon not," Perley agreed, "but it looks a lot better'n the one I found her in."

"There's a new store opened next to the Bella Union Saloon," Julia said. "You should go there. I've heard they plan to carry men's and women's clothes, so you might get a better price since they're probably trying to get their business started."

"It doesn't matter how good their prices are," Lena interrupted, "I ain't got no money."

"Don't you worry, honey, Mamie's gonna take care of you," Mamie cooed playfully.

Perley smiled, enjoying the warm, friendly atmosphere. It appeared he had wasted any moments he had spent worrying about Lena's welfare.

After breakfast, Perley and his grandfather decided to do a little sightseeing on the crowded street outside the hotel. Grandpa insisted he could walk in spite of his wounds, declaring that a little physical activity would speed up the healing. Perley had a strong notion that his grandfather's real incentive was to finally feel the throbbing pulse of the teeming streets of Deadwood, the place he had ridden so hard to see. It would have been a shame for his grandfather to come so close to seeing Deadwood, only to turn back before getting a good look at it.

Perley had to admit that he found the beehive of miners, merchants, drifters, whores, even outlaws, fascinating as well, but he would be glad to leave it in the morning. After he had checked on prices for some of the supplies he needed, he decided to wait until after they left Deadwood to buy what he needed. He and Grandpa resigned themselves to simply sightseeing.

"Lena!" Belle Tatum blurted without thinking when she spotted the young girl coming

427

out of J. J. Wallingford's.

"Where?" Lucy Drover responded, as Belle grabbed her arm and pointed to the door of the general mercantile store across the street. "Well, I'll be damned . . ." she drew out, then immediately whispered, "Don't let Mott see her!"

It was too late. "Well, as I live and breathe, ain't that a sight for sore eyes? Looks like our little family is back together again, don't it? Come on," he said and immediately started across the crowded street, pushing anyone aside who happened in his way.

"She's got somebody with her," Belle said, distressed over having blurted out Lena's name. "Maybe we'd best not bother her."

"Maybe you'd best not tell me what to do," Mott came back at her. "Ain't nobody with her but that old lady, and I aim to claim my property." He continued to plow through the people crowding the street.

Mamie looked up to see the huge man bulling his way toward them and stepped to the side of the boardwalk. "Move over, or you might get run over," she said to Lena.

Lena looked behind her and froze in shock for a moment before she could utter the one name she detested: "Mott!" Seeing the leering face of the monster she hoped she had escaped, her only thought then was to take flight, so she ran past Mamie, her eyes wide with fright.

Mamie immediately recognized the name Lena had muttered and acted at once to intercept the raging beast. She stepped in front of Mott and grabbed his shirt in an effort to stop him. Although a large and husky woman, she proved no match for a person of Mason's size and strength. One blow with his fist sent her sprawling, to land on her back, and barely slowed him down in his craze to recapture his property.

Lena, slim and quick, could outrun the clumsy man chasing her, but her luck ran against her when she collided head-on with a miner coming out of a saloon. Mott was on her before she could scramble back up onto her feet. With one huge hand around her throat, he lifted her up to stand her on her feet.

"Hello, darlin'," he slurred triumphantly. "Did you really think I wasn't gonna find you? You put me to a helluva lot of trouble, and I aim to take it outta your hide."

"Let me go, you son of a bitch!" Lena cried, and began flailing away at his chest with her fists. It seemed to bring him a great deal of satisfaction and served only to tighten his hand around her throat until she could no longer breathe. When she could fight no longer, she began to fade away, giving in to the threat of death. She lost consciousness before she could hear the command.

"Let her go."

The spectators, who had crowded around to watch the altercation between the man and the girl, hurriedly cleared a wide path to avoid getting in the way of any gunfire that might erupt.

Standing at the other end of that path, Mott saw the man who had challenged him. He immediately released Lena to free his gun hand, and she crumpled to the ground. Without taking his eye off Perley, Mott ordered the two women who came up behind him to drag Lena away and make sure she didn't run again. "Who the hell are you?" he then demanded of Perley.

"I'm the man who's gonna stop you from harmin' that girl," Perley said. "You've tormented her for the last time, and I'm givin' you a choice — clear out of here and leave her be, or I'll shoot you down."

He meant what he said. He had never threatened to intentionally take another man's life before. It was against his nature, and he knew he would take no satisfaction in it, but there was no other choice. If he didn't stop Mott Mason now, Lena would

430

never be able to live without torment and fear, forever on the run.

There was a brief standoff while the two men stood taking the measure of each other. Mason sized up the young man challenging him and concluded that he was not a serious threat. He didn't wear his handgun low in a fast-draw holster, and he lacked the look of a killer, so Mott decided Perley was most likely emboldened to vie for the girl's life because he was sweet on her. Convinced that that was likely the case, Mott decided to work on the young man's nerves.

"You the son of a bitch that stole her outta my camp?"

Perley didn't answer, so Mott continued, thinking the longer he talked, the more nervous the young man would become.

"She didn't tell you that I bought her from her old man, did she?"

Perley made no reply.

"And now she's got you so worked up that you're fixin' to pull on a man that will outshoot you six days a week and twice on Sunday." Mott shook his head as if amused by the standoff. "I don't think I'll even waste a bullet on a tenderfoot like you."

The outlaw shrugged and shifted, as if about to turn and walk away, but suddenly reached for his pistol instead, thinking to catch Perley off guard. A fraction of a second later, he doubled up in pain, struck in the chest by the .44 slug from Perley's Colt, Mott's gun having never cleared his holster. The look of pure shock on his face was reflected in the faces watching the duel.

"Damn . . ." Lena exhaled, having recovered enough to have witnessed the shooting. "I never thought he could do anything like that."

She looked at Belle Tatum kneeling beside her, who was equally amazed. They were joined in moments by Mamie Dance, who was sporting a swollen lump beside her left eye.

"Are you all right?" Mamie asked, relieved to see that Lena was conscious. When Lena said that she was, Mamie asked, "Did you know he could handle a gun like that?"

Lena answered by slowly shaking her head.

Equally impressed, for he had not read that quality in his mild-mannered grandson, Grandpa walked over to stare at the body of Mott Mason.

"I swear, he's dead — shot through the heart," he announced, then looked around him at the spectators crowding in to get a look. "I reckon ever'body saw it. He drew his weapon first. It was self-defense."

"You're right, old man," one of the spectators said. "He drew first, but I never saw the young fellow draw at all."

The sound of gunshots had brought the acting sheriff and a deputy to investigate. There were plenty of witnesses willing to testify that the shooting was in self-defense, and the sheriff was happy to accept their word, but he suggested to Perley that he should move on to some other town. Perley assured him that he was leaving the next morning.

Lena, of course, was free of ever again having to worry about the threat of Mott Mason. She was somewhat concerned about the situation Belle and Lucy now found themselves in. Mott had been their only means of support, and now that he was dead, what would they do?

She was to find that their attitude was not one of despair at all. In fact, they felt a considerable measure of freedom now that he was not there to command their every move.

"We ain't worried," Belle told her. "We've got us a horse and wagon and everything in it. Me and Lucy will make out all right."

There was a celebration of sorts that evening at the Gaines Hotel to salute Lena's freedom, and a farewell supper for Perley and his grandfather. Mamie once again prepared a meal to remember on their way back to Texas, serving up deer meat, bacon, and coffee. In a way, it would be a rather sad farewell, for in the short time they had all been together, they had begun to feel like family.

After supper, Perley and Grandpa retired to their room, wishing everyone good night. The next morning, Mamie and Lena came down early to prepare a fitting breakfast for the travelers, only to find them already gone. Lena, especially, was sorely disappointed to find that Perley had not waited to say good-bye.

"That man saved my life," she cried. "I had so much to thank him for. I wanted him to know that."

"He knows, honey," Mamie said. "That's the reason he left before we got up, 'cause he hated to say good-bye." She had no idea if that was true or not, but Perley struck her that way, and it seemed to make Lena feel better.

CHAPTER 18

"You know, boy, I weren't sure you had much gravel in your craw when you first found me up yonder in Mamie's shack," Grandpa confessed as they sat by a campfire halfway between Deadwood and Hill City. "I reckon what they say about judgin' a book by its cover is true."

He was seeing more and more of himself in his grandson, and he was genuinely looking forward to the long trip back to Texas. They would first return to French Creek to recover the treasure buried there. Then they would head home with enough gold to help salve Grandpa's conscience for leaving his son so many years ago.

When they struck French Creek, they ran up on a dozen deer drinking at the water's edge, and when Perley yelled, "Let's go huntin'," Grandpa saw it as the very thing he was thinking. The deer bolted, but not before Perley brought one down with his

Winchester. And when the rest of the herd scattered, Grandpa bagged a doe that veered across in front of them.

"Good shot!" Perley called out.

"You didn't think I just came to watch, did ya?" Grandpa called back, grinning from ear to ear.

He decided that he liked his grandson very much, and he liked to imagine that Perley's father had been much the same kind of man. Perley won more of his approval when he suggested they should camp there a day or so longer — whatever time it took to smoke the meat and dry the hides some. Perley said it wouldn't be right to shoot the deer if you weren't going to use the meat for food, which Grandpa also approved of. They ended up camping there for two days before continuing on down the creek toward the claim and getting back to the business of retrieving the gold.

"Buck must remember this place," Perley commented when the big bay whinnied as they approached the site of the fight with the two claim-jumpers. He reined his horse back to take a look around before riding down from the ridge to the creek below. Buck might have been trying to tell him something else.

Anxious to recover the gold, Grandpa

pushed by him and rode on down to the edge of the creek and dismounted. Perley had no choice but to follow.

While Perley stepped down from the saddle, Grandpa walked over to stand beside a large rock that protruded out over the water. He patted the boulder and said, "Those two skunks snooped around here waitin' to see which one of these rocks me and Lem was gonna start diggin' under."

"Is that a fact?" The voice came from behind them, startling them both. "That's right, Mr. Quickdraw, go for that damn gun. I owe you for this hole you put in my shoulder. Now turn around real slow. You, too, old man. I've done killed you once, and it would pleasure me to do it again."

They had no choice but to do as he instructed, so they turned around to confront Sam Ingram, his shoulder crudely bandaged, brandishing a double-barreled shotgun.

"Do like I tell you and I won't shoot you. I've got a little work for you two. You're gonna dig that gold out from under that rock." He paused to add a devious chuckle. "I'd help you if it weren't for this bad shoulder, and if you're thinkin' 'bout testing me, this shotgun's got a hair trigger. By the way, I 'preciate you leavin' the horses and guns for me, Quickdraw. Now, with your left hand, both of you, unbuckle those belts and let those guns drop on the ground."

Perley's brain was swirling as he considered his options, only to conclude that there were none. His only hope was to get an opportunity to catch Ingram off guard while he and Grandpa were digging under the rock. He and the old man were alive only because of Ingram's bad shoulder, and as soon as the gold was unearthed, they would be executed. *I should have paid attention when Buck tried to warn me that somebody was hiding down here,* Perley thought as he began to unbuckle his belt, unprepared for what happened next.

Sick inside for having blundered into an ambush, Grandpa cursed himself for losing the fortune he had intended to pass on to his family. His grandson had paused on the ridge to look things over. He should have waited, too. He decided to take the only option left to him. Having witnessed Perley's confrontation with Mott Mason on the street in Deadwood, he was confident of the outcome of his intention. With that in mind, he suddenly reached for the .44 he wore on his side.

The blast of the shotgun covered the

sound of Perley's instant reaction. The old man was knocked several feet backward, landing on his back, while Ingram doubled over and fell on his side.

"Grandpa!" Perley cried out in anquish, and put another round into Ingram, this one in his head. Then he hurried to kneel by his grandfather. The close-range shotgun blast had torn a terrible circle in the old man's torso. He lay still, the only sign of life a fluttering of his eyelids as a pool of blood began to spread under him.

"Grandpa," Perley said, "you gotta hang on till I can help you." Even as he said it, he knew there was nothing he could do to save his grandfather. It made Perley sick to think about it — the old man had committed suicide in order for Perley to live.

"Grandpa," he continued to plead, "can you hear me?"

The old man's words came in short gasps as the blood now flowed from his mouth when he tried to talk. "Get gold . . . for family."

"To hell with the gold," Perley said, "I wanna see if I can get you somewhere for help."

Grandpa gripped Perley's shirtsleeve tightly and repeated, "Get gold . . . for family. Promise."

"I promise," Perley said. "Now, don't try to talk." He felt the hand gripping his sleeve relax and knew the old man was almost gone.

"Not rock — rooster," were the dying words that came from the old man's lips in his final exhale, words that had no meaning for Perley. He could only guess that his grandfather was past conscious thought when he spoke them.

Perley unsaddled the horses and unloaded his packhorse, thinking he might as well let them rest, since he would be there awhile.

He picked a site near the top of the ridge for his grandfather's grave, under the trees, then went to work digging it. When he had finished, he laid the old man's body into it as carefully as he could manage. When the grave was filled and covered with rocks and branches, Perley tried to think of something he could say. He was never much with solemn words, so he just thought about what a shame it was that the old man had been so happy about the prospect of going home to meet his family, only to end up in a lonely grave over a played-out mining claim.

When Perley returned to the edge of the creek, he stood staring at the man who had

440

killed his grandfather. After a long moment, he grabbed the body by the boots and dragged it over to the gully where he had found Lem Wooten's body before. With a silent apology to Lem, he rolled Ingram's body over the edge of the gully.

He was inclined to saddle up and head for Texas and to hell with the gold. Too many had been killed because of it, but he had promised his grandfather that he would dig it up and take it to his family as Grandpa's atonement for leaving his wife and child.

"Ah, hell," Perley cursed, stripping down and entering the water with a shovel.

All the rest of that day was spent in knee-deep water, digging the dirt out from under the big rock his grandfather had walked up to when they first came to the site. At the end of the day, Perley had to conclude that there was no gold under the rock. Tired and hungry, he was done with the treasure hunt. He remembered the old man saying there was one more thing he needed to know in order to find the treasure, so whatever it was, he'd never know.

Perley built a fire and cooked some of the smoked venison he was packing. He would camp there overnight, then decide what to do with the extra horses he was now in possession of. His initial feeling was that he didn't want the horses that had belonged to his grandfather's killer. He was inclined to unsaddle them and let them go free.

By morning, however, Perley had decided the horses probably held no ill feelings toward his grandfather. So, with horses to sell as well as extra guns and saddles, he decided to return to Deadwood, where there was a better chance to sell them. He was in no particular hurry to return to Texas now, since he wouldn't be taking Grandpa home.

With that settled in his mind, he drained the last cup of coffee out of the pot and stood there gazing at the ill-fated mining claim below him. *It looks peaceful enough now,* he thought. *But it claimed a hell of a lotta lives, and no gold to show for it.*

"That's the way things work out sometimes," Perley said with a sigh, and walked down to the edge of the creek to rinse out his coffeepot.

Then he stood staring at the big rock that had become a symbol for wishful thinking, while he finished the coffee in his cup. When that was done, he rinsed it, too, and decided to take one last look at his grandfather's grave. He walked up the slope and stopped before the grave, thinking about the funny little man buried there.

Out of the corner of his eye, he noticed a jagged rock about the size of a large gravestone, only a few yards away. He hadn't taken notice of it before.

"If I didn't care if anybody found your grave," he said to his grandpa, "I coulda buried you over there and used it for a headstone."

Taking another look at the rock, it occurred to him that it kind of looked like a rooster from that angle. His grandpa's last words struck him then. *Not rock — rooster.* "Well, I'll be damned . . ." he muttered, when he could speak again.

ABOUT THE AUTHORS

William W. Johnstone is the *New York Times* and *USA Today* bestselling author of over 300 books, including the series Preacher, the First Mountain Man, MacCallister, Luke Jensen, Bounty Hunter, Flintlock, Those Jensen Boys!, Savage Texas, Matt Jensen, the Last Mountain Man, and The Family Jensen. His thrillers include *Tyranny, Stand Your Ground, Suicide Mission,* and the upcoming *Black Friday.*

Visit his website at www.williamjohnstone .net.

Being the all-around assistant, typist, researcher, and fact-checker to one of the most popular western authors of all time, **J. A. Johnstone** learned from the master, Uncle William W. Johnstone.

The elder Johnstone began tutoring J.A. at an early age. After-school hours were often spent retyping manuscripts or researching his massive American Western History library as well as the more modern wars and conflicts. J.A. worked hard — and learned. "Every day with Bill was an adventure story in itself. Bill taught me all he could about the art of storytelling. *'Keep the historical facts accurate,'* he would say. *'Remember the readers — and as your grandfather once told me, I am telling you now: Be the best J. A. Johnstone you can be.'* "

The employees of Thorndike Press hope you have enjoyed this Large Print book. All our Thorndike, Wheeler, and Kennebec Large Print titles are designed for easy reading, and all our books are made to last. Other Thorndike Press Large Print books are available at your library, through selected bookstores, or directly from us.

For information about titles, please call:
(800) 223-1244

or visit our website at:
gale.com/thorndike

To share your comments, please write:
Publisher
Thorndike Press
10 Water St., Suite 310
Waterville, ME 04901